The Marquess of Cake

BOOK YOUR PLACE ON OUR WEBSITE AND MAKE THE READING CONNECTION!

We've created a customized website just for our very special readers, where you can get the inside scoop on everything that's going on with Zebra, Pinnacle and Kensington books.

When you come online, you'll have the exciting opportunity to:

- View covers of upcoming books
- Read sample chapters
- Learn about our future publishing schedule (listed by publication month *and author*)
- Find out when your favorite authors will be visiting a city near you
- Search for and order backlist books from our online catalog
- Check out author bios and background information
- Send e-mail to your favorite authors
- Meet the Kensington staff online
- Join us in weekly chats with authors, readers and other guests
- Get writing guidelines
- AND MUCH MORE!

Visit our website at
http://www.kensingtonbooks.com

The Marquess of Cake

HEATHER HIESTAND

KENSINGTON BOOKS
Kensington Publishing Corp.
http://www.kensingtonbooks.com

KENSINGTON BOOKS are published by

Kensington Publishing Corp.
119 West 40th Street
New York, NY 10018

All Kensington titles, imprints and distributed lines are available at special quantity discounts for bulk purchases for sales promotion, premiums, fund-raising, educational or institutional use.

Special book excerpts or customized printings can also be created to fit specific needs. For details, write or phone the office of the Kensington Special Sales Manager. Attn.: Special Sales Department. Kensington Publishing Corp., 119 West 40th Street, New York, NY 10018. Phone: 1-800-221-2647.

Kensington and the K logo Reg. U.S. Pat. & TM Off.

First Electronic Edition: July 2013
eISBN-13: 978-1-60183-111-8
eISBN-10: 1-60183-111-0

First Print Edition: July 2013
ISBN-13: 978-1-60183-129-3
ISBN-10: 1-60183-129-3

Printed in the United States of America

For Michael, Katherine, and Fenimore Hiestand

ACKNOWLEDGMENTS

Many eyes reviewed all or portions of this novel, making it better each time. Thank you to Viola Estrella, Shoshanna Evers, Eilis Flynn, Mary Jo Hiestand, Delle Jacobs, Joleen James, Judy Laik, Isabel Mere, Gina Robinson, and Jacquie Rogers for your thoughts. Thank you to Andy for the many hours spent in front of cake decorating television shows. I wouldn't have written this story without them and you. Thank you to Leander, Mary Jo, David, Pat and Katie, and Elizabeth and Delle, for supporting this writer in all her endeavors. Lastly, thank you to Peter Senftleben and the Kensington team, and Pam van Hylckama Vlieg and the Larsen Pomada team, for making this book (and series) a reality.

Chapter One

November 1886

Michael Shield, Marquess of Hatbrook, breathed in the mouth-watering scent of pastries drifting through the open iron gates of the corner shop at Oxford and Regent Streets. The window display of scones and shortbreads, sponges and meringues, and wafers and biscuits, reminded him of all the exquisite flavors to be had within.

He paused for a moment to admire the arrangement. A young woman, who was sheltered head to toe by a dark cloak, jostled his arm. She smelled like cake.

"My apologies." She glanced in his direction, so that he received an impression of fierce, dark eyes, then turned her head to her companion. "I won't be ordered into the country like I'm some sort of ornament for a hunting ball."

"Too right, Alys," agreed the shorter girl, striding briskly alongside. She, not as well dressed as the first girl, wore a shabby jacket and bonnet.

"I like my work too much to leave it," said the cake-scented girl as the pair swept through the shop gates.

Cake. Redcake's Tea Shop and Emporium was heaven right here in London. Heaven and hell, because if he partook of such a treat his hands might stop trembling and his thoughts might clear, but then, in less than an hour, the cycle would begin anew. A minor medical matter, to be sure, but an irritating one.

Only vigorous exercise kept his body trim, thanks to his frequent indulgences. Still, one small bun, perhaps a slice of fruitcake?

He caught the door with the hooked handle of his umbrella as the women dashed toward the bakery on the right. As he moved through the entryway to the tearoom on the left, he took a deep breath of yeasty goodness.

"Hatbrook, you degenerate! Just the chap I need!"

He spotted an old Oxford chum waving from a window-side table and made his way through the afternoon crowd. His friend, Theodore Bliven, mahogany curls in careless disarray as usual, moved a stack of newspapers, clearing a space for the bill of fare. A pert waitress, or "cakie" as they were called, placed the sheet in front of Michael before he'd even had time to remove his hat.

"Best girls in town, aren't they?" Theo said. "I tried to hire one away to staff our house, but old Redcake pays them too well for that."

"He isn't being knighted for being a stupid tradesman."

"He isn't being knighted for being a good one either," Theo chuckled. "I hear it's because the queen can't resist his Scotch trifle."

The trifle was a rather extraordinary Christmas treat. "Why are you following the investiture lists?"

"It seems they'll knight anyone these days." Theo poked his finger into the newspaper. "That name sounds familiar."

Michael made a face. "My man of business."

"Truly?"

"Yes. When we were up at Balmoral this past summer, he fished one of the young princes out of the lake."

"Why did you invite him to Scotland?"

"He brought me some figures regarding my winery expenses. I needed the information and his expertise."

"A pity. That knighthood will give him airs."

He did sense a change in the air at his solicitor's office today. "What did you need me for, Theo?"

"You're an old Sussex man. I need a recipe for cockles. It's revolting what they do with them at my club."

Michael reflected. "I like them in a pie, myself, with salt pork and onions. But why are they serving peasant food?"

"Hmmm. Some of the old men like them, I suppose. They're always in a revolting white wine sauce."

"Maybe they use cheap wine?"

"Like the kind that comes out of your vineyard?" Theo poked Michael's leg with a damp boot.

Michael moved his leg to the left. Just because his piece of England was the sunniest part of the country didn't make it the best spot for grapes. Still, his vineyard turned a small profit these days.

"Gentlemen?" asked a cakie in a businesslike tone. "What may I bring you today?"

Michael considered her. The young woman with elfin features didn't look familiar, but she smelled delicious. With a start, he realized she'd been the cake-scented girl who jostled him just a few moments ago outside. He wondered why she'd prefer waiting tables to a trip to the country.

Michael forced his eyes from the avowed city girl's generous curves, which were ornamental indeed. He couldn't get that blasted Scotch trifle out of his head. The memory of that heather-honey flavor of the Drambuie in the sponge, reminding him of simpler times, had his mouth watering anew.

"A dish of the special holiday trifle, if you will, and coffee."

"I'm so sorry, sir. We're all out." The cakie's voice didn't change tone as she delivered this tragic news.

"That's 'your lordship,' young miss," Theo said, mischief dancing in his eyes. "You can't refuse trifle to the Marquess of Hatbrook."

A woman at the next table gasped and nudged her neighbor, whispering, "A marquess, that is!"

The cakie swallowed sharply, but then her pointed chin went up. "I'm sorry, your lordship, but it's all gone to Buckingham Palace for a celebration."

"Buck House," whispered the other gossip at the next table. "How fancy!"

"Very tiresome," Michael said, enjoying the cakie's show of spirit. An attractive girl with heat in her eyes was as welcome as Scotch trifle. He wondered if she ever put those rosy lips to use in other passionate endeavors. "Instead, I'll have a plate of scones with honey."

"Would you like some Drambuie with that?"

A gasp went up from the other table. "Did she just offer his lordship spirits? I thought this was a respectable place?"

The cakie flushed scarlet, but her chin stayed up. Her gaze had regained the besieged fire he saw outside.

"That won't be necessary."

"Yes, your lordship."

Her clipped tone had him glancing at her again. Those eyes were as dark as Theo's, but the high color and pursed full lips told him of her pique. Though a cap covered most of her hair, he could see, not surprisingly given her temper, that her hair was a carroty red, though smooth and shiny at the part. All together, a young woman with spark, and he wondered again why she would want to spend her days here. Of course, times were hard, and poverty sent many girls into the workforce. Since the girls wore black dresses of a conservative cut with white aprons, they offered no hint of individuality, though he thought this particular girl was the least subservient cakie he'd ever run across.

The girl's gaze captured his and he realized he'd been staring.

Her forehead and cheeks flushed crimson. "I-I'll get your order for you, your lordship."

She darted away, skirts fluttering, offering a glimpse of trim ankle. Fetching, very fetching indeed. He wondered what she'd look like in a ball gown under gaslight, with her hair aglow and her pale skin enhanced by golden glamour.

He started, the smell of pastry and Theo's grin reminding him where he was. Only the cakie's delectable scent of cake and, yes, orange flower water, had him thinking these sensual thoughts about a working girl. He had no time for romance, either marriage or dalliance-minded, not with the time it took to float money from holding to enterprise to mortgage, as he rebuilt his family fortune from the mess his father's gambling had created.

"Are you staying in town through the holidays?" Theo inquired.

"Yes. My mother wanted to come in to shop and then my cousin Laurence is being knighted tomorrow. Smythe, my man, is being knighted at the next investiture in three weeks."

"Maybe you'll get some trifle tomorrow then."

"I'm sure the royal family will hoard it to their collective bosom," Michael said.

"I once thought you might marry into the royal family," Theo said. "Since you are an intimate."

"Ah. The queen's children are all married off now."

"Your mother must be disappointed," Theo observed.

"She'd like someone very grand for my sister, at least. Beth is seventeen now, if you can believe it."

Theo winked. "She's much prettier than you. I'll take her off your hands."

"No, thank you," Michael said. "You aren't very grand."

Theo sighed theatrically. "I have prospects. Only three elderly bachelor cousins have to die before a title comes to my side of the family."

"Oh?"

"Yes. There's a good chance I'll be an earl by the time I'm fifty."

"Plan to live that long, given your propensity for trouble?"

"Fifty does seem terribly old," Theo admitted.

"My mother is forty-seven," Michael said, toying with Theo's plate. It was covered with crumbs and he wondered what Theo had been eating. It looked like a red, seedless jam had been involved.

"I'm sure she looks much younger."

"She does try. All that trying is quite expensive. I think I'll marry a woman who isn't obsessed with her appearance."

"They make women like that?"

"My plan is to tell her how beautiful she is on a regular basis, so she doesn't get any ideas that she is losing her looks."

"Sound in theory, but do you think women really listen to their husbands?"

"Mine will. I'll only marry a sweet, biddable girl, not a termagant like Mother." Remembering the cakie, he added, "One who enjoys rusticating far more than the hustle and bustle of the city, like I do."

His stomach rumbled in anticipation when their cakie crossed the floor, holding a plate of scones with a small dish of honey and a cup of coffee on a tray. As the girl passed the table with the gossips, one of the ladies gesticulated wildly. Her arm caught the tray. The cakie jerked back nimbly enough, but the tray dislodged from her hands when the lady threw up her arm yet again. The cakie rocked on her heels and, in seeming slow motion, began to fall backward.

Michael leapt up, his thigh slamming the edge of his table as he caught her by the apron, then found purchase for his hands around her hips. The tin tray clattered to the floor as he pulled her curvy hips flush against his legs. Her body pressed against him. He scented that delectable perfume of hers. *Eau de Redcake's.*

The ladies at the table shrieked and another employee ran toward them, a cloth in her hand. Michael glanced down and saw the cakie's large, brown eyes staring into his, confusion evident.

He blinked at the girl. "How beautiful you look today." He peered at the black embroidery on her apron. "Alys."

Her entire body vibrated. She stepped away from him almost before his lower body reacted to the sensuous press of her substantial bosom against his chest. Her cheeks were scarlet, which made the freckles high on her cheekbones stand out adorably. Given a choice between a display of cake and her, he might just stare at this girl.

The other cakie exclaimed and helped Alys gather up the ruined food, broken cup, and saucer before running for a mop and bucket. The gesticulating woman at the next table rose, muttering about the falling standards of the tea shop. The other tossed bills on the table and departed with a last frank stare in Michael's direction.

He sat abruptly as the injured muscle of his thigh contracted, reminding him he had slammed his leg against the table during his rescue.

Theo guffawed. "You do have a way with women."

He stared at the departing gossips. "How rude, when they caused the accident."

"Your mother would have reacted the same way and you know it."

"It's so depressing to realize she's not the only horror in the world."

"It's no problem, sir," the cakie with the mop said, looking up. "We'll get you another plate immediately."

Alys rushed away. In less than two minutes she had returned with fresh dishes.

"I do apologize for my clumsiness, your lordship. Of course, there will be no charge." Mouth pursed, color high, she had a damp stain down one arm.

"Quite all right. Not your fault." Even underneath her starched white apron, he could see her bosom was as magnificent as it had felt against him for that tantalizingly brief moment.

"I should have been more careful."

"Not at all. Please do give me the bill. I won't hear of it being otherwise." He rather liked this Alys and didn't want the bill to come out of her salary.

She blinked and shook her head. "I'll see about that."

She rushed away, leaving Michael quite bemused by her pride.

"It was about time Mother hired us a dressmaker," Rose Redcake opined loudly from her pose in front of a floor-length mirror as Alys dashed into the shared dressing room.

Their other sister, Matilda, nodded from her perch on a rich, red velvet sofa.

Rose continued, twisting her thick locks into a knot at the top of her head. "Father must allow us to dress for our new position in society."

Their father had been spending a great deal of money lately, and not just on their mother. He had bought this Georgian house on St. James's Square just two years ago from an earl. Last week, he'd purchased a country estate in Sussex, a parcel of property the Duke of Devonshire had been discarding. Alys found this purchase worrisome. She couldn't understand why her father would buy a home so far away from his industrial base in Bristol, the mills and baking factories that had made him wealthy. The Tea Shop and Emporium she adored was merely the diamond in his crown.

"The shops are lovely here," Matilda argued. "I've found the most beautiful dresses at Liberty and Co."

"Ready-made," Rose sniffed. "Machine lace."

"Eighteen and already a snob," Alys sighed, dropping onto a padded ottoman next to her youngest sister.

"Please change out of that uniform before you leave Redcake's," Rose said. "You look like a maid."

Alys looked down at her sensible dress with affection. One of the best perks of holding a position was wearing comfortable clothing much of the time. "At least I don't have to lace my corset so tightly that I risk swooning, unlike some young ladies I know."

"One must suffer for fashion," Rose wheezed.

The discussion was cut short by their mother's entrance, along with a short, stout dressmaker and her two frightened-looking assistants.

"The girls need reception gowns for an affair at Buckingham Palace." Ellen Redcake floated her left hand next to her cheek, as graceful as any dancer.

"Sensible," Alys said. "Something we can wear again, in our regular lives."

"Silk," Matilda insisted.

"Fit for the Palace." Rose made a grand gesture with her pinky pointed.

"Everyone at this investiture is on the rise," their mother said. "Who knows who you might meet there?"

"I know what I would like," Matilda said.

"No pink, Matilda," their mother said. "It clashes with your hair."

"But I love pink," Matilda cried.

"No man will find you attractive in pink. You're twenty-one now, dear, it's time to be careful." She raised a hand. "Alys, twenty-six isn't too old to wed."

"I don't want a husband," Alys muttered. Her mother could even dangle that handsome marquess from Redcake's in front of her and she'd still say no.

"All women want husbands. You simply require a very special man." She tilted her head into a dreamy pose.

Alys focused on the dressmaker, hoping she could be measured first. She had a new idea for a wedding cake decoration she was dying to experiment with before a wedding consultation the next day.

Unfortunately, the dress discussion went on for hours, as Matilda wanted romance, Rose wanted something fit for a duke's daughter, and Alys wanted something severely tailored.

With their mother's assistance, they settled on kilted skirts of silk, with velvet bodices and tunics due to the time of year. Matilda found a forest-green silk in the dressmaker's samples and matched it to a velvet decorated with yellow flowers. Rose, who could wear pink, chose a pink silk skirt and cream velvet. Alys insisted on a delicate gray for both of her fabrics. They also argued over the size of the bustle but their mother agreed with Alys and kept it relatively small.

"You will all be a credit to your father, girls," their mother said approvingly.

"Perhaps we might order another few dresses?" Rose asked. "I have nothing to wear on calls to new friends, and what if we receive party invitations, Mother?"

"I have work to do," Alys muttered, and left the room as quickly as she could, impeded by the tightly laced corset her mother had forced her to wear.

Three weeks later, Alys smoothed her dove-gray gown over her hips as she listened to Rose and Matilda argue next to the fire.

Her twin brother, Gawain, recently of Her Majesty's army, and her inventor cousin, Lewis Noble, paced the drawing room, looking very handsome in their morning coats. Her brother's limp made a thump, slide, thump noise against the parquet as he stomped around the edge of the rug. They stopped in front of a family portrait painted by their mother. The watercolor depicted smiles all around, quite a contrast to today's mood.

"Look, Gawain," Lewis said, pointing to the brass parrot on his shoulder. Dear Lewis, always trying to cheer people. He might never be precisely fashionable, since he cared little for his appearance, but he never had an unkind word to say to anyone. "She talks. Pretty, isn't she, Alys?"

"Cracker," said the parrot's deep, ghostly voice. Its metal wings fluttered, sounding like the tinkling of tiny bells.

Rose laughed, then coughed. The pestilential London fog bothered her lungs fiercely at this time of year, and Alys suspected the greenery decorating the room did her no good either. Their mother had ordered Rose to keep her corset loosened at all times, but Alys knew her sister insisted their maid tighten it whenever she left the house.

"How did you make that silly thing speak?" Matilda asked, drowning out Alys's, "Very pretty."

Lewis grinned at her, his teeth shining through his slightly inadequate blond beard. "It's a secret."

Ellen Redcake glided into the room in a long, purple-and-green flowing gown more suited to the medieval age than the modern era. Mrs. Nettleship, her mother's dressmaker, often designed for the theater and it showed.

"The carriage is waiting, ma'am," Pounds, the butler, said, entering the room.

"Where is Father?" Alys asked.

"We'll pick him up at Redcake's. The weather is simply dreadful."

Her mother's hands fluttered. "Why did the queen have to schedule this investiture today?"

"She can't predict the weather, Mother," said Gawain.

"You poor dear," Mother said, rubbing her hand along Gawain's sleeve. "You must find this so very trying, after India's warmth."

"I'm happy to be home." Gawain glowered at her, despite his words.

A trio of housemaids entered with outer garments for everyone. An extra carriage had been hired for the occasion and it was agreed Alys and her brother would go to Redcake's while the others went on ahead.

Would anyone at Redcake's recognize her in these clothes? She looked like a lady. Would his lordship, the Marquess of Hatbrook, think she was his social equal in clothing like this? She'd found it hard to forget him these past weeks. Had the sensation of his hard chest and strong thighs flush against her body made such a lasting impression? It seemed so. That saucy friend of his no doubt was a gentleman as well, but as lively and naughty as he'd been, she preferred the more austere character and looks of the marquess. Though admittedly, he'd had the hungriest eyes she'd ever seen. She shivered at the thought.

How exciting that such people came to the tea shop now. To think it had started as so small an operation that she'd been the one to suggest many of the menu offerings, including the Scotch trifle her father's mother used to serve at Christmastime. What happy memories those had been, when their older brother, Arthur, was still alive and learning the mill business, before Gawain had gone into the army, before she'd learned not everyone was kind.

Now Arthur was dead of some horrible wasting disease that had claimed him at twenty years of age, and Gawain had a patch over his ruined eye and a permanent limp. His career had been ended by the injuries, though Father hadn't been sorry to see his only living son safely back at home again and ready to work at Redcake's.

She pressed her lips together and tried to return to happier thoughts. How could she not admire the marquess, with his wavy, brown hair just touched with a hint of the sun, despite the time of year? She thought his eyes must have been a stormy sea blue, though of course it was awfully hard to say since she had tried not to stare.

The carriage entered the alleyway behind Redcake's, where their father waited on the loading dock. He worked entirely too hard, but she understood why. She loved Redcake's as much as he did. The tea shop and emporium part at least. She wasn't so fond of the factories.

Bartley Redcake nodded to his son and kissed his daughter's cheek as he entered the carriage, bringing the scent of flour and vanilla with a backdrop of tobacco. He was a hands-on manager still and she didn't doubt he'd checked a measurement and stirred a pot or two today.

"Are you nervous, Father?" she asked.

"Oh, the queen isn't so different from you or me," he said heartily, adjusting his topcoat over his substantial stomach.

The buttons strained and Alys made a mental note to tell her mother so she could alter the garment.

"Still, it's something, isn't it? Really something."

"We're all so proud of you," Alys assured him.

Gawain said nothing, just took out a cigar and began the ritual of preparing it.

"I'll take one of those, son."

Without a word, Gawain passed him his cigar case.

An hour later, she held hands with Matilda and Rose as they craned their necks for a view of the spectacle. Queen Victoria entered the richly decorated, polychrome ballroom in Buckingham Palace, attended by two Gurkha orderly officers and various support staff.

The queen, a short, elderly woman dressed in black with touches of lace, wore a style of gown in fashion when Alys was a baby. She wore a lace veil to indicate her widowed status and her thick fingers were covered in rings. In one bow to contemporary fashion she wore a velvet band around her neck, black of course, from which dangled a diamond pendant that caught the light.

The dais held five members of the Yeomen of the Guard, dressed in their Tudor finery of red and gold. The room was enormous and Alys could well believe it the largest room in London.

"I like their hats," Rose giggled, poking at the feathers in her hair. "Too bad the Yeomen are all such old men."

"Isn't that usher adorable?" Matilda said from the other side, lifting her chin toward a young man dressed in black, his curly, blond hair surrounding a face still encased in more baby fat than Alys could find attractive.

"I think that's the Earl of Lathom with the queen, he is Lord

Chamberlain presently," Mrs. Redcake said, turning from her position just in front of them. "What is he thinking with that beard? So unattractive."

She stopped speaking when "God Save the Queen" began to play. Afterward, the earl announced the first recipient and his achievements. Another man bent to whisper in the queen's ear as an elderly man doddered forward. The queen took a sword from a servant. Alys felt it an incongruous sight to see a large sword in the hand of such a grandmotherly figure.

She watched as an usher helped the man kneel on the investiture stool and receive his accolade from Queen Victoria's sword.

The elderly man stood as the queen stepped back, seeming taller than before. Alys could have sworn he held his shoulders straighter, and he certainly walked better. As an usher announced his name the elderly man smiled, appearing almost handsome.

"How different the knighting has made him seem," Matilda whispered in her ear, echoing Alys's thoughts.

Then, their father's name was called. Alys scarcely breathed as her father strutted toward the stage. Her mother clasped her hands to her throat as Bartley Redcake knelt and became Sir Bartley Redcake.

"Lady Redcake," she heard her mother whisper under her breath.

Yes, this altered her mother's status greatly. What would happen to the rest of the family? Alys liked things as they were. Comforts, yes, and useful work too. But this knighthood changed everything. Whether she wanted it or not, her family's new status would redraw her entire life.

Chapter Two

Michael watched from one side of the ballroom as his man of business's name was called. John Smythe received an actual smile from the reserved queen, who knew one of those closest to the throne would now be buried in a chapel in Scotland if not for his quick actions a few months previous.

He hoped the knighthood wouldn't change Smythe too much. The man was reliable, dependable, quicksilver smart. He'd been well trained for five years by the now-deceased solicitor who had handled the Hatbrook business affairs previously. But he knew he'd soon lose the man to a duke, or even to the royal family. Or to government. That wouldn't surprise him at all. Sir John might be a member of parliament in a few years.

Michael would have to find a new man of business and quickly, before his affairs again sank into disarray. Why hadn't he encouraged Smythe to take on an apprentice?

His hand trembled and, suddenly starving and nauseous, he wished refreshments were being served. But he'd looked, and no sign of the Scotch trifle or any other treat was to be found. Nor were any of the younger set of royals at the investiture, someone he might have leaned on for afternoon tea.

When the ceremony was over, the group of honorees was ushered into the Inner Quadrangle and reunited with their guests.

"Congratulations," Michael said heartily, as Sir John joined him with a broad smile. He would kill for a scone right now.

Sir John rubbed his hands together. "What an auspicious occasion, your lordship."

"Indeed," Michael said, his vision seeming to narrow as his hunger increased. "I must take my leave now, but all congratulations due, my good man."

Sir John's gaze shifted to a point beyond Michael's shoulder. "Oh, but first, your lordship, if I might beg your indulgence. May I introduce you to my fiancée's father, Mr. Thomas Cooper?"

A heavyset man with long, graying mustaches lumbered toward them, followed by a lady of equal girth and a pale slip of a girl dressed in a white gown with a disturbing number of flounces. She had a fox's shrewd eyes however, belying her silly clothing and demure appearance. Some men might think this girl pliant, but Michael could see she'd be in command of her home.

"Of course," Michael said, tightening his hands to fists to control the slight shaking.

After introductions Sir John said, "The Marquess came specifically to support me, sir. I am overjoyed to have such a friend in him."

Michael had only come because he knew to decline would have cost him an excellent man of business almost instantaneously. Sir John, to be sure, had a hint of the toady about him, which would make him even more desirable to a royal.

Cooper bowed. "Very pleased to make your acquaintance, your lordship. I'm in the cotton textile trade, you know."

Michael nodded. "I've never ventured into the cotton side of things. I do have cattle and sheep, of course, in Sussex." Recent purchases, that had yet to make profit.

"Excellent, your lordship. I believe I've drunk Hatbrook wine?"

"Yes, I have a winery too. And Sir John helps me manage a tile-works, my fishing boats, and an inn or two in Eastbourne." Even a pot of stew at his Seaport Inn sounded scrumptious at the moment.

Mrs. Cooper clasped her hands together and sighed with ecstasy.

"You must regard him highly," Cooper remarked.

"Indeed. You are lucky to have him joining your family," Michael said honestly.

Sir John grinned at Miss Cooper. The smile took years off his face. Her expression remained serene. The lady already knew she'd chosen well.

"Smart as a whip," Cooper said. "And not least because he offered for my daughter as soon as word of his investiture was made known. He'll run my business one day, since I have no sons, you know."

As Cooper was not young and quite corpulent, Michael feared that day would come soon. "I'm sure he will do your legacy proud."

"Indeed, sir, indeed."

"Well, my man, you are certainly coming up in the world, taking a wife and all that. You'll need to gather in a good apprentice too, the sooner the better, I'd say."

Sir John coughed.

"My wife has a few cousins in London. Meant to look them up, you know. Maybe one of them will do," Cooper said.

"Yes, sir," Sir John said.

"On that note," Michael said, "I shall take my leave. Please interview these young cousins as soon as is prudent, Sir John. A pleasure to meet you all." Before anyone could speak again, he strode toward the doors. A footman stopped him to hand him a note. The queen probably wanted a word.

Matilda's squeal broke Alys's reverie. She'd been watching men shake hands with her father, all the titans of industry and politics who'd been knighted or received other awards alongside him.

Rose squealed too and Alys turned to both of them. "Whatever is going on?"

"Do you think now that Father is a knight we might be courted by someone like that?"

Thankfully, neither Matilda nor Rose pointed their fingers, but Matilda lifted her chin toward a tall, austere gentleman in a perfectly tailored black frock coat, moving toward the doors and a waiting usher who held out a note.

As he walked, an elderly lady with tall plumes in her hair jostled him. When he turned to steady her, his beaver top hat slid off his head and hit the floor.

Alys caught a glint of sun-streaked hair, an off-kilter lift of the upper lip, the broad half circle of manly chin. Hatbrook! Her heart skipped a beat.

His handsome head turned and his glance seemed to catch hers. Did he recognize her from the tea shop, despite her finery? Had she said his name aloud?

"That's a marquess," she hissed at her sisters without looking away. "You two must be mad."

"I don't believe I've ever seen a marquess before," Rose breathed. "How handsome he is."

His gaze moved on. He said something to the elderly lady and she grinned at him like a schoolgirl. Had she looked at him like that at Redcake's, with those same mooncalf eyes?

"How do you know? Have you met him?" Matilda demanded.

Hatbrook looked their way again, raising an eyebrow. Alys turned away this time, blushing furiously because he'd caught her staring.

She put her hands to her cheeks. "I served him at Redcake's last month. Another customer knocked me over but he caught me before I could fall."

"It's a pity he met you under such lowering circumstances, Alys. There's no hope of greeting him as an equal now, even if you have been introduced."

"Really," Alys muttered, taking a quick peek in his direction again. "How would someone like me have ever even met a marquess unless I was serving him?"

Hatbrook bowed to the lady as two middle-aged women came to rescue her, then picked up his hat. After he spoke to one of the women, a footman handed him the note that had fallen to the floor and opened a door. Hatbrook glanced in Alys's direction again briefly, narrowing his eyes as if trying to recall her name, then opened the note. When he had perused the contents, he left without another glance at anyone.

"We're terribly rich now," Rose said. "Any number of titled gentlemen might find us appealing. We're pretty and wealthy."

"Gentlemen with empty pockets are not appealing," Alys said. Although she could see how someone as handsome as Hatbrook would entice even if his fortune were squandered. He was quite the most attractive man she'd ever laid eyes on. "They are likely to love money more than you. How would you ever know their true motivation? Besides, you haven't any money of your own. It's all Father's."

"I'll know when someone loves me, and I'm not going to be a cakie for pocket money," Rose said. "I'd ruin my hands and probably my complexion too. Father gives me all the money I need."

Alys smiled. "I make a real salary and I could rent a little cottage and hire one of you to be my companion if I wanted. I mostly supervise our wedding cakes and do the decorating. I haven't been a full-time cakie in over a year."

"It must be shocking to find yourself twenty-six. You had so many years without prospects that you are quite spinsterish, and I understand why you must work," Matilda said. "But since Father's fortunes have improved so nicely, we have opportunities you did not."

Alys found herself open-mouthed at her sister's effrontery. Had the five years between them made such different people? Perhaps, but she suspected her work experience had made the larger difference. That and other things she didn't care to remember.

"Beauty fades. Just remember love, respect, and companionship are more important than a title."

"The queen married a prince and he was lovely from all reports," Matilda said. "I am sure there are wonderful titled people, and I can fall in love with one of them just as easily as I could fall in love with a baker."

"The queen married her cousin," Alys said tartly. "And besides, she could have had anyone. She had the pick of the world's most eligible men, so why wouldn't she have found a good one?"

"I want to live in a mansion," Rose said dreamily. "With all the latest furnishings, and fine paintings and a carriage of my own."

"We live in a mansion now," Alys said.

"I don't care to live in something less now that I know how lovely it is to have a mansion," Rose said.

"What will the two of you do with yourselves all day once these great marriages have been found for you?"

"Pay calls, throw parties," Matilda said.

"Babies," Rose said, "who will have the best of everything."

Although Alys loved Redcake's, she felt a pang at the thought of babies. But, she had decided at fifteen that marriage and family were not for her.

"May I introduce my daughters, your lordship," Alys's father said, walking over to them with none other than the unfortunately bearded Earl of Lathom.

Alys saw Rose covering her mouth with her hand, clearly hiding a giggle, as her mother curtsied.

She and her sisters followed suit as her father presented them to the Lord Chamberlain. Her brother and cousin bowed.

"My girls will never want for anything," her father boasted. "Next we need to find them husbands, eh, Lady Redcake?"

He grinned at his wife while the earl nodded stoically.

"I've bought an estate down in Sussex. Good place to find a husband who isn't aware of my elder children's lack of fine finishing, eh?"

All the heat drained from Alys's face and she swayed where she stood. Gawain caught her by the shoulder, steadying her, and she forced herself to be strong, because she knew her brother couldn't hold much of her weight due to his bad leg.

The earl raised a bushy eyebrow.

"Yes, it's unfortunately true that my eldest children started working in my factory up north at the age of eight. You won't find that kind of past in the aristocracy, but it made Gawain and Alys strong. Good sturdy blood, they have, and with Alys's dowry, we ought to be able to find her someone."

Alys noticed her father didn't mention her oldest brother, Arthur, who hadn't been so sturdy, and had died. She held herself still as the earl blandly named off a couple of widowers with minor titles and large debts. She had learned a lot from reading the assortment of papers customers left behind in the tea shop each day. Matilda and Rose's eyes grew wide with the notion that they might be fit wives for these titled men, but it just made Alys feel ill. Was she not her father's able assistant? Did she have no value other than to be a potential wife who would raise her father's status?

"As long as she finds a good husband, that is what matters," Redcake said. "Otherwise I've failed her."

Alys opened her mouth to speak, but her mother clamped her hand to Alys's free arm. "Look, there is Lady, er, Calves-foot. Come Alys, we must thank her for her kindness."

Gawain released her other arm and Alys allowed herself to be towed away while giving her father the evil eye. It was better to glare than cry. She was a woman of dignity and wouldn't lower herself so.

"Do not even think to show disrespect for your father in front of others," her mother whispered when they had come to a stop out of the eyesight of the earl.

"What about me?" Alys said. "How can Father think he's failed me unless I marry? I don't want to marry. I'm happy as I am."

"A woman's role is to marry and have children," her mother said.

"It is too large a sacrifice," Alys argued. "I don't wish to give up my position."

"What position?"

"Mother!" She was outraged. Did her mother think she played at Redcake's all day? "I've worked very hard. Our wedding business would be nothing without me."

"It is kind of him to humor you," her mother said with a wave of her hand. "It's obvious you are overheated. I'll call someone to bring our carriage so you can leave."

Alys turned, but her mother stopped her with a touch. "Do not move an inch until I return for you, young miss."

She wanted to scream, but her respect for her mother stilled both her voice and her feet. How humiliating to know how competent one was, yet still be a child to one's parents. Or at least someone of no more value than Matilda, or heaven forbid, Rose. She had bigger dreams than they did, but her parents couldn't see that. They only saw failure.

Michael strode through the gates at Redcake's the next day, intent upon finally procuring a large portion of Scotch trifle. Surely the Palace would have let some slip from its iron grasp, since the queen should have returned to Windsor by now. He hadn't seen any on the tea tray in the private rooms of the palace the day before. The queen had been kind enough to invite him by note after the investiture. If Scotch trifle was unavailable today, he'd order a bowl to be delivered to Hatbrook House in Belgravia and eat the entire thing himself since his mother didn't like sweets with liquor in them.

He smiled, remembering when his younger brother, Judah, was a child, he'd suffered from sore throats on a regular basis and he'd been served copious amounts of hot tea laced with whisky, which he'd drink while nibbling on the shortbread their tutor always had, since the under-cook was sweet on him. They'd both developed a taste for alcoholic sweets as a result.

But today, he had more on his mind than just the trifle. He wanted to show a photograph to the staff of Redcake's and see if they recognized a young man in a group photo of the Second Battalion of the Royal Sussex Regiment. Judah had mailed it to him because he was clearly visible in the front and thought their mother might appreciate the image.

Michael thought he'd seen another of the young men pictured recently, however, and at Redcake's. The man had a long, hawkish nose that had a distinctive hook at the tip. How many men could sport that same unusual proboscis?

He didn't see any friends of his this time as he entered the crowded dining room and seated himself at a table. A cakie soon approached and he was thrilled to hear his trifle was available now.

"It's just come on the special tariff this week, sir, now that it's close to Christmas."

"Excellent. And I wonder if you could have a look at this?" He produced the photo from a portfolio case and handed the cakie a magnifying glass. "Do you recognize this young man?"

The young woman frowned. "Are you a constable or some such?"

"Not at all," he assured her. "This young man at the bottom left is my brother, who is in India. But I believe I've seen this other young man at Redcake's and I wondered if he had any stories to share about the Battalion."

"Oh." Still with two furrows between her brows, the cakie took a look through the magnifying glass. She straightened with a jerk. "I'll see if I can find one of the family, sir."

"Family?" Michael asked, confused, but the young woman had darted off as speedily as if he'd pinched her bum. She hadn't even written down his order, and he was unsure if he'd see his trifle anytime soon. He should have come earlier in the day.

After a minute of waiting, the mingled scents of pastry, clotted cream, jam, and tea were driving him mad, so he took up his magnifying glass and perused the photograph. It depicted his brother with nine other Englishmen in uniform. The photograph was similar to a famous photograph of a group of officers who had all died during an attack in Kabul shortly after the photograph was taken, more than half a decade before. His brother was posed in profile at one side, one hand resting on the hilt of his sword. A heroic posture to be sure, but it had caused Michael to have nightmares after the first time he'd seen it, something he blamed on an overrich chocolate cake he'd had after dinner that night.

Judah was twenty-five now and it had been six years since Michael had seen him. He'd gone to Egypt first, then to India. His brother's frame was spare now, but broad-shouldered and very straight in carriage. He looked like a man to be leaned on, a man to trust, a leader of men. Certainly someone an older brother could be proud of.

The man he was convinced he'd seen recently was also standing in the photograph, on the opposite side behind seated senior officers. He wore a sergeant's uniform and looked about Judah's age.

"I was told you needed to see me?"

Michael glanced up to see none other than the owner of Redcake's himself, Sir Bartley Redcake. Besides a smudge of flour on one sleeve, he was resplendent in clothing as fine as Michael's own.

Michael stood. "I'm Hatbrook," he said, and offered his hand.

"Yes, your lordship. I believe I saw you at the investiture yesterday."

"Yes, my man of business received a knighthood."

"Ah, yes, Smythe, I believe?"

"Quite. But I haven't come about him. I hoped to discover the identity of this sergeant in India. You see, the photograph includes my brother, who is in the Black Mountain region now, but I could have sworn I saw this distinctive young gentleman right here at Redcake's recently."

Sir Bartley Redcake took the magnifying glass Michael offered and bent over the photograph. His hand moved slowly from the top down, covering the bleak and stony ridges of the Hazara country backdrop, then to the faces of the men.

He tapped the face Michael knew. "My son, your lordship. He was injured in a brawl with those blasted Pathans very late last year. Lost his eye and damaged his hip, so he's been discharged."

"I say, how dreadful," Michael said. "I did wonder. This photograph must be older than I had been led to believe."

"You can ask my son, of course, but it was likely taken as soon as they arrived in the village where they are headquartered."

"I would like to speak to him. Curious, you know, to understand what my brother's life is like there. If he seems happy enough in the army. I could just afford to bring him home now, if he wishes, to live the life of a gentleman. Wasn't true when he went in. Finances in disarray."

"My father spent time in debtor's prison," Sir Bartley said. "I know all about repairing family fortunes."

"I wonder if Judah would like to come home, but it's so difficult to say from letters, and one never knows who might be reading them as they pass through."

He nodded. "I expect Gawain can help you. He's apprenticing to be a bookkeeper in our offices upstairs. Would you like to speak to him now?"

"If it is no trouble. Or I could make arrangements."

"Not at all."

Michael was gratified to see a dish of trifle coming his way, though it was delivered by none other than the pretty carrot-haired cakie who had failed him in the trifle matter a few weeks before. As she set down the tray, her arm brushed his, setting off a reaction thankfully hidden under the table, as he smelled her delectable perfume.

"Oh it's you again, your lordship," she said pertly.

Sir Bartley's bushy, orange-gray eyebrows shot up in outrage. "Alys."

"Quite acceptable," Michael said, not wanting to get the girl in trouble. "We have a history. My friend, Theo Bliven, gave her a very hard time when we were here last." He wouldn't mention how sensual her curves had felt against his body, when he'd held her, though he could hardly forget. He'd dreamt about that moment.

"Ah, Mr. Bliven," Sir Bartley said with a smile. "He is a jocular young fellow. I know his father. We're in the same club."

"We were schoolmates," Michael said. "I'm glad to see Buckingham Palace has not stolen all the trifle again."

Sir Bartley smiled graciously. "We are thrilled to be under Her Majesty's warrant, of course, but I do apologize that her needs superseded your own."

"Quite all right," Michael assured him. He caught the cakie rolling her eyes as she turned away. What a personality that one had. "Could I have a pot of tea, Alys?"

Sir Bartley retired with a promise to deliver his son as soon as possible.

Michael's thoughts had been on family and they drifted to his impossible mother while he waited. She was lucky to have been born into a good family and with the beauty to marry well. With her personality, she would never have been able to hold a position. She could never bend and always had to slip her point of view in somehow, and it frequently had a bite to it. He could well imagine her rolling her eyes like Alys had, but she'd also have made some cutting remark that devalued the queen's fondness for Redcake's pastry.

As always, when faced with thoughts of family, he said a little prayer for Judah's continued well-being. Since Michael had Judah as his heir, he hadn't had to rush into marriage to provide one. Anyone his mother brought to his attention had been utterly unsuitable, the most unattractive, bluestocking type of female. His ideal was a girl with limited imagination, the kind of horselike, country sort so opposite to his mother that she wouldn't even comprehend the older woman's barbs. He'd never met a girl like that and had no idea how to find her, but he wouldn't marry until he did.

"God bless Judah," he muttered.

"Excuse me, your lordship?"

Michael looked up to find the photograph come to life.

The young man, whose face was now marred by an eye patch that almost hid a fresh, horizontal scar reaching down to his cheek, nodded at him and set down a tea tray. "I'm Sergeant Gawain Redcake."

Michael pushed back his chair and shook his hand. "Sergeant Redcake. I had no idea you were who I was seeking." The cakie must have given him the tray. A pity. He'd have liked to have Alys brush up against him again.

"So Captain Shield is your brother?" The young man sat across from him and poured two cups of steaming black tea.

Michael took the offered cup and added sugar. "Indeed. You must have seen action not too long ago."

"That part of the Black Mountains is always in great unrest. Fierce tribes there, want the British out. Small skirmishes there from time to time." He shrugged. "I had some bad luck there."

"I see you did. Is bookkeeping to your liking now?"

He raised the eyebrow over his good eye. "I don't mind the work at all, but I'd rather it was for some other business. Still, when I've become competent, I can find other work."

"Family complicates everything."

The fervent tone in which he expressed this sentiment brought a smile to the sergeant's mouth.

"My late father complicated my life greatly," Michael said.

"As you can see, my father is firmly at the reins."

"Yes, and I don't mean to keep you from your work, but tell me, when last you saw my brother, was he well and happy?"

Redcake took a sip of his undoctored black tea. "He is a natural soldier, I believe, and I do not recall him ever being wounded. A crack shot, knows how to use his bayonet to maximum effect, decisive."

"All good things. Is he in constant danger?"

"As much as any officer. They are not in the same level of risk as a common foot soldier, but any man can fall. I was with supplies, working in the Officer's Mess, having the background I do, yet I found myself in a battle thanks to a surprise attack. There are no guarantees in the army."

"No, that is clear. Do you think he would want to come home, given a reasonable allowance?"

"I've never known him to discuss money, my lord. I couldn't say."

"I am sorry for your wounds and I thank you for your time."

Redcake nodded and took his leave. Michael watched him limp away, wondering if his brother's fate would be the same. One had to wonder if he'd been safer in Egypt. He resolved to make money as quickly as he knew how, so as to provide added inducement for Judah to return home soon.

Chapter Three

"Make certain all the shilling factory-made cakes are close at hand. With Christmas so near, they are sure to sell," Alys directed, pointing to a full rack in one of the storage rooms underneath the tea shop.

Ralph Popham, the bakery manager, made a face. "I wish we didn't have to sell them nasty things."

"They aren't so bad. At least they come from a Redcake's factory. All the ingredients are wholesome." Some appalling ingredients from bad milk to laundry dye to fake butter found their way into baked goods, but never at Redcake's. Customers knew their goods were safe to eat at any price point.

"I'm sure you're right, Miss Redcake," Popham sighed and groomed his mustache with his fingers. "Now that's a lovely bit of work." He pointed his chin toward a wedding cake on the counter.

The three-tier cake was resplendent. Alys had used her best, most expensive recipe and the results smelled divine, a mix of candied citron and orange peel, raisins and currants, almonds and exotic spices, but best of all, the fresh lemon zest combined with rum and brandy to give it a heady essence.

She'd spent hours on the design, starting with a silver-edged board and topping the design with the aristocratic bride's choice of a raised gum-paste basket complete with a scrollwork handle. Wild-flowers cascaded down the sides of the cake, which she'd worked with scrolls around each tier, and her famous threadwork at the top and bottom of the tiers. The wildly lovely design would be consumed early this afternoon at a post-wedding luncheon, held at the bride's family home.

"Ready to transport?" asked Simon Hellman, their delivery manager, as he came into the room.

"I think so. The pastries and smaller cakes are already boxed."

Simon gestured to two apprentices and Alys left the room with the bakery manager.

"Always a flurry of activity at this time of year," Popham said.

"Yes, and I'll be out this afternoon at that luncheon. The bride's mother asked me to be on hand to make sure the cake is displayed and cut properly."

"Don't they have enough servants?"

"I don't mind," Alys assured him. "It gives me a chance to discuss cakes with guests and bring in business. After all, we're nearly done with the October to December wedding rush. We won't be busy again until the April to June wedding season."

"I should think the name of Redcake's is all the advertising we need."

"Not if we want the best sort of customer." Alys's eagle eye caught a misaligned tray of shortbread in the display case and she quickly restacked the rectangles so they displayed perfectly.

"I'll take your word for it, miss. But don't wear yourself so low you damage your constitution."

Alys grinned. "The only thing that tires me is playing cakie. I'm much happier when I can stay out of the tearoom."

"Those girls do put up with a lot from our gentlemen guests," he agreed. "I prefer when my daughter reports most of her trade was from the ladies."

"Yes, sometimes men do behave like they are in a pub, but overall, I think we do a good job with the atmosphere. People expect ladies to be safe here and act accordingly."

"I'm glad Sir Bartley had the idea of the tea shop. There's nothing else in London quite like it."

"I believe it was my mother's idea, but my father enacted the idea beautifully. I expect we'll be copied in time."

Four hours later, Alys was dressed in her best, the reception gown she'd worn for the investiture, and stood next to the wedding cake in a corner of the second best ballroom in a duke's Belgravia home. The bride was his granddaughter and she was marrying an up-and-coming member of parliament, someone sure to have his own title one day.

When a footman opened the door and signaled to her, she put on her apron. The wedding ceremony must be nearly over. Various family retainers entered to serve beverages and pastry.

She wondered if this would become the new style. Normally, bride's families had a luncheon after a morning wedding and the cake would be served at the table, but this wedding had been far too large for that. Instead, the wedding had been at two P.M. followed by dessert.

The wealthy did set trends, after all. And this way of doing things wouldn't hurt her business at all. In fact, it might enhance it as the cake would be on display longer.

Since a receiving line had been set up in front of the ballroom doors, in order that guests might receive a bit of good luck by touching the bride or groom, guests began to spill into the ballroom in small groups.

The scent of evergreen from boughs hung under the gaslight sconces began to be overset by that of perfume and warm bodies. Alys fended off the guests who went right toward her cake and sent them to the coffee, tea, wine, and pastries. The bride and groom planned to cut the cake together to symbolize their first task as a married couple, and feed each other a bit of cake to symbolize their commitment to provide for one another.

"How beautiful," an elderly woman said, clasping her hands to her bosom. "Who made that lovely cake, dear?"

"I did." Alys smiled. "This is a Redcake's three-tier masterpiece."

"Ah, Redcake's. I do love their marmalade. How does one order a wedding cake?"

"If you come to the Emporium bakery, we can show you drawings of cakes and help you design what you need."

"I may just do that. My daughter is marrying in April."

"We'd love to assist," Alys assured her. "If you send us a note in advance or come in to schedule an appointment, we can have tasting cakes ready."

"Wedding cakes are very traditional. Doesn't everyone do the same cake?"

"No, ma'am, we have different options depending on what kind of fruit is used, how much butter, the kinds of alcohol in the cake, and so forth."

"Fascinating." The woman was joined by an acquaintance and they asked numerous questions about frostings and decorations.

"Orange water is most traditional for frosting flavor," Alys told them, and was about to suggest alternatives when her gaze was caught by a tall, austere man entering the room, his arm gripped by an angular lady in a rose-colored gown.

She wondered why she'd noticed him, until she saw the way the gasolier revealed a hint of sun in his hair. *Hatbrook.* Her entire body tingled traitorously as she put name to the broad-shouldered, impeccably dressed gentleman.

Of all the guests who might enjoy a slice of cake, he'd likely take the most pleasure in it, with his keen appreciation of Redcake's. She'd heard the cakies gossip about how often he came into the tea shop. Most of their clientele was female.

"I'm sorry," she said, when one of the ladies repeated a question. "Yes, of course we could make a mint-flavored frosting."

The second lady put her hand to her ear. "Speak up, please."

Alys repeated herself at twice the volume.

The woman nodded. "But only for the groom's cake. Chocolate mint, my son would love that."

"Are your children marrying each other?" Alys asked with a wink.

The ladies tittered.

"No, no, my dear. Two separate ceremonies, I assure you."

"Wonderful. Can I answer any more questions for you?" She pulled out a cake-ordering pad and wrote down the specifications of each as she had been told them, then handed the sheets to the prospective customers. "If you bring these in with you we won't have to start again."

"Very thoughtful, Miss Redcake," the deafest of the two said loudly.

At those words, Lord Hatbrook's head snapped up, as if he was a bloodhound going on point. Alys's attention had never really left him and even though he was several feet away, his glance met hers.

He nodded in her direction and she mimicked the motion, pleased with his recognition, though it made her breath catch in her throat. She hadn't expected such a gentleman to notice her.

"I look forward to seeing you both at the Emporium," she said. "I'd suggest quite a bit of notice, especially if you find you want this particular cake, as the alcohol needs to soak in for some time."

"Do you keep cakes on hand?"

"Yes, but since your son's wedding is at the height of the nuptial season I can't guarantee the best cake with less than a month's notice."

"We will order well in advance," the first lady said. "Let's get a cup of tea, Mrs. Minter."

Alys smiled at the ladies and kept her smile pasted to her face as Lord Hatbrook approached. "Your lordship."

"Hello." His gaze drifted to the wedding cake, then back to her face.

"It's Alys," she said quickly, realizing she didn't have her name tag and of course he wouldn't remember a cakie's name. Or perhaps he recognized her from the investiture instead of from the tea shop?

"You told Lady Burnham you were Miss Redcake," he said with a frown.

"I am. Alys Redcake, the eldest daughter of Sir Bartley Redcake." She stood taller, proud to represent her family at a prestigious event.

"I see. I must have met your brother then. Sergeant Redcake?" His gaze moved down, then back up to her eyes again.

Or did he not remember her at all? "He's my twin."

"You don't look anything alike." He seemed fixated on her nose.

With difficulty, she refrained from scratching at it. "He takes after my mother. I have three living siblings. Matilda and I look like Father, and Rose and Gawain have Mother's hair and build."

"And all of you work in the business?"

The angular lady joined them.

"Ah, there you are, Mother."

"How tiresome," Lady Hatbrook said, her fingers worrying at a fold on her fashionable gown. "Why ever are you speaking to this person?"

Alys watched as Lord Hatbrook's eyes briefly pinched closed, as if his mother's mere voice gave him a headache. "Miss Redcake's brother served with Judah, Mother, until he was wounded last year shortly after the Battalion moved to India. He is in that photograph Judah sent us recently."

"I see. I'd like a cup of tea."

This last was directed at Alys, but the mother of the bride had begged her not to leave the cake, for fear that a certain mentally challenged guest would slip away from his supervision and thrust his fist into her creation.

"Yes, your ladyship." Alys raised her hand and waved, hoping to catch one of the servant's eyes. When that didn't work, she craned her neck, hoping to see a footman, but they were all blocked by the crowd.

"Whatever are you doing, girl?"

"I am so sorry but I've been asked not to leave the cake."

Lady Hatbrook offered no response other than a bored expression.

"I'll get it, Mother." A slight smile fluttered one side of his lips.

The marquess dashed off. Alys had the impression he was thrilled to leave her with his mother.

"Do you like wedding cake, Lady Hatbrook?" she asked.

"Not particularly." Her nose went into the air. "I prefer soda crackers. Better for the digestion. Huntley and Palmers makes an excellent product."

"Yes, like Redcake's they serve the royal family, I believe," Alys said.

"They have a warrant here, as well as for various European royal families," Lady Hatbrook said. "Does Redcake's?"

"No, we are a domestic concern," Alys said.

Lady Hatbrook sniffed. "I see."

"It's more difficult to transport our baked goods," Alys said, feeling the need to defend Redcake's.

Lady Hatbrook sniffed again. Thankfully, her son returned with a cup of tea.

"With milk, just as you like it," he said.

Alys noticed telltale crumbs at the corner of his mouth. She'd never really noticed his mouth before. He had a beautifully plump lower lip. His top lip was thinner, though pronounced, but his mouth was very nearly oversized. She wondered if he'd have dimples in his cheeks if he smiled, to match the slight cleft in his chin. Overall, it was a very sensual mouth. How would it feel against her lips?

"Did you enjoy the wafers, your lordship?" she asked politely.

"I do not enjoy the flavor of lemon as much as some others," he admitted, "but it is purely a matter of personal taste."

"It is the bride's favorite flavor," she said. "You can also find small strawberry jam tarts at the table."

"Sadly, they have all been eaten and the servant must go back to the kitchen for more," he said.

"How tiresome," Alys agreed, glad not to force her smile any longer.

"This is tiresome," Lady Hatbrook said. "I'd like to sit now. It's not as if her brother is here to discuss the army with you, and I don't understand why you find it so interesting. Sometimes I think you wish you were the second son so you could have gone to India."

With a mother like her, Alys could understand why. "It was a pleasure to meet you, Lady Hatbrook. Would you like me to see if we can procure a plate of soda crackers for you?"

"No thank you," she said, raising her chin and walking away. Lord Hatbrook shrugged in Alys's direction and followed her.

Alys permitted herself a small smile. Her mother might be dramatic and dreamy, but at least she was pleasant.

Alys entered her shared dressing room at home, intent on removing her damp uniform and putting on a warm dressing gown. A cup of tea in front of the fireplace with *The Vanished Diamond* by Jules Verne, a book she wanted to read for the simple reason that the heroine's name was Alice, were her plans for the rest of the afternoon. She wished her mother would allow her to change how she spelled her name, but her mother found "Alice" too common. She found "Alys" to be silly.

Instead of solitude, she found her sisters bent over one of their new dresses, laid out on the dressing-room floor. As it was a rather small room, she had to edge around the rug to reach the wardrobe.

"Is something wrong with the dress?" At least the fire was going and the room was toasty. She unpinned her hair in hope that the damp edges would dry.

"Change into something suitable," Matilda hissed. "We have a caller."

"You do?"

"Yes. Lady Lillian sent a note around. She's coming for tea."

Lady Lillian Cander was the youngest daughter of Earl Gerrick and had been at finishing school with Rose, though she was around Matilda's age. Alys suspected her of being a bad influence, though she'd never actually heard her say anything truly inappropriate. Still, many a conversation ended abruptly when she entered a room when the girl was in town.

"I don't need to join you," Alys said. "I just want to relax with a book. You have no idea how beastly the weather is today."

"If it wasn't so bad I'd have gone shopping," Rose said. "Lily is bringing us an invitation to a musicale. We're trying to decide if this dress is suitable."

"I should think not. It's a ball gown."

"What do you wear to a musical evening?" Rose fluttered her hands. "Oh, Mother should have prepared us for this."

"She may not have been invited to many musical evenings herself," Alys pointed out. "I think your dinner dresses should do nicely. The new ones you ordered in October?"

"But they aren't new. We'll be meeting fashionable people. There will be Americans there, most likely. We can't be dressed in old rags when American heiresses are in new gowns."

Alys blinked. Rags? Hadn't her sisters ever seen what poor unfortunates wore compared to them? "Matilda, can you help me with my buttons? I'm soaked."

Her sister helped her disentangle herself from the damp fabric while Rose continued to fret.

"Are we in direct competition with Americans for some reason?" Alys inquired in a low voice.

"Rose feels our future husbands are probably the sort of British gentlemen who might marry an American shipping or mill or banking heiress," Matilda said in an equally low tone. "I believe she is right, and since we don't have the mystique of an American at least we'd better dress properly."

"Ah," Alys sighed.

Matilda helped her strip down to her combinations, then found fresh stockings and a tea gown suitable for an aristocratic caller. Before Alys knew what was happening, she was dressed for Lady Lillian instead of Jules Verne.

"You have the most spinsterish taste in clothing," Rose said. "Combinations? Really?"

"They're comfortable," Alys said. "And don't tell me I need to suffer for fashion. I don't spend my days swanning around like you two."

Matilda had opened her mouth to protest when a housemaid knocked.

"Your guest is in the parlor," she informed them.

Rose squealed and rushed from the room, followed by the others. As Alys entered the parlor behind Matilda a few minutes later, she heard another squeal as Rose greeted Lady Lillian.

The young woman had an air of refusing no pleasure life had to offer. Overly plump, wearing jewels more suited to an opera performance, she dressed in a gown so lacy and flounced she could have been trying to imitate a wedding cake.

If wedding cakes were decorated in that shade of plum.

Her hair was raven dark and curled into separate sausage ringlets that dangled unattractively around her cheeks. But, her smile was genuinely warm as she greeted them.

"Did you secure us the invitations?" Rose gasped.

"Oh, yes. I called on Mrs. Lennox this morning with Mama and she said she would send Lady Redcake an invitation in tomorrow morning's post."

"How thrilling," Matilda said, clasping her hands above her bosom.

Alys narrowed her eyes. Something had changed with Matilda's silhouette. She gasped, then put her hand over her mouth. Nothing could be said with a guest present, but was her sister wearing a bust-improver? Good heavens. She really should have stayed for the rest of that dressmaker visit. The bustle was quite enough artificiality, thank you.

"Are you a music fan, Miss Redcake?" Lady Lillian fluttered her eyelashes at Alys as a maid brought in a tea tray.

"Certainly, when it is well played."

Lady Lillian giggled. "There's no hope of that. The Misses

Lennox are frightfully tone deaf, but have such a china doll prettiness the most handsome young gentlemen come to such evenings."

"Gentlemen with titles?" Rose inquired.

"Gentlemen with money?" Matilda asked.

Lady Lillian giggled again. "The Lennoxes have good dowries, enough so that some of the men could be fortune hunters. You must be prepared to listen to the gossip and decide who might be most suitable for you."

"A fortune hunter with a title might be fine," Rose said. "As long as he has property. I'm sure Father plans to give us good dowries."

"Has Father ever said anything to you, Alys?" Matilda inquired.

"Certainly not." Alys bit savagely into a buttered scone.

"Of course not, because you don't want to marry," Matilda sighed.

"Is Sir Bartley going to insist on Alys marrying first?" Lady Lillian asked.

"He'd better not," Rose said. "Otherwise we'll all be spinsters. I'd like to marry by the age of twenty, so Matilda needs to find a husband this year."

Matilda choked on her tea. "Not just anyone, Rose. I want to fall in love."

"Make sure he's suitable," Rose said. "So we don't waste time with objections."

Alys rubbed her forehead. It was beginning to hurt. Lady Lillian looked at her with confusion. When Alys moved her hand back to her forehead she discovered she'd left a smear of butter.

"Oh, Miss Redcake," Lady Lillian said, handing her a handkerchief. "I'm forever doing that. Be careful, or you'll develop spots like I do."

That explained her application of powder. "Do you have hopes of marrying in eighteen-eighty-seven?" Alys inquired.

"Oh, I'm already engaged," Lady Lillian said carelessly. "He's nearly fifty and lives in Yorkshire, but he's the heir to an earldom. Pots of money, but quite the miser, I've been led to believe. I'm in no rush to actually marry him."

"How did you come to be engaged to him?" Alys asked.

"He's my cousin. Third, I believe, which is actually a rather distant connection in my family. We marry in and out of three or four different titles, keeps all the money in the family."

"Do you find that to be true of all noble families?" Matilda asked. "Is it so hard for someone like us to break in?"

"If you're wealthy you'll find someone who needs your money," Lady Lillian said. "I'd introduce Rose to my brother as he would certainly find her looks appealing, but he doesn't need the blunt."

"Not very romantic," Matilda whispered.

"Maybe you shouldn't look for a title," Lady Lillian said. "A politician might be wiser. They are often given titles because of their service. And they are often connected to the best families, or at least are very intelligent."

Matilda nodded. "I wonder how we would meet such gentlemen?"

Lady Lillian waved a plump hand. "I'll help you search. I have all the time in the world. There's no chance of my fiancé visiting London."

"Oh, you are the best of friends," Rose squealed and gave her a hug.

"We saw the most distinguished man at the investiture," Matilda said, when the friends had disengaged and were holding their teacups again.

"Oh? Do tell."

"Alys said he's the Marquess of Hatbrook. Is he attached?"

Alys sat forward in her chair, desperate for relevant gossip. She remembered his lips with longing, a strange sensation for an avowed spinster.

"No. He's an odd sort, completely focused on making money out of his properties in Sussex. Stays down there a great deal. You'd think he'd leave everything to his man of business but he's not the usual sort of marquess."

"Surely he needs to marry." Matilda smiled.

"He has a brother," Alys said, to keep the conversation about Hatbrook going. "The brother knows Gawain, actually. They served together in India."

Rose's eyes widened. "You didn't tell us?"

"I didn't know until today. He was at the wedding." She felt a thrill of triumph that she had seen him and her sisters had not.

Rose dropped her head into her hands. "And he saw a Miss Redcake playing the servant? Oh, Alys. You need to leave your position!"

Her pleasure was trumped by indignation. "I like it."

"She's right, Miss Redcake. You don't want to hurt your sisters' chances for matrimonial bliss."

"Matrimony, perhaps, but certainly not bliss. You aren't anticipating such on your own behalf."

"Oh, Monty and I will rub along well enough," Lady Lillian said. "It's the family way."

"But no love," Matilda said.

"We love our family. We'll have children. That's enough. But I wouldn't dream of wasting my efforts on someone like Hatbrook. He's very reserved. Not likely to fall head over heels in love."

"His mother doesn't seem the sort to find him a wife," Alys observed, remembering that most difficult lady.

"I've never been introduced to her," Lady Lillian said. "She doesn't move about in the best society circles. Some old scandal from before I was born."

"You seem to know a great deal about the marquess," Matilda said.

Not nearly enough. The thought had Alys frowning. How silly to find a marquess the least bit interesting. The next thing you knew she'd be as ridiculous as her sisters, and her far too old to make a match, even if she wanted to, which she didn't.

"I promise I will attend the musicale, in such spinsterish garb that no one could possibly think me marriage material. That should allow you two to flourish despite my existence," Alys said. "Now, may I go read my book?"

"I regret to inform you that I will be moving to Manchester next month," Sir John told Michael as they sat in his office on the gloomy Tuesday morning before Christmas.

Michael's jaw popped as he ground his teeth together. "Had you planned this all along?"

The man blushed, despite his mature years. "It seems I will be marrying by special license directly after the holiday, your lordship."

He's gotten the girl pregnant. Michael wondered if she had schemed, once she knew he was being knighted, in order not to lose him. "I'm sorry to hear that. I mean, congratulations, of course."

Another gesture was clearly expected, given Smythe's air, so he stood and shook the man's hand.

"I do wish you'd found an apprentice."

"I am sorry. But I'll be happy to pass your affairs on to Mumford and Egglesworth. They are an excellent firm and will serve you well."

"Yes, they have a distinguished reputation," Michael said. "Thank you for smoothing the way."

"There is one thing I wish I'd had time to do," Sir John said. "You have a bit of cash available at the moment, and really should invest it so it works for you."

"Absolutely. What is your idea?"

"At the investiture, it was rumored that Sir Bartley Redcake is planning to sell his tea shop and emporium in London, now that he's bought that property from the Duke of Devonshire. I believe he intends to be a gentleman of leisure."

"Redcake's, eh?" He would be proud to own such a place. It did a brisk business and sold exactly the sorts of things he liked. He could imagine mentioning it when he saw their cakes and things at parties, horrifying the snobbish aristocrats who thought being in trade was terrible. Being in hock was worse, in his opinion. Besides he needed to do more with his time than spend it in an endless round of sport and parties.

"Should I ask Mumford to make inquiries? I do suggest you work with him. The senior Egglesworth is quite ill, and the heir is only twenty-five. Very intelligent but not so experienced, whereas Mumford is a solid forty years of age."

"Very well." He had a fleeting thought of lively Alys Redcake's pride in her wedding cake business, and wondered if she knew of her father's plans. She did not seem to be the sort of female who craved leisure.

"Once again, I am sorry."

"No, no. Your future is in Manchester. Even a solicitor must follow his heart." Where would Alys Redcake's heart lead her if she lost her business? Silly to wonder, but she was an uncommonly pretty girl. Natural for a man to think of it.

Sir John's mouth widened into a smile. He had quite lost his businesslike mien since being knighted. "Indeed, your lordship. I wish you the best, and if you ever have any interests in the north, I will be happy to offer my services as ever."

"Thank you." Michael shook his hand again and walked out of the office, bemused. While he had expected something like this, he'd thought he had months before it became a reality. Still, his step quickened as he thought of owning Redcake's himself. The queen would never keep all the Scotch trifle from him again.

His left hand trembled, reminding him it was rapidly approaching luncheon. He decided to visit the tea shop, perhaps meet with Sir Bartley Redcake on his own behalf. It would be best to take a more active hand in things while he was in town and didn't know his new man of business. He was sure Sir John wouldn't set up a meeting until after the holidays.

Chapter Four

Alys was bringing out a rack of the factory-made Christmas cakes early that afternoon when she heard a plummy, aristocratic woman's voice say loudly, "I want to speak to that girl."

"What girl, madam?" inquired bakery manager Ralph Popham, who was spending the day out front helping, since so many people were buying treats for holiday gatherings.

"That extremely orange-haired person."

Alys saw Popham scratch the back of his head as she turned the corner with the rack. "I'm afraid you'll have to be more specific, madam. We have more than one orange-haired female working at Redcake's."

"You may call me 'my lady,' young man. I am the Marchioness of Hatbrook."

"Ah, my lady."

Alys heard Popham clear his throat as she lifted a cake from the rack, neatly packaged into one of their distinctive pure-white boxes embossed in gold and tied with red ribbon.

"May I inquire as to where you encountered the orange-haired person?"

"At Viscount Manater's daughter's wedding," she said. "The girl said she had designed the cake and made the pastry order. My son, the Marquess, is excessively fond of the tarts that were offered there."

Alys dropped her cake. Lady Hatbrook was asking for her? Oh no! She couldn't waste the cake. She fell to her knees and delicately untied the ribbon and checked the cake. Good. The box had protected it. She switched it for another cake at the bottom tier of the rack and picked that one up instead.

"Ah, you must be referring to Alys Redcake, my lady."

"Redcake, you say?"

"Yes, she's a daughter of the family."

Alys took a deep breath and stepped out from the back room, holding the cake box as a kind of armor. *Please, don't let her have found a hair in her cake slice or something of the sort.* "My lady. What a pleasure to see you again."

Lady Hatbrook sniffed. "I thought your father was wealthy. Why ever are you employed?"

Alys heard a little gasp from one of the girls working the counter on the opposite side. "I like what I do, your ladyship. I love making cakes."

"Did you make that one?" The marchioness indicated the box that she held.

"No, ma'am. This was made in our factory up near Bristol. I did work there when I was young, before we moved to London. This is a shilling Christmas cake."

Lady Hatbrook sneered. "I hope you can do better than that."

"Ma'am?"

"For my ball."

Alys tried to follow. "You'd like Redcake's to supply your ball, your ladyship?"

"Yes. December thirty-first. About three hundred people, I think. I'd like a tiered cake appropriate to the occasion and pastries, the kind the marquess likes."

"He likes trifle best," Alys said.

The marchioness raised an eyebrow.

"Your ladyship. But I've seen him eat scones as well. And you said he liked tarts."

"Were you listening to my conversation with this employee from somewhere secret? Not a very attractive quality."

Alys swallowed. "I was around the corner performing my duties, ma'am. I'm sorry if I overheard part of the conversation."

She waved a thin hand. "Can you do it?"

"Oh yes, my lady. Let me get my book."

Popham moved behind her and started unloading the Christmas cakes into the display case while Alys discussed the cake with the marchioness. They decided on four tiers, three of which were very large and one small decorative one at the top made of chocolate batter, while the rest were fruitcake.

"That way my son can offer chocolate to his cronies if he wishes," she said.

"An eight-inch round will serve about twenty guests. Will that be enough for his lordship?"

"Yes, I think so. The majority will accept what they are given."

"And the rest of the cake should serve about two hundred and ninety," Alys said, after figuring the sums in her head. "Now, let us discuss the cake topper."

"Not Christmas or wedding," the marchioness said with a sniff.

"Of course not. I could design the year in marzipan." Alys sketched quickly, showing how she should anchor them upright.

"I like that," the marchioness said. "Now, about the pastries."

She had strong thoughts on that, making sure the marquess would have all his favorites. Alys felt faintly alarmed at the list because he seemed to eat a great deal of pastry for one who wasn't portly. Did his clothing hide stays? She wondered if she would hear creaking when he moved.

No, she couldn't believe that. He moved with too much ease, too much intensity.

"Is that everything then?" Alys inquired, scribbling notes on the order, trying to push thoughts of the handsome marquess aside.

"Quite. You may send the bill to my son's man of business."

"Yes, your ladyship. Are there any further instructions?"

"No, simply have everything delivered that afternoon. We have plenty of staff so you needn't be present."

Alys nodded. "That is the usual way. I shall put this on the delivery list for the afternoon of the thirty-first. Thank you for your order, ma'am."

Lady Hatbrook sniffed and turned away, then stepped back. "Before I go I think I'd better have one of those cakes."

"Which ones?"

She pointed to the case holding the shilling Christmas cakes. "Those."

"Would you like to see how they are decorated?" Alys pointed to a displayed cake on a stand inside the glass case. "They all look like this, then we can personalize them."

Instead of responding, Lady Hatbrook opened her reticule and pulled out a shilling and dropped it on the counter. "I believe this is the price?"

"Yes, ma'am." Alys took a box from the rack behind her, opened it to make sure the cake was in perfect condition, then handed it over.

The marchioness sniffed again, took the box and turned smartly, then marched away without another word.

Alys wondered if her ladyship was as addicted to cake as her son was to Scotch trifle. And if so, how did she manage to stay so thin? She didn't look healthy. In fact, her skin hung loosely at her neck and her rose gown didn't appear to fit properly, loose in some places and stretched in others. Perhaps she meant to give the cake to her maid.

The next afternoon, Ralph Popham found Alys piping "Holiday Wishes" on a fancy Christmas cake order.

"Your father sent word that you're to come up and see him," he said.

"I have to finish this," she said, not taking her eyes off the red frosting.

"I'm told Sir Bartley is in quite a mood," the bakery manager said dourly.

"He is always terribly concerned that we won't sell out of the shilling cakes each year, but is so jolly at home on Christmas when we do," Alys confided. "Can you believe it is only two days away? The season has passed quickly."

"I don't know if it is that," Popham said. "Word came down that he's in one of those red-faced rages he has."

"Oh, dear. I hope one of Mr. Hellman's apprentices didn't tip over the delivery wagon again." Alys set down her pastry bag and rubbed at an itchy spot over one eye. "Betsy, can you finish for me, please?"

Betsy Popham closed a box lid over a cake and came over eagerly.

Alys knew she wanted to learn cake decorating so she could leave being a cakie behind.

"It only needs an 'e' and an 's' there at the end," Alys said. "You can see the lettering I did. Just match that and it will be ready to pack up."

"I'll be very careful, Miss Redcake," Betsy promised.

"Good girl," Popham said. "Now, Alys, you'd better get upstairs."

"Thank you, Mr. Popham." Alys removed her apron and unfolded her sleeves, then rebuttoned her cuffs. One thing that had changed over the years was that she had to appear the lady in front of her father, instead of as an employee. He had yelled at her on the factory lines just like any other young person when she'd been a child; there had been no special treatment then. Not for Gawain or Arthur either, but unlike Arthur, she and Gawain had been good at their jobs.

Frosting had been her assignment and no one had ever done the job faster. Her brothers, however, had worked the batter mixing line. She remembered the bruising on their hands. Arthur had even broken a finger and somehow it had become infected, preventing him from working for a time. At least he'd had a family who wasn't desperate for the income, unlike so many of their fellow workers. Now her cousin, Lewis, had invented machines to simplify the process, helping to make her father wealthy.

Alys climbed the staircases to the third floor where her father's offices were. Certificates naming Employees of the Month lined the wood-paneled walls. Redcake's and her family had come far from those early days, when her father inherited a mill mired in debt.

"Miss Redcake." Ewan Hales, her father's secretary, stood. A man of about her age, though rapidly balding, she suspected he had romantic notions about her.

She nodded. "My father wants to see me?"

Ewan stepped out from behind his desk. "Yes, miss." He opened the heavy, paneled door for her.

"Hello, Father," she said cheerfully, stepping in. "I haven't seen you downstairs. Normally you are all fired up during Christmas week!"

Sir Bartley looked up from the papers he was perusing on his large, untidy desk. His hair, so like hers though faded, matched the mess, as if he'd been running his hands through it. The difference was his sack suit was clean. Not a bit of flour nor sheen of butter darkened the coat or vest. His tie was knotted and tucked perfectly, not askew like usual.

"Sit," he said.

Alys had a sinking feeling, and wished she could remain standing. Her hands moved behind her back and she clutched her fingers together. Now what? Had her sisters complained about her?

Her father stared at her. After a moment of eyes locking, she cleared her throat and sat down in one of the two chairs in front of his desk, grabbing at the armrests with icy fingers.

Her father lifted his hand. She turned, realizing Ewan still stood in the room. Good heavens, had he spoken to her father about marrying her? No. She breathed a sigh of relief as Ewan walked out.

But then, confusion resumed when Ewan returned a moment later, followed by Ralph Popham. If he was joining her, why hadn't he said so? If this was to be a sales meeting, she wasn't prepared.

"My accounts?" she said. "Perhaps I should find my journal."

"That won't be necessary," her father said. "Ralph, sit down."

Mr. Popham's expression was even more hangdog than usual as he sat next to her. She raised her eyebrows at him, hoping he could communicate to her somehow, but he shook his head slightly and turned away.

She bit her lip and looked at her father.

"You've worked at Redcake's for, what, fourteen years now, Alys?"

"Eighteen," she said sharply. "I'm twenty-six."

"Quite right," her father said. "A long time."

"Yes, it is my second home."

"To be sure. But we have a better home now, don't we, girl? We've come a long way up in the world. And now, I have a knighthood to match."

He spoke as if to himself, more reflective than Alys was used to her father being.

"I'm very proud of you, sir."

"Thank you, daughter. I need to tell you of my disappointment."

Alys swallowed. She had done nothing wrong, she was certain of this. "Sir?"

"You are a Miss Redcake. That means something now."

"Of course it does. I'm very proud to be connected to Redcake's."

"Not to Redcake's," her father said, steepling his fingers. "To me."

She'd never seen him make that gesture before. It was as if he changed before her very eyes. "You aren't proud of me, Father?"

"You do not behave as a young lady should."

She wondered if this was about Ewan after all. Or, she thought in horror, of Ralph Popham. He was widowed, after all, but she was only eight or nine years older than Betsy.

"I am a hard and efficient worker, sir. I am proud of my accomplishments."

Her father stood and pounded on the desk with one fist. The reverberation made her chair shake. "They are the wrong accomplishments, miss. Your sisters, they are young ladies. You, on the other hand—"

"What?" she whispered.

"I understand you are promoting yourself and your cakes, among the aristocracy, of all things. Do you never think of your sisters, their prospects?"

"I was trying to grow our business! You know our quiet time is coming, and I did get orders from the Manater wedding. A marchioness, no less, came to make a large order. Mr. Popham was there!"

"Exactly," her father said.

Ralph sank lower into his chair. Alys fancied he wanted to become invisible.

"I did a good thing," Alys insisted. "Nothing different than before, except that as Redcake's becomes more prominent, our opportunities are better. I had to refuse Lord Hatbrook his order just last month, because the queen had ordered all the Scotch trifle we had on hand."

"A Miss Redcake cannot be having these conversations, my dear. The daughter of a knight should not be a shopgirl."

"I'm not a shopgirl. I am responsible for the wedding cakes."

"Not any longer, my girl. You shall return home at once. Your prospects have changed. Your mother shall decide what to do with you."

"But I'm grown," Alys said. "I have my own money. I'm capable."

"You are my daughter," he said. "I will not have you displaying yourself as little better than a servant. Your mother is Lady Redcake. You have a substantial dowry."

Alys wondered what her young, factory-girl self would have said to that, to hear her father firing her and telling her she had a large pot of money available to her, when she'd cried herself to sleep for months after her father sent her to work, before she decided she liked it better than going to the village school.

"I'm happy here," Alys said. "I could get lodgings, leave the household so that Matilda and Rose aren't affected by me."

"Don't be ridiculous," her father snapped. "You no longer have employment. Return home to your mother at once."

"Would you speak so to Gawain?"

"Gawain will inherit my business one day."

"But I'm the one who loves it," Alys said.

Ralph shifted in his seat.

"You don't understand business. You are a cake decorator," Sir Bartley said dismissively. "Do not presume you know more than you do."

"Gawain has no more education than me."

"And no more than me, either. My fortune makes changes now. No daughters of the Redcake family will ever need to work again!" he shouted.

"But what if we want to?"

"You only think that because you've never known a better option."

"I'm happy here."

"Do not behave so unbecomingly," he said. "Now, go."

Alys stood, her back very straight. Without looking at Mr. Popham, she turned and stepped to the closed door. She left the offices without looking at Ewan.

As she reached the outer door, she heard the secretary say, "Goodbye, Miss Redcake."

With a hot rush of shame, she realized he'd known what her father had planned to do to her. Furious, humiliated, she stalked downstairs to collect her coat, hat, and reticule.

Ten minutes later she stepped out the back door next to the loading dock. She hadn't said good-bye to anyone. Surely this wasn't over yet. After Christmas she'd change her father's mind. He'd see how unhappy she was embroidering with her sisters. He'd miss her sure hand in the cake department.

As she walked down the street toward home, she realized the timing meant she wouldn't receive her Christmas bonus on Friday along with everyone else.

"Blast him!" she muttered under her breath. She kept her head down in the hope no one heard her unladylike outburst.

The air was thoroughly foul and she nearly wished her father had waited until the end of the day to ruin her life so she could have taken the carriage home with him. Instead, she had to tramp home under the darkening sky. A fleck of snow dampened her nose from time to time as she walked, while the revoltingly fetid, wet pavement wetted her black skirt. At least she'd never have to wear this particular dress again. It was her cakie uniform, worn for those times when she dashed into the front of Redcake's on some mission.

Blast Lady Hatbrook! This was all her fault! Alys swung her reticule savagely in the air. It slammed back into her side just below where her corset ended along her hip. If only the marchioness hadn't made such an unpleasant scene, called for her so loudly.

She knew her father had a good head for business. If he'd made mistakes before today she hadn't known it. But still, didn't he realize she'd made the firm an excellent profit?

"Blast him," she said again, catching a hint of surprise on the sooty face of a lamplighter.

By the time she made it home, she too had soot on her face. It seemed the very sky had pressed down upon her, bringing foul odors and making a clear vision of the streets all but impossible.

Pounds opened the door for her. She entered quickly and handed him her coat and hat as soon as she could wrestle the damp garments from her body.

"I'd like a bath, please."

"I will tell Lucy." Pounds bowed and left her in the foyer.

Alys stared down at the marble floor for a moment, then glanced up to find herself staring at a white marble statue set into a recess between two fluttering gas lamps. The statue was of a shepherdess.

"I wish my life were as simple as yours." She saluted the statue like a simpleton and climbed the steps to her dressing room, hoping tears would refrain from dripping down her face until she reached privacy.

Alys couldn't wear mourning to the musicale the next afternoon, but she certainly felt the loss of her position as keenly as any death. Rose had told her she looked pale as a phantom and that she should pinch her cheeks and possibly apply the lightest touch of rouge to her lips.

Alys hadn't replied to the unladylike suggestion. Her father hadn't come home for dinner and he'd left for Redcake's early. She'd have faulted him for avoiding her, but knew how busy the emporium was just before Christmas. Her place was there too!

She wiped snow from her nose in the Lennoxes' foyer and tried not to stare at Matilda's enlarged bosom when her sister removed her heavy mantle. Dear God, was this to be her main concern now? Not orders and customers but her silly sister's clothing mishaps?

When they were all tidied, they followed Lady Redcake through the house to the music room. The large, carpeted space held a low dais for performers. Alys saw a piano and a harp and wondered if the sisters played as badly as they were reputed to sing.

Rose caught Alys's sleeve. "He's here!" she whispered.

"Who?"

Rose lifted her chin. "That marquess! Lady Lillian was right, the most handsome men do come here."

Alys followed the line of her sister's chin and saw Lord Hatbrook, in profile, deep in conversation with another young man who looked vaguely familiar. Then, the second man's lips curled at one corner in a mischievous, dimpled grin and she recognized him as the customer who had tormented her the day she'd met Hatbrook.

The marquess folded his arms across his chest and tapped his booted foot against the floor, even though there was no music as of yet. He seemed twitchy to her. Perhaps he was as uncomfortable in society as she, though that seemed unlikely. She glanced around the surrounding faces to see if she could spot his mother, but didn't see her.

"Oh, Miss Redcake," Lady Lillian said, coming toward them with outstretched hands. "Is this not the dampest Christmas you can remember?"

"Foul beyond belief," Alys agreed.

"But it's Christmas," Rose said, taking her friend's hands. "And it's so pretty inside."

A *Tannenbaum* stood majestically in one corner, decorated with tinsel, gingerbread cookies, and lit candles. A wreath was hung at each window. Though it was very faint, Alys could hear carolers outside. Ivy and holly were entwined below the gas lamps.

"Mistletoe!" Matilda gasped, coming up beside them.

Alys squinted, and finally saw a small bunch almost hidden beside the Christmas tree.

"Can you imagine the scandal?" Matilda said, almost wistfully.

"Don't squint. It makes you look like an old maid," Rose whispered balefully.

Just then, Lord Hatbrook's friend turned and stared straight at Alys. He looked confused for a moment as if he couldn't place her, but he was staring so directly that she bobbed the tiniest curtsy. He bowed his head then returned to his conversation, but a moment later Hatbrook turned. His gaze caught hers and she felt a flutter in her chest. Rose caught at her arm and opened her mouth, but then Alys saw Lady Hatbrook appear in the open doorway between the tree and her son.

Her eyes narrowed when she saw Alys. Alys turned toward Rose and drew her sister a few steps away.

"What is it? Your mouth was hanging quite open. You must be more discreet."

"I just saw Lady Hatbrook," Alys confessed, feeling a lump in her stomach that even a strong cup of tea might not dissolve. "Oh Rose, I have played the servant with that family, and now Father has taken away my position. But it might be too late to save you or Matilda!"

"What are you babbling about?" Lewis said, coming toward them.

Alys noticed her cousin's white-blond hair was damp, hiding its natural curl.

"Did you forget your hat again, cousin?" Rose asked.

Lewis ignored her. "What is too late, Alys?"

Alys tried to smile. "How can my sisters make good marriages when I've been serving the aristocracy at Redcake's? We reek of trade."

"Uncle Bartley is a tradesman," Lewis said. "We aren't aristocrats and it is silly to think our status has really changed."

Rose opened her mouth, her nose wrinkled in outrage, but Alys appreciated the good sense. What did she care if Lady Hatbrook recognized her? Lady Lillian might belong in this room, but she and her family did not. They were the interlopers and Lady Hatbrook could do what she liked.

Then she glanced up and saw Lord Hatbrook only two steps away from her. His mother was nowhere in sight, but his friend stood at her elbow.

Hatbrook turned slightly to her left and spoke. "Sergeant Redcake, I am happy to see you again."

Her brother must have come in with Lewis as he stood there now. He shook the marquess's hand.

"A pleasure, sir. May I introduce my sisters, Alys, Matilda, and Rose, and my cousin, Mr. Lewis Noble?"

"I have had the pleasure of meeting Miss Redcake a time or two," the marquess said. "May I make my friend Theodore Bliven known to you all?"

After introductions were made, the marquess said, "The sergeant here served with Judah until recently."

"You must have some tales to tell, Sergeant," Mr. Bliven said. "Don't envy you, man."

"Better forgotten." Gawain scowled. "I work at Redcake's now."

Mr. Bliven grinned. "Ah, then you are the envy of Lord Hatbrook. I do believe Redcake's is his most favorite spot in London."

Lord Hatbrook caught Alys rolling her eyes and the corners of his eyes tightened as if he held back a smile. She flushed.

"I trust business is excellent for the season?" Hatbrook inquired.

Alys found herself fighting tears. "Excuse me, your lordship. Something in my eye." She turned away.

"I'll take her," Lewis said, grasping her by the elbow as Alys put a hand to her cheek to stop any tears from dripping. This forestalled her sisters from having to leave the conversation, as they most assuredly did not.

As they walked away, Lewis said, "You're going to have to be stronger than this, Alys."

"He took away what I love," Alys sniffed. "And I'm afraid he did it so someone at the emporium can offer for me. I had the strangest looks from Popham and Hales. I thought they considered me an equal, but now this!"

"You don't have to marry any of them, you can marry me," Lewis said.

He stopped walking. Alys bumped him, stunned, her tears forgotten. She looked up and realized Lewis had halted directly underneath the mistletoe. On purpose.

"Don't be silly," she chided. "You don't want to marry me."

"How can you know that?" Lewis said, in a low voice.

He bent his head as if to kiss her, and she stepped back quickly. Cousin or no, no matter how he felt, she wouldn't let him kiss her at a public event.

"I'm sorry," he said quickly.

"I must not embarrass my sisters," she said, wishing her excuse hadn't put that look of hope into his eyes.

Chapter Five

Alys waited with the rest of her siblings in the back parlor to receive her Grandmother Noble and Uncle Jacob. They had decorated their *Tannenbaum* earlier in the afternoon. Due to the chill of the day and the oppressive sensation of a coming storm, her hands had been clammy and chilled. Lewis had stayed out of the house and no one knew where he was. She worried about him, feeling guilty because her initial reaction to his proposal had been to tell him he was being silly. His expression had told her he had been serious after all.

Alys's view of the tree, with its candles, popcorn, and cranberry rings, blurred. She couldn't clearly see the outlines of the paper-snowflake cutouts Matilda had made a few years ago. Lewis had carved the bird ornaments from weeping-willow scraps and she had painted the tiny blue eyes that stared accusingly into hers now.

Where had he gone on Christmas Eve? They had resolved nothing the night before and she had the sick feeling of dread to show for that. What was she going to do? She couldn't marry him. Not only was he her cousin, but he had no income of his own and hers had been stripped from her. Even Ralph Popham would be a better match from a practical standpoint, ill as the thought made her.

Pounds opened the door and male voices disrupted the quiet. Her stomach clenched, then she recognized the high tenor of Uncle Jacob, her mother's only living sibling. The scent of roasted chestnuts drifted in along with the odor of wet wool from outer garments. Her uncle, tall and slender with a magnificent snowy beard, and resplendent in a bright green waistcoat, was two years older than her mother and had never married. He lived with his mother in Reading. Twelve years before, when her aunt had died, the Redcakes had accepted her son Lewis, then seventeen, into their household, and her uncle had taken in Grandmother Noble.

"We drove by Redcake's," Uncle Jacob said as he walked into the room with her father, followed by her mother and grandmother. "Most impressive edifice."

"Thank you, brother," her father boomed. He always grew louder around Uncle Jacob, as if his more gentle tones brought out the bombast.

"Oh, dear, I do hate to travel," Grandmother Noble said, sinking down into a wingback chair near the fireplace. It was their father's favorite chair, but Grandmother Noble was one of the few people who Sir Bartley allowed to do as she pleased, despite his newly elevated place in the world.

"We're so happy you made the effort, Mother," Ellen Redcake said gently.

"Would you like a fur wrap to cover those old bones, madam?" Sir Bartley boomed. "Or a dish of tea. Or whisky, perhaps?"

Since Grandmother Noble didn't treat him with respect, Sir Bartley made an effort to expose her little foibles, like drinking more than was polite.

Alys sighed. She loved her family, but enjoyed escaping into her business world as often as possible. She felt a stab of pain in her palm and realized she was digging her fingernails into the opposite hand. If she didn't figure out a plan, she'd be sharing the whisky bottle with Grandmother Noble by the end of Boxing Day.

"Where is my handsome Lewis?" Grandmother trilled, after receiving her whisky.

Silence ensued until Alys looked up and realized everyone was staring at her. Why? What did they know? She shrugged.

"Did he say anything to you at the musicale last night?" her mother asked. "I haven't seen him since I saw you speaking to him there."

Alys felt her cheeks heat. "No, Mother. He didn't tell me of his plans."

"He left rather abruptly," Matilda said, her eyes narrowed.

Alys caught her father's glance and looked away. She would only stay civil over the holiday if she didn't speak to him.

Had Lewis said anything to Father? If so, she was doomed. Clearly, he wanted to marry her off to get her out of the way of her sisters and their potentially greater success on the marriage market. Could Lewis have been his choice all along?

The evening droned along, with a large, nap-inducing dinner followed by Bible and sermon readings. By the time Alys went to bed, she was desperate for solitude.

On Christmas morning they all went to church, then returned home to exchange gifts. Lewis still hadn't appeared and many comments were made about his eccentricities.

Grandmother Noble planned another series of Bible and sermon readings. Alys pleaded a headache and went upstairs to lie down. As she opened the door to her room, quite dark despite it being the middle of the day, she heard a melodious chirping.

A footstool tripped her as she moved to the window to rearrange the curtains the maid had been too busy to draw. When she visited, Grandmother Noble's needs always caused everyone else in the household to be neglected. Alys stumbled forward and pulled back the heavy, beige velvet drapes. This gave her enough gray light to find a candlestick and stir the fire to life. She hummed "O Little Town of Bethlehem" as she worked.

To the side of her fireplace she saw a glint of emerald green. Confused, she stopped humming. She moved closer and lifted her candlestick.

An emerald eye winked at her. She stumbled back, hearing the pretty chirp again.

"Oh," she breathed, realizing. It wasn't a person, but a bird!

Another of Lewis's fantastic mechanical birds. The feathers looked amazingly lifelike in shades of green, orange, and gold.

"What is your name, pretty thing?" she crooned, touching a metal feather gently.

The bird opened its tiny beak and a lovely song poured out. She didn't recognize it. Could Lewis have composed the tune? The bird's claws clung to a metal branch of a bronze metal tree. When she looked closer, she saw a tiny sign tied onto the branch with twine. It read HEART'S DESIRE.

"You are a beauty," she whispered, when the bird had finished its song. Lewis was so talented, and this would be a gift greatly appreciated by anyone who loved him.

Sadly, she didn't love him in the way he apparently wanted. She sighed and stroked the bird's feathers again. The song restarted.

Neither of them had what they wanted at this point in time. She had no idea what Lewis's ambitions even were, other than an allowance from her father to continue work in his machine shop. Lewis built equipment for Redcake's, which is why her father supported him, though his partner did most of the practical work.

Both of their lives were ruled to a great degree by her father's whims. As a woman, could she break free? Lewis could find employment, but if she did the same, she'd embarrass the entire family. Already, it might be too late to redeem her younger sisters from their working-class taint.

She sat in a comfortable tufted chair by the fire and knitted a pair of children's socks she'd promised to the vicar's wife, deep in thought about her future prospects. Not the merriest way to spend the holiday, but she supposed it was as good a day as any to consider new beginnings.

She had fallen into a light doze when a knock came on her door. The almost-finished second sock fell from her lap as she knuckled her eyes and went to the door through semidarkness.

"You have to come down," Rose said, between coughs. "It's time for our Christmas wishes."

Each year, the Redcake children wrote a Christmas letter and cast it into the fire, a tradition passed on from the Noble side of the family.

Alys thought of protesting, but she could use all the help she could find for her future, so she followed her sister's candle down the stairs and hallway to the back parlor.

Only the women were in the room, she was happy to see. She sat next to Matilda and took up her pen, writing that she wished her father would change his mind, that her sisters would be happy, and Lewis and Gawain too, but she found her thoughts drifting to the handsome profile of Hatbrook.

Could she wish him for one of her sisters? No, she was too drawn to his stern male beauty to want him for someone else, even if she didn't desire to marry.

She folded her letter. Then, with a second thought, she opened it again, and wrote, "Hatbrook happy, too, please. And his mother will have a good party with the best cake ever."

Content with those slightly juvenile wishes, she folded her letter. When her sisters were done, they stood at the fire, united in a goal for once. Wrapping their free arms around each other's velvet-clad waists, they bent forward in unison and dropped their letters into the fire.

Alys took in their faces, shiny with heat and burnished by the fire. "I love you both dearly."

Rose held up her hand. "Don't tell us your wishes," she croaked. "Or they won't come true."

Alys shook her head. "I know that. I'm the one who told you that."

"I think that was my mother's idea, actually," Grandmother Noble said, stirring in her chair. "But I'm glad to see the tradition has been passed down. Where are Gawain and Lewis? They have their own letters to write."

"I haven't seen Gawain since we ate," Rose said.

"Lewis was here, but he left again," Alys said, remembering the metal bird.

Matilda yawned. "This weather is making me so sleepy."

"Don't fall asleep now," Rose warned. "You promised to play backgammon with me."

Sir Bartley entered the room and for Alys, the holiday spirit vanished.

"Everything in good order at Redcake's?" her mother asked. The emporium remained open as most shops did despite the holiday.

"Fair enough," he said, rubbing his hands together.

"I have to finish my socks." Alys swept past him toward the door.

* * *

An extremely bad snowstorm overshadowed Boxing Day. All morning long, Alys could hear trees cracking outside as the weight of snow overpowered them. Her father had taken Uncle Jacob to work by foot so they could discuss new mill equipment, and Grandmother Noble had stayed in bed, claiming a sore throat and chest pains. Would this be the first of many days to come just like this one, minus the *Tannenbaum,* with novels Matilda and Rose took turns reading aloud while the Redcake women knitted charity socks?

"I do wish we could take a walk," Rose moaned. "My head simply aches."

"It's the storm. I always have the headache when it snows," their mother said. "Do you want some willow bark tea, dear?"

"Yes."

Alys knew Rose's head must really hurt. She despised the bitter brew. "I'll get it."

She lit a candle to find her way down the dark hallway from the dining room to the kitchen. Her father had installed gas lighting in the kitchen but hadn't done so for any of the hallways or staircases mostly travelled by servants.

"Miss Redcake?" Pounds's large body loomed over her quite unexpectedly at the kitchen door.

She bit back an alarmed cry when her candle rattled in its saucer. "Miss Rose desires some willow bark tea."

"Very good, miss. I'll have it brought in."

"Thank you." She stared as he returned through the door. If she were in Redcake's, she'd have been able to go into every room and no one would block her way or question her. Here, in her home, servants had their own domains. She wasn't free to roam her own house. Her hand went to her chest. Her corset seemed to be cutting off her air. She was used to living in looser clothing most of the time.

This wouldn't do. She needed to speak to her father.

For the rest of the day, she stilled her tongue, but on Monday, she rose early, before Lucy had even come in with her tea, and went downstairs in the simple black cakie uniform she could dress herself in without assistance.

As she expected, her father was in the dining room, drinking black coffee and having an egg before he left for the emporium. She had been at his side not too long ago.

What she hadn't expected was that Lewis would be right next to him, pointing at a complicated diagram on a piece of paper in front of them.

"Father, Lewis," she said.

"We're discussing some potential upgrades to Uncle Bartley's mills," Lewis said. He smiled at her.

She realized she hadn't seen him at all since the musicale, except for dinner last night when he was placed at the opposite end of the table. "You must have been busy designing over the holiday."

His smile widened, showing pleasure that she'd noticed. "Uncle Jacob made some comments that gave me wonderful ideas. I couldn't stop drawing."

This also gave him the excuse to avoid the interminable sermon readings Grandmother Noble enjoyed so much, welcome since Lewis was not the religious sort.

"I'm happy you were so gainfully employed," Alys told him.

"I could explain my design to you," Lewis offered.

"No, thank you." She kept her shudder to herself. Mills held no appeal to her. "But I loved your latest bird."

"I'm glad."

Sir Bartley set down his coffee cup. "Did you need something, Alys?"

"I wondered if I could go in the carriage with you this morning."

"Whatever for? You need to get packing." He stared at her uniform.

"Packing?"

"Yes, you and Mother and the girls are taking the train down to Eastbourne later today, and setting up the household at Redcake Manor."

"Redcake Manor?" Train? Eastbourne? Her brain seemed to shut down.

"I've renamed the property. Since we're going to be spending a great deal of time in Sussex, I want it all ready for me when the holiday rush is over."

"But everyone's in town now," she said.

"Go pack, Alys."

"I'd like to go into Redcake's," she pleaded.

Sir Bartley picked up his cup and put it to his lips. He frowned when he noticed it was empty. "You are no longer welcome there, Alys, unless it is to take tea with a friend."

Alys felt anger boiling up and couldn't care that Lewis witnessed her shame. "I did an excellent job for Redcake's, Father. I love it there."

He raised his hand. "I'll take no more nonsense from you, young lady, not in my own house. Am I not master here?"

"Yes, Father." Irritation made her bold. "But the least you can do is offer me a letter of reference. I deserved better than to be let go without a reference."

Lewis's eyes widened.

Her father pushed back his chair and stood. Silverware clattered against the table. "While there is breath in my body, girl, you will want for nothing. Even after, you will be provided for."

"I want my position back," she said. "Or a reference."

His nostrils flared. "Lewis, wrap up those papers, you are coming with me. Alys, I will not speak to you again until we meet in Sussex."

Alys stood her ground, not moving until her father and Lewis left. Her father stepped around her without a second glance, but Lewis kissed her cheek. Clearly, her cousin had said nothing to her father about his offer. That would have only made things worse. When she heard the outer door close, she sank to the ground, letting her skirts puff around her knees as she knelt.

"Darling!" Her mother shrieked, coming into the room. "Smelling salts!"

Slowly, Alys pulled herself upright with the aid of a table. "My apologies, Mother, I was being dramatic. Father has just made it clear that not only am I forbidden at Redcake's, I am to live in the country."

"Yes, he wants us to leave today, but Pounds says the trains aren't running due to the storm. I think I can persuade him to leave off the travel until after the first of the new year."

"And my position?"

Her mother shook her head. "You have to let that go, Alys. Your father insists that you marry, not stand in the way of your sisters. Perhaps it might have been different if Gawain hadn't returned, but now that he has a son in the business again—"

"He doesn't need me," Alys finished.

"I'm afraid that's how he sees things. He feels we've gained a new position and he's proud of that accomplishment. He wants his family to reflect his place in the world."

"Even if we're not happy about it?"

"You and Gawain are the only two who are unhappy," her mother said in a slow, thoughtful tone. "But you both must make your peace. Your father is the parent God chose for you, and he knows what is best."

"What does Gawain want?"

Her mother toyed with a long necklace for a moment. "To be miserable, I think. But that will change in time. He suffered a terrible shock when he was injured, you know."

"I don't want to marry, Mother. I can't, I just can't." Her knuckles began to burn and she realized she still clutched the edge of the table.

"You'll feel differently when we find the right man for you."

"Don't I even get to choose?" She knew she shouldn't use that bitter tone with her gentle mother, but that clawing, suffocating feeling was taking over again.

"I won't let your father force you to marry someone you dislike."

"To think I have to satisfy myself with that, when I was so very good in my position. I am ill-served by this, as is the bakery."

"You can still make cakes, darling. I'll explain to Cook that it's your special hobby. Perhaps you can have a little kitchen of your own in the Sussex house."

"You mean Redcake Manor?"

An impish expression crossed her mother's face. "Even so. Let your father be proud, Alys. He's worked so very hard for us. You can't imagine how he started."

"Unlike you, Mother, I was in the mill working as a child. I know very well how he started since things didn't improve very much until the past ten years."

"But you've always had a family to support you, brothers. He had no one," her mother said gently. "Be kind."

"I'd like to go to my room now," Alys said, because she felt anything but kind.

Her mother nodded. "I'll have Lucy bring you a tray."

Alys shrugged and stepped around her. To think it had to be worked out with Cook so she could be allowed to bake in her own home. No home of Sir Bartley's was really hers. And the only escape? How ironic. *Marriage.*

* * *

Michael shook the snow off his top hat before entering Mumford and Egglesworth for the first time on the Tuesday after Christmas. Sir John Smythe was meeting him here, unable to resist being a part of such a conference.

When he shut the door behind him, he immediately took off his muffler. It seemed the blasted thing had sucked in moisture from the snow and packed it around his neck instead of protecting him from the chill. Leave it to his mother to give him a gift with negative effects.

"My lord." Sir John came toward him, hand outstretched, nose red from the cold.

Michael shook his hand. "I cannot believe a deal was reached with such rapidity."

"Just so, my lord. You will be pleased."

A few moments later they were ushered into an oak-paneled room. Gaslights sizzled on the wall and an elegant marble fireplace warmed the space. Plush chairs were arranged around a table.

Settled in the chairs were Mr. Mumford, Sir Bartley, and two other men, who Michael assumed were Sir Bartley's man of business and accountant. Another man entered behind him, his arms full of papers.

After introductions were made, Mr. Mumford said, "As you are interested in the Redcake's Tea Shop and Emporium, we have only examined the books of this enterprise, though you must understand that Redcake's mills and factories have been major suppliers to the business and therefore could affect its health."

"What did you find?" Sir John said.

"Nothing to concern us," Mumford said. "The enterprise is five years old at this location. Start-up costs prevented a profit at the start, but it has done well for three years now."

"This document here lays out the various departments and their profit margins," said the man who'd come in laden with papers.

"We find the tea shop is lucrative because of the markup, and the bakery is lucrative because of the volume of business relative to the size of the space needed to operate it," Sir Bartley said. "A very good business, poised for expansion."

"Then why do you not expand it?" Michael asked. "It's your name above the gate."

"I am retiring to the country," he said. "I plan to learn to ride and shoot."

"You're going to take up the life of a country squire?" Michael wished someone had thought to bring a tray into the meeting. Samples from the bakery would be nice.

"Yes. I've had a lifetime of labor and I'd like my daughters to experience a different lifestyle. London is not good for any of them, year-round."

"The weather is most unhealthful," Michael agreed. "I try not to spend more than a couple of months at a time here."

Sir Bartley nodded. "I plan to spend my time between Sussex and Somerset, where I have my other businesses."

"My estates are in Sussex as well," Michael observed.

"I am relocating there more by accident than design," Sir Bartley observed. "The right property became available at the right price."

"You won't regret it. And it is easy to get to London from there, these days."

"Yes, my travel should be quite convenient." He rubbed his hands together.

"Sir Bartley is anxious that this business be completed as soon as possible," one of the men said.

"One thing." Michael lifted a finger.

"Yes?" asked Mumford.

"What about Sergeant Redcake?" he asked, still turned to Sir Bartley. "I believe your son said he worked as an accountant for the emporium?"

"I do not believe he enjoys this employment. You can of course offer him a job if you desire, but I hope he moves with us so I can train him for my other businesses, since I don't intend to sell them."

"You simply wish to be quit of London."

Sir Bartley nodded.

"And Miss Redcake?" Michael asked, wondering about Sir Bartley's city-loving daughter. "Who does the cakes?"

"She is no longer involved in the enterprise." Sir Bartley's mouth folded into a tight line.

"Is she well, sir?" Michael asked quickly. She seemed to be the blooming sort of person who never took ill.

"Of course, my lord. Never doubt it."

He nodded with relief. The girl had been so enthusiastic about her cakes, but it seemed more than the holiday had transpired over the past few days. He was well versed in family complications. Could she have run off with a man? "Very well. If we can come to terms on price, I am very interested."

"Not concerned about entering trade?" Sir Bartley asked.

"I will not concern myself with day-to-day operations," Michael said. "But I cannot deny a sense of personal satisfaction at owning such a charming business." Even if it would be somewhat less than charming without Miss Redcake in his employ. He had wanted to speak with her again, see if the same sparks ignited, not that he intended to act on his attraction, but she probably had an excellent dowry, something to keep in mind if a man needed funds, not that he ever planned to be in that position again.

Sir Bartley placed his hands on the table. "While it no longer suits my interests, it has been an excellent business and you'll find cheerful, honest employees. Hales there has a list of key men."

"Give the list to Mumford," Michael said to the sallow man who held up a paper. "He'll be hiring a general manager."

"We have several candidates, my lord," Mumford said. "Some recommended by Sir Bartley himself."

"Excellent. I shall leave you all to work out the details," Michael said, rising. "Best of luck to you, Sir Bartley."

The older man stood and shook his hand. "And the same to you, my lord."

Michael left the room, trailed by Sir John.

"Anything to concern you?" Michael asked, when they were back on the street.

"Not at all. Redcake is a fool to sell. You could develop a string of tea-shop emporiums across the better shopping districts in England with such an idea. Lots of ladies out and about, these days."

"It's a new age," Michael thought again, remembering Miss Redcake and her keen professional interest. "But I agree about Redcake. A man's home is his castle and all that, but I've met the eldest daughter and I can't imagine she is pleased to lose her cake business. Have you heard what happened to her?"

Sir John shrugged. "Perhaps she is getting married. Women do, you know."

Michael rubbed at his face, and told himself the sudden itchy sensation, as if hives were developing, was due to the wet wool around his neck. "Of course, that is most likely. Alys Redcake to domestic life, and Gawain Redcake to the counting desk at the Somerset mills. I'm sure Sir Bartley has his family's future all planned."

"Either way, none of our business."

Michael nodded. Though he found himself unaccountably curious about the siblings.

"Coffee?" Sir John suggested. "I have one or two points to bring up with you before you meet Mumford again."

"Very well. I'm seeing him on Friday." Michael fixed his hat more firmly on his head and they set off together for the nearest coffee-house.

"Who'd have thought, with the conditions of things when your father died, that you'd be able to casually buy such an enterprise?" Sir John commented.

"It's a testament to both of us," Michael agreed. "Maybe we can open the second branch of Redcake's in Manchester."

"My bride would love that," Sir John agreed. "She loves a good cake, same as you, my lord."

Chapter Six

"Are you certain you do not want to go on calls with us?" Matilda said in a wheedling tone. "Lady Lillian is taking us to the home of two countesses."

Rose coughed. "And a baroness."

"Don't you think you should loosen your stays?" Alys asked. The weather had stayed foul, so much so that her mother had persuaded their father to drop the subject of travel for now.

Rose sniffed. "I am perfectly fine."

"You look delicious," Matilda said, twisting this way and that in front of their dressing-room mirror. "I do love this blue silk."

"It brightens your hair," Rose observed.

"How dare you!" Matilda squeaked.

"You are a dream in blue," Alys said, to keep the peace.

"Lady Lillian is downstairs," Lucy announced, coming into the room, her nostrils still sore and chapped from an ague she'd been battling since Boxing Day.

"Oh, we must be off." Matilda pecked Alys on the cheek and

rushed out of the room, followed by Rose, her mouth covered by her handkerchief as she coughed again.

Alys met Lucy's gaze.

"Maybe you should leave London for a time, miss," Lucy said. She twisted her reddened hands into her apron. "I know it is impolite, but I've been here four years, and I have never seen you sad and sour before now."

"I'm sure we will depart as soon as the snow melts," Alys said. "But for now, I'm going for a walk. Once we're in sunny Sussex, I may miss these overcast skies."

"I doubt that, miss. But I'll bring you your things."

"Thank you."

When she was snugly dressed in a mantle, bonnet, and new green-striped gloves and muffler knit by her sisters as Christmas gifts, she left the house. She walked toward Piccadilly Circus without quite meaning to do so. From there, it was pleasant to window-shop her way along Regent Street.

She stopped for a moment in front of a banqueting hall, imagining it as a cake shop, with ALYS REDCAKE emblazoned above a smartly painted front door. Wouldn't that be something, to have a shop? Of course, it would have to be in Eastbourne, or in whatever small village Redcake Manor was nearby. Having had no interest in her father's real estate acquisitions, she had no exact idea as to where the new house was.

Probably though, opening her own bakery would cause a catastrophic break with her father. Maybe she could interest Gawain, but, bitter though he was, he'd likely learn to side with her father over time, since he was the heir.

And then there was Lewis, but she couldn't see marrying him. He'd served as brother to her for nearly half her life now. No hint of a romantic connection had ever passed between them, not on her side anyway. When he appeared long enough to resolve things between them, she doubted he'd be in the mood to provide a front for her bakery idea. Plus, she assumed he wouldn't be moving to Sussex with them since his machine shop was here.

She walked up the street, passing a cacophony of businessmen talking, ladies gossiping. A man in a ragged coat pushed in front of her holding a sheaf of bills, trying to hand them out, though the damp would soon ruin them.

"No, thank you," she said, stepping away from him.

Bootblacks on opposite corners shouted out their prices to passersby. A locksmith clanked by on some rescue mission farther up the street.

"Baked potatoes!" cried a man pushing a wheelbarrow down the side of the street.

"Roasted chestnuts!" boomed another.

Her attention was caught by the display inside a bakery. Egg wash made the pastries in the window glisten. If she had a bakery of her own, she'd have to hire staff to make other confections, since she really only liked to make cakes. Did she have a head for business? She had no idea. She didn't have the education her sisters did since she'd begun to work so young, but reading had seemed to close many gaps in her knowledge. Her father never said anything about business in her hearing that she couldn't understand.

Perhaps she'd try one of those raisin buns. The cool air had her longing for the feel of something warm in her mouth. She put her hand on the door handle.

"Redcake's carries a much superior product," said a gentleman's voice behind her.

She turned. "Hatbrook," she exclaimed with pleasure. He was ever present in her thoughts as her sisters compared every man they met to his handsome face. But to see him before her struck her anew with attraction to that lopsided smile.

"Miss Redcake." The marquess lifted his top hat slightly. "What are you doing outside a rival bakery? Comparing merchandise?"

"It is no rival to me, your lordship." Alys fought to keep her tone casual.

"I had heard you were quit of the Redcake enterprise," the marquess murmured.

"From whom did you hear that?" Alys asked, shocked. Were the cakies gossiping to customers? Or, could he have asked about her?

"You contracted with my mother to do some work for her party the day after tomorrow."

"Are you afraid the order won't be fulfilled? I assure you, sir, I won't let that happen." A certain spark left her when she realized he only cared about the party order, not her personally. She'd have to sneak back into Redcake's to make certain the order was up to standard. Thankfully, she had baked the cakes before her expulsion, but they needed to be frosted, assembled and decorated, not to mention the pastry order. Oh, what had her father done? All those weddings had been booked too, and nothing had been started. If she wasn't there to manage and decorate, it might all fall apart, damaging the reputation of the firm more than any mere Redcake daughter working there might.

"Is it in your power to make that promise?" The skin around his eyes tightened.

It seemed to Alys that he regarded her with some special interest. "I-I still have friends and family in the enterprise, my lord. And the work was begun before Christmas."

"What happened, Miss Redcake?"

She moved away from the door to let a customer go inside. "My sisters have formed a connection with Earl Gerrick's youngest daughter and it has greatly expanded the family's social opportunities. My father fears I may hurt their reputations if I am behaving as a working-class person."

"I thought you might have become engaged over the holidays."

He must have seen her with Lewis at the musicale. His interest intrigued her anew. "No, I am quite unattached."

He tilted his head, keeping his steady gaze on her. "What are your future plans?"

Alys laughed, to relieve the discomfort of his penetrating attention. "I have my sisters' happiness at heart, always, sir."

"That is not what I asked."

She shook her head, realizing his question was sincere. "It doesn't matter. We are moving to Sussex next month, so my employment would have ended then."

"Oh?"

"My youngest sister suffers from a minor lung ailment, however it does plague her at this time of year in London. I do not suffer the same, but," she hesitated. "My place is at her side."

"The air is highly insalubrious," the marquess agreed. "I applaud your family feeling."

"Thank you. It is in our best interests to leave London for a while, though I'm sure she'd rather stay here and attend parties." She swallowed hard, thinking that no one but her father was pleased by the arrangement, necessary though it might be.

"As your sister's keeper, you may wish to be warned that Lady Lillian does not possess a spotless reputation."

"She is a bit flighty," Alys said cautiously.

The marquess raised an eyebrow, making his expression even more remote. "I would not want to see innocent girls take up with her, as I assume your sisters must be."

"Can you be more specific, my lord?" She wanted direct speech from him.

"She is wasteful of money and careless of people, Miss Redcake. I would not speak so if you weren't so new to society and if I didn't feel a certain kinship to the Redcakes knowing that your brother served in India with my brother."

"T-thank you, my lord," she stammered, shocked to think he felt himself to be on any kind of equal level with her family. "I am not fond of her, but she is my sisters' special friend. I shall implore them to take care."

"The family has plenty of money, and I suppose yours does too, so perhaps it doesn't signify."

"We are too new to money to be casual with it."

"There is a brother without attachment. Is he being considered for you?"

"Not for me, certainly. Are you saying he gambles?"

The marquess winced. "I am, Miss Redcake. I enjoy spending money, but only on what I consider valuable."

"Whereas I secret mine away for no reason I can understand." She sighed. "It is very rude to speak of money, is it not?"

"Yes, it is. And certainly it is rude to damage young ladies' reputations as well."

"Then I must consider you a friend, to be so honest with me, my lord."

"You must," he agreed. His shoulder jerked and he clasped one gloved hand with the other. "I must be off, Miss Redcake, but I do hope you will accept my personal invitation for you and your family to attend the New Year's Ball. I understand the refreshments will be excellent."

"I assure you they will be," she agreed, matching the twinkle in his eye with her own, while simultaneously wondering why he had become so twitchy all of a sudden. "Are you sure your mother will welcome us?"

"It will be a large crush," he said carelessly. "Perhaps your sisters will make new friends. It can only be for the best. Since we are based in Sussex as well you might even make friends from that part of the country."

"That would be so pleasant," she said. "It would be lovely to have an acquaintance already in place."

"Then we are agreed. I'll have an invitation sent to your mother and you will persuade her to accept."

"It is quite agreed."

He bowed his head in her direction then pulled open the door of the inferior bakery and walked in. She stared, bemused. Why would he want to purchase items from this bakery when Redcake's was nearby and he'd told her this bakery was inferior?

Men. She couldn't understand Lewis's motivations and she'd known him all her life, so how could she expect to understand the actions of the Marquess of Hatbrook?

With great purpose, she ignored the snow that fell lightly and made her way to Redcake's. She went in the front entrance, which felt terribly strange, and took a table in the tea shop. When one of the girls waited on her, she ordered raisin buns and tea and asked her to send in Betsy Popham.

"Of course, Miss Redcake. I'll find her. Are you certain you don't want to go into the back?"

So her father hadn't let the staff know he'd cast her off? That would make things easier on Friday. "I'm very cold," she said. "If I don't get a cuppa into me I'm liable to become an icicle."

The cakie laughed. "Back in a wink."

Alys hadn't lied. Her teeth chattered as she unwrapped her muffler and she noticed her hands shook when she took off her gloves, not dissimilar to the marquess. Yes, he could have been shaking from the cold, though admittedly he hadn't looked cold, clad as he was in thick winter wool.

She wished he had come with her to Redcake's, though perhaps he wished to remove himself from her presence. After all, like Lady Lillian, he could have a fiancée tucked away in the country somewhere. She didn't like that idea and spun a delicious fantasy of his paying court to her. But she wasn't sure that offered the private moments with him she craved, so she thought about kissing his fascinating mouth, until she felt very warm.

The cakie brought her tea and buns and Alys warmed her hands on the teapot before pouring. She glanced around at the clientele while she ate her first bun. Lovely to see so many ladies out enjoying a day of shopping. She saw string-tied parcels at the feet of many customers and everyone seemed wrapped in that holiday spirit that made this time of year bearable despite the London fog.

Here and there, she did see a young woman alone, some dressed in quite modest stuff. The better shopgirls perhaps, having a Christmas treat, or spending their Christmas bonus on a taste of a higher class of life. She so easily could have been one of those girls if her father hadn't spent all the profit from the mill he inherited to build a factory, and then another mill with that profit. After that, the money seemed to earn itself and he brought them to London to create a flagship bakery. Or maybe he'd just been fleeing from the place of Arthur's death. What does it do to a man to lose his heir? Would he sacrifice the dreams of other children to save one? She wondered how Rose's health came into her father's thought processes, or if that was a womanly concern. Surely the marriage market was better in London, if his only concern was to find his daughters husbands.

"I'm sorry I was so long, Alys," Betsy said, coming to her table in a flurry of flour, sugar, and salt. "I had to change my apron since it was covered in frosting."

"Sit down, please."

Betsy glanced around nervously, perhaps making sure her father hadn't slipped in, then sat across from her.

"Do you want a bun?" Alys asked, holding up the plate.

"No, thank you."

"Are you sure? They're really good today. Must be just out of the oven." She shook it enticingly.

"No, I don't like raisins."

"And you work here?"

"Father procured the position for me. It's a wonderful place to work, even if I don't like all of our goods."

Alys tried to hold back a laugh. "Did you have other dreams?"

"You know I want to decorate cakes."

"But before."

Betsy waved her hands. "Oh, art of course. I longed to have time to paint. But Mother was ill and I cared for her until she passed, and then Father found me this. I'm luckier than most."

"I'm sorry you lost your mother, though. But I'm glad you found a way to express your love of art, here. Are you going to be able to take over from me?"

Betsy's eyes widened. "There isn't anyone else with the eye for it. I don't think anyone had planned for you to leave. My father has been quite upset each time he checks your papers."

"I didn't choose—" Alys paused, realizing once again that no one seemed to know what had really happened. "Listen, Betsy. We are only two days away from the Marchioness of Hatbrook's event."

"I saw the cakes. They smell lovely."

"I need to be sure the pastries are on the schedule and the cake is finished. Can you frost the layers? Then if you let me in the back on Friday morning I'll do the decorating with you and make sure Simon and his boys get the shipment out."

Betsy's freckled face broke into a smile. "Are you sure? You must have other things to do, now that you're a lady of leisure."

"The marquess especially asked me to make sure the job was done right," Alys said. "I can't say no to a marquess."

Betsy put her hand to her forehead. "Good heavens, Alys. Of course you can't."

"Then it's settled? You'll check on everything and let me in through the back on Friday morning?"

Betsy nodded. "Of course."

Alys felt as though an anvil had been lifted from her chest. She knew once her mother saw the invitation to the marchioness's ball that they would be attending and she'd be so embarrassed if the special cake and pastries never arrived. Then she would have to bury herself in the country until she was old and gray.

Two hours later, she had arrived home again. Lucy dressed her in a tidy navy-blue sateen gown, suitable both for dinner and the modest place Alys saw as hers in this world.

Her sisters stumbled into the dressing room like a couple of young pups, red-cheeked from the cold. Or was it from the cold? She smelled a strong hint of sherry wafting through the air.

"I do not think we shall go down for dinner, Lucy," Matilda said, pronouncing each word very carefully.

"I have a headache," Rose said, with a cough.

And a wheeze.

Alys closed her eyes. Her sister sounded worse.

"Undress Rose immediately," she said to Lucy. "I'll fetch Mother."

Matilda sank down on the vine-patterned love seat next to the fire. Her expression was goofy and vague.

Alys swore in quite an unladylike fashion under her breath as she went toward her mother's suite. The marquess had been correct. What kind of calls had Lady Lillian taken her sisters on, that they drank spirits instead of tea?

She knocked on the double doors leading to the suite and her mother's maid, Edith, answered the door.

"Yes, miss?"

"Is Mother available? It's important."

The maid nodded and stepped aside. Alys entered the art-filled room and found her mother sitting in front of her fire, reading a book of poetry.

"Darling," her mother said. She looked up, then frowned. "Your hair, Alys. Do I need to speak to Lucy?"

"She wasn't finished yet," Alys said, touching the windblown mess on top of her head. "Matilda and Rose came in from their calls. I'm worried about Rose."

"Oh?"

"I'm worried about both of them, because they seem worse for drink, Mother, but Rose is wheezing."

Her mother tossed her book aside and stood. "Edith, have a can of hot water and some lavender oil brought to the girls' room immediately," she said.

"Yes, my lady." Edith went to the bell pull while Alys followed her mother out of the room.

"Drink, you say? That can make breathing worse. You won't remember Lewis's mother, but she was much the same. What have those two featherbrains been doing?"

"They were on calls with Lady Lillian, Mother."

"And you stayed at home?"

Alys ignored the implied rebuke. "She doesn't have an excellent reputation. I heard this from an unassailable source."

"You haven't been spying on your sisters, Alys."

"No, Mother. I merely mentioned the Gerrick name in passing and the information came my way."

"Alys, I hope you are not becoming jealous of your sisters. It is unfortunate that you aren't younger now that things have changed so much for our family, but it is no fault of Matilda's or Rose's that they are younger."

Alys rolled her eyes. "Mother, I am not in the least jealous of them. I am merely sad that my own pleasures have been taken from me, but I am happy to make sacrifices for their happiness, of course."

Her mother sighed. "I wonder if that is true. The way you have lived has perhaps developed a more masculine personality than a feminine one."

"Mother!"

"It is true. That frightful rag you are wearing, for instance. Is that a mended tear at the hem? And I swear Grandmother Noble might have worn that pattern in eighteen-thirty-six!"

Alys couldn't quite hold back her giggle. "Only family is dining."

"You are the daughter of a knight now, Alys. Dining with family is a bit more consequential than before."

"Yes, my lady," Alys said, with a little curtsy.

Her mother sighed. "Come, we must deal with your sisters. Let us hope we can find a niche in society more salubrious than Lady Lillian's."

"And suitors better than the Earl of Lathom mentioned at the investiture, Mother. None of them are worth having."

"And I wonder how you would know that?"

"From the papers, Mother."

"I should not have thought you in the habit of entering your father's study. You know he dislikes that."

"At Redcake's, Mother. There is always a great deal of reading material available there."

"I see. Be assured that your father will investigate the background of any man interested in his daughters. He will do well by you."

"Me? I thought we were speaking of my sisters."

Her mother gave her an unreadable glance as they reached the sitting-room door. They opened it to find an unspeakable mess, courtesy of Matilda, on the stone flags before the fireplace.

Their mother sighed. "Rose, dear, you might feel better if you do the same."

Already looking green in the face, Rose complied. The smell was such that Alys felt ill herself. She hastened to open a window while her mother reached for the bell pull. Lucy came running with towels and a basin of cold water and did what she could to clean up the mess.

When a housemaid entered the room, her mother said, "Bring the tincture of lobelia and one of Sir Bartley's cigars."

Soon, Edith arrived with the hot water and lavender. Her mother applied the lavender to a handkerchief, then made Rose breathe in the steam and the scent with her head under a shawl. When the tincture and cigar arrived, she mixed the medicine with hot water and lit the cigar.

"The tincture has alcohol in it," Alys said.

"If she vomits again it is all to the good," her mother replied. "Otherwise the medicine should help."

Alys sighed. "I'm going to get Matilda to bed."

When her mother nodded, she and Lucy undressed the swaying young woman and cleaned her face.

"Could you put a brick in her bed, please," Alys asked the housemaid who had brought the water. She pulled a nightdress over Matilda's yawning head.

A few minutes later, she had her sister tucked into bed. As the housemaid stirred up the fire, Lucy fetched a basin and set it by Matilda.

"In case you need it, miss." Lucy coughed.

Matilda yawned again.

"Go to sleep, Matty," Alys ordered.

"You sound like Mother," her sister said softly.

"Then obey me like you would Mother."

Her sister smiled and closed her eyes. Alys judged it was safe to leave her and went back to help her mother. At least Matilda's health was sound.

The next evening, everyone was in the back parlor just before dinner, except Rose, who was confined to bed until her breathing recovered, and Sir Bartley. Matilda looked pale, but composed. Even Lewis had come in, though he stared at the fire instead of speaking to anyone.

When Sir Bartley made his entrance with Ralph Popham, Alys wanted to run upstairs and crawl into bed with Rose. Her father had never brought any of the employees to dinner before, even when he was plain Bartley Redcake. He introduced Popham to the family. She could tell Popham was nervous from the way he groomed his mustache. He always fingered it when he was upset or emotional. A man of strong opinions on subjects he knew nothing about, he could be most tiresome, though he was good at his position and the bakery thrived under his care. He loved nothing more than to persuade customers to buy a more expensive cake than they asked for, which nicely increased profit.

She had never thought to judge his age, though he must be about forty years old since he had a seventeen-year-old daughter.

Popham walked over to her place by the pianoforte and offered her his hand. She'd never touched him before, but was not displeased to find his grasp firm and palm dry. "Miss Redcake, so pleased to see you again."

"Until recently you saw me almost every day," she pointed out.

"Yes, and I've missed your shining face."

Shining face? What was she, a tidied street urchin?

"I can't deny I miss my position," she said. "Have my notes made sense to you? About the scheduled events?"

He glanced at her father, then spoke. "I understand you are soon to leave for the country?"

"Yes, London does not agree with my sister."

"I am sorry to hear it. I have always considered you a rather urban sort of person."

"I do believe I thrive here," Alys admitted. "But it cannot be helped."

"Perhaps your father would allow you to stay here," Popham said, touching the left side of his mustache. "If you had a reason."

Alys knew where this was going, but proceeded, even though it felt like ripping at a fresh scab. "And what reason do you believe I would need?"

"If you were affianced to a London businessman, for instance," he suggested.

"Alys is not interested in marriage," said Lewis loudly, turning from the fire.

Matilda gasped and put her hand over her mouth.

"Every woman is interested in marriage, I believe, sir," Popham said.

"Not Alys. I ought to know," said Lewis. "She has yet to respond to my proposal, yet I know she loves me."

"Lewis!" said Sir Bartley.

Alys fought to keep a smile from her lips. While she felt terrible for her cousin, she could not suppress a sense of pleasure at the way Popham was being put in his place. She only hoped Betsy heard nothing of this.

"Is this true?" her father thundered. "You think to marry my daughter, though you are dependent on me?"

Lewis put his hands on his hips. "More like you are dependent on me, sir. If I hadn't improved your ovens and your mixers, your factories would not have been profitable. You'd never have come to London and received your knighthood from the queen. Just because you haven't paid me fairly for my efforts doesn't mean they aren't worthy or valuable."

Her father's face had reddened noticeably during Lewis's speech. He pointed one finger toward the parlor door. "Out of my house."

Lewis bowed. "Alys, you may find me at my machine shop. I have a cot there." He walked out, his back very straight, his head held high.

Alys felt faint. She put a hand to her stays. Her mother moved to her side and put an arm around her waist. As her heart fluttered, she realized she'd never seen such a virile show from her cousin. Though he'd never be more than a brother to her, she knew he'd make some woman magnificently happy. Just not her.

She stared at the back of Popham's head. His lank, brown hair had gray strands floating up from it. He was too old for her. How could her father think they would make a match? And did he think a man of stature would be inclined to marry into a family that included Popham? No, this merely spoke to her father's desperation.

"I find I have the most appalling headache, Father," she said. "Would you please excuse me?"

Matilda's horrified expression spoke volumes. She might not want to be the only Redcake sister at the table, but Alys couldn't talk Redcake's business with Popham and she had no other interest in conversation. She had more to discuss with the Marquess of Hatbrook than she did with Redcake's bakery manager now.

"Go," her father said, his face still reddened, his eyes narrowed under bushy, graying eyebrows.

Alys fled the room. She couldn't be sorry to go to bed early since she needed to sneak out in the morning to finish up the Hatbrook ball order.

At four A.M. the next morning, she was leaving the house by the servants' entrance, when a broad-shouldered male body loomed in front of her.

For a moment, she was afraid it was her father.

"Alys," the man whispered.

She recognized Lewis's voice.

Chapter Seven

"Cousin," Alys whispered. "What are you doing outside? It's so cold." For a moment, she wondered if he meant to kidnap her like some ancient Scottish laird.

"A little bird told me you'd be sneaking over to the bakery this morning," he said. "Come."

Alys held up the lantern she'd brought to light her way through the morning fog. In front of her was a large, black-painted carriage, suitable for at least six passengers. Yet only one horse stood in front of it.

"How does that work?" Alys asked. "Did you mean to drive me there?"

She saw Lewis's teeth flash in the lantern light. "I've made some improvements. The carriage does much of the work itself. Come inside. I'll show you."

She let him help her climb into the carriage, then Lewis took the driver's seat. She knelt on the seat, and hooked her lantern onto a sturdy nail. Lewis bent down, doing something with metal levers. Then she heard a low belching and rushed to the back window to see steam exiting the back of the carriage, mixing with the fog. The carriage jerked and she fell back into the seat. They were off.

She judged there was some kind of steam engine in the undercarriage. What a treat this warm compartment was in comparison to the walk she'd expected on this chilly winter morning. Just a few minutes later, the carriage clop-belched to a stop behind Redcake's. The carriage shuddered, then Lewis must have disengaged the motor because the shaking stopped. A moment later, she felt Lewis jump down, then the door opened and he came into the compartment.

"It will be warm enough for a few moments in here." He hung his lantern opposite hers.

"Where did you get the money to buy this?" she asked.

"I scraped money together for the first one from my allowance from Uncle and a few clocks I repaired, upgraded, and sold," he said. "I sold the first carriage to a collector of curiosities in Edinburgh. The second went to a German aristocrat. This is the third, and I think it will sell to an American businessman who has expressed interest."

"I had no idea," Alys said.

"We live in the same household, but I think we rarely speak."

"Since Gawain has come home you've had a male companion, and of course I've my sisters."

"Yes. The household has become increasingly formal, I find, as your father has risen in the world. It is not entirely to my taste."

"No, I should think you've spent your last night there." She shuddered at the memory of the previous night.

He leaned forward. "You cannot be happy, Alys. I know you too well to think you would enjoy life as a lady of leisure. You care for me, don't you? When I sell this carriage I'll be able to afford the rent on a cottage. You can bake to your heart's content and I'll eat a slice of every cake."

"There's a lot more to running a household than eating cake."

"I'm afraid you'll have to do much of the work yourself. But I'll make sure we have a maid-of-all-work, and hopefully better soon. I have an idea for a new kind of clock, and a member of the royal family came to look at one of my birds the other day. I'm hoping for a commission."

"I'm glad you are doing so well." She leaned forward and took his hand. "And I do appreciate your offer, all the care you've taken. I know Father's precipitous decision about me probably tipped your hand prematurely."

"You don't have a firm grasp on his character," Lewis said, putting his free hand over hers. "He had planned this ever since you came from Somerset."

"I hope he hadn't planned to marry me to Popham all this time!"

"No, Popham's wife was still alive then. But no doubt he wants you married to someone who can run the businesses, in case Gawain flees the nest."

"I can run them," Alys said. "If he'd train me."

"It's not a woman's place, my dear," Lewis said. "But you could run my household. I'd never question you. We'd have a nice little family."

"I'm sorry, Lewis, but as well as you know me, there are pieces you are missing. I'm neither willing nor fit to be a wife." At that moment, the increasing pressure of his hands was too much, too demanding. She felt nothing for him beyond sisterly friendship and his grasp reminded her of darker times.

"I find that hard to believe, if the right man came along."

She pulled her hand gently from his grasp. "I'm not fit," she said.

"You are far more feminine than you think," he argued. "You can find contentment in the running of a house, I know it."

"You are missing pieces of me," she repeated. "It isn't possible, and even more importantly, I don't want to marry you, Lewis. You are like a brother to me. I'm sorry. Perhaps my sisters do not see you that way, but I do."

"Your sisters won't be marrying the likes of Popham or me," Lewis said.

"Probably not," she agreed. "I can only hope they find men as worthy as you, dear cousin."

His mouth twisted as she named him thus. "So that is all?"

She nodded. "I'm sorry."

"Very well. You know how to find me."

"Of course. And in a week or two, you should come to dinner. I'm sure Mother will talk Father out of his temper."

"You'll be in the country by then, I think."

Alys pressed her rapidly chilling lips together. "Yes, of course, I had forgotten."

"I think you have blocked all the unpleasantness from your mind. But I see you hate the thought of leaving London less than you hate the idea of marrying me, or Popham."

"Rose will need someone sensible about her," Alys ventured.

"Even so. You'd best get your work done before your father realizes you've been in the bakery," Lewis said.

"Thank you. The ride here was exhilarating," Alys said.

"I'll send you a note when I've upgraded to carriage number four."

"Good luck with the American. And the bird automaton commission."

"Thank you."

She smiled, a bit painfully, then he opened the door and fixed the step into place for her so she could step down.

A few hours later in her decorating room, the Fancy, in the basement bakery, Simon Hellman loaded the Hatbrook cake onto a cart for delivery later. Betsy had a list of pastries required and was checking them off in the bakery, since Alys didn't want Ralph Popham to see her and report back to her father.

She supposed she should be irritated that she hadn't received a day's wages for a great deal of work, but she was happy to be done with it. Her father would likely recognize the cake as her style at the ball tonight, but wouldn't be able to react in public and would have calmed down by the next morning. What was the worst he could do? Exile her to the country? He was already going to do that as soon as the weather improved.

"Is that the cake?" The Marquess of Hatbrook strode in, dressed in a handsome suit with a waistcoat of red-striped silk.

The sight of him in the Fancy was so incongruous that Alys had to blink a few times. She tried to brush flour off the cakie uniform she'd worn to blend in, but realized the white mess was buttercream when she smeared it into the fabric.

"Your lordship?" Her heart beat out of rhythm.

"Yes." Hatbrook drew out the word in a most superior fashion.

"Alys, I checked off every pastry as it was packed." Betsy trotted into the room, waving a sheet of paper. "It's all done!"

Hatbrook turned. The girl blushed nearly purple and dropped the packing list.

Alys snatched it from the floor. "Thank you ever so much, Betsy. Please remember, I was never here."

"Of course." Betsy's eyes were wide. "I—I—"

Alys made a shooing motion. The girl dropped a grateful curtsy and ran.

"Friend of yours?" Hatbrook inquired.

"Yes, actually. Though I don't think I'll be able to continue the friendship." Alys stared at the list, but it might as well have been gibberish for all the sense she made of it.

"That my list?" Hellman asked, reentering.

"Yes. Betsy says it is all there."

"Excellent," Hellman said, taking it. "We'll get it all there in perfect condition. I have no fear on that account, your lordship. We take pride in our work."

Hatbrook nodded. Alys glanced between the two, wondering why Hellman would recognize the marquess since he never entered the tea shop. What was the marquess doing in the back rooms?

"Are you on a tour, your lordship?" she asked. "Did you lose your guide?"

Hellman coughed and exited the room, walking backward as if Hatbrook were an Oriental potentate.

"I did receive a tour, yes, thank you, but I was allowed to explore on my own after."

"At ten in the morning?"

"It is nearer twelve, Miss Redcake."

"Oh, dear. I hadn't realized." Alys untied her apron and tossed it into a bin. "I had better leave before I'm noticed."

"You are quite noticeable to me."

"I mean by Upstairs." Heavens, but she was tired. And nervous. He quirked a brow.

"Management." No response. She tried again. "My father?"

"Ah. Defying his orders by being here?"

She tapped her foot. "I promised your mother the job would be done right."

He smiled, causing his cheekbones to pop in a most sensual manner. "Is my mother a higher power than your father?"

"I believe my father would see it so, were I not involved. The customer comes first."

"A noble sentiment."

"You wouldn't make the decision I did to get the job done?"

He considered. "You might have sent a note to other workers here."

"I'm the only one who decorates the fancy cakes," Alys said. "I was training Betsy, but she's not ready yet."

"You're saying your departure leaves a hole in the smooth running of this bakery?"

"I believe so. I can't say what other arrangements my father might have made." She knew he had done nothing, but didn't want to admit it.

A discreet cough came from just inside the door. Alys thought the man looked vaguely familiar, but certainly she couldn't place him as a person who belonged in the bakery.

"Do you feel this changes anything?" said the man.

Hatbrook shook his head. "No, I was aware."

Alys noticed he had gone a little pale.

The other man nodded. "Shall I wait for you?"

"No, Sir John. You can walk back to your office. I'll be taking the carriage back to Hatbrook House."

The other man nodded and left.

Alys didn't understand, but whatever was going on, it seemed to involve her. "Your lordship?"

"You should speak to your father."

"I'm sorry you are a witness to my most undaughterly conduct, sir, but I have explained to you the reason for my actions. I apologize if I have given you cause for concern for your mother's party." She felt sick that he might not take her at her word that all would be well.

He grasped a counter with his hand. "You wouldn't happen to have a spare slice of cake around here, would you? I haven't eaten in hours."

"Of course." She kept a small assortment of tasting cakes for undecided customers and brought him a slice of the best available.

Hatbrook ignored the fork she offered and stuffed a large piece into his mouth. She hoped he wouldn't choke himself and risked leaving the room to find him a cup and water.

When she returned, she found the slice of cake had vanished, and Hatbrook had seated himself upon the stool she used when doing fine work.

"Here." She thrust the mug of water into his hand.

His fingers trembled as he took it. "Thank you, Miss Redcake." He drained the glass.

"It's very hot down here," she ventured. "The men tend to work in shirtsleeves."

He smiled wanly. "I can see why. How can you stand to wear black?"

"This dress is far less confining than what I wear at home." She blushed at the intimate subject matter. "I do forget everything but my work because I love it so."

"I am most impressed by your dedication."

She sighed. "I wish my father had been."

"If someone had the power to return you to your position, would you do so?"

"That would all depend on the cost." She wondered if Popham would have let her work if she married him.

"I see from your expression that you have an unacceptable cost in mind."

"My father brought Mr. Popham home for dinner last night. He's the bakery manager and Betsy's father. I love Betsy, but I don't want to be courted by someone so much older than me." She put her fingers to her lips. Why was she telling him this?

"Had he come courting?"

She nodded, not daring to speak.

"Why would your father bring him when you are out in society now? Surely he can find you a higher class of husband than one of his own employees."

"Mr. Popham is a very nice man," she said quickly. "He was very kind to his wife when she was ill. He has been in Father's employ for fifteen years or more."

"So your father thinks you need a husband who would be kind?" The corner of Hatbrook's mouth lifted in what might have been a sneer in a less aristocratic face.

"I believe he simply wants me to have a home of my own before it is too late. I am twenty-six. Popham is reliable."

"I am twenty-eight and do not feel close to death yet," he deadpanned.

"I am happy to hear it, sir. I find myself somewhat concerned by you."

"May I confide in you?"

"Of course, sir." She stepped closer to the table, thrilled that he wanted her confidence. This close, she could smell the scent of lime soap from his skin and fruitcake from his lips. She remembered her fantasies of kissing those sensual lips.

"I become rather ill when I haven't eaten in a few hours. It is quite temporary. I eat, then the feeling goes away after a while. Something about being in the city makes the sensation worse."

She was absurdly pleased by his confidence. "Has it always been like this?"

"Yes, I believe so. It is easy enough to hide simply by eating regularly, but I was busy with meetings this morning and didn't take care of the matter."

"Your color is better now. Is this condition common in your family?"

"I suspect my mother has a similar problem. Her temper flares before meals quite often." He smiled wryly. "It may be that her temper flares are normal, however."

"She is a spirited lady," Alys ventured.

"I'd have put an adjective before the word 'spirited,' but I am ever a dutiful son."

Alys bit back her smile. "I don't think I have ever had a conversation quite like this one, my lord, outside my family."

"It is nice, isn't it?"

They smiled at each other. After a moment, Hatbrook placed his boots firmly on the ground and stood.

"Thank you for accepting my confidence, Miss Redcake."

"It was my pleasure."

He was still so close. Her gaze fixated on his plump lower lip, where a crumb clung. She lifted her hand—

He licked away the crumb. "I will see you at the ball this evening?"

"Of course. My family would not miss it." Instinctively, she licked her lips too, and tasted buttercream. She remembered the mess on her apron.

"Then I look forward to a waltz with you?"

She smiled at the incongruous nature of his request. "By all means. I promise to avoid your toes."

He inclined his head. "What are you going to do about Popham?"

"As little as possible, my lord."

He nodded and went to the door. She handed him another piece of cake she'd wrapped. He accepted it with a smile and took his leave.

It wasn't until he left that she realized he'd never quite disclosed why he had been in the back part of Redcake's.

Simon Hellman popped his head in. "Your father wants to see you, Alys."

She gulped. Who had told him she was here? Oh, she should have left sooner!

Michael felt his brain clearing as the fruitcake and water had its effect on his body. He blamed the fogginess of his thoughts for his bizarre questioning of Alys Redcake. Who was he to give a trades-man's daughter courting advice?

He stood in a dank corridor lined by racks. Gaslight flickered every few feet along the walls. So far his tour had shown Redcake's to be fresh and modern. Employees were active and full of purpose, and he already knew the clientele was enthusiastic. He'd seen no rea-son to turn him from his purchase, nor had Sir John or Mumford in their research. At least no reason other than the more time he spent here, the more the luscious baking smells would drive him to eat sweets. A continued relationship with Redcake's factories would sup-ply product, both raw and finished, though he'd have his staff keep an eye on rival companies to keep the prices reasonable.

A pity Alys Redcake wasn't a man. Dedication to one's position was laudable and he knew she had excellent bakery skills, though perhaps she wasn't the best cakie. Still, he had to accept any Redcake family member would have gone to the concerns that stayed in their father's empire. She wouldn't have been in his employ for long re-gardless of her sex.

Perhaps the fact that she'd come so close to being employed by him was why he was so concerned for her well-being. Yes, that was it, not her lithe form or puffy, kissable lips. And even though he liked her, she had far too much personality for a wife, possibly too much even for a mistress. She'd be one to complain if she were unhappy. No patient forbearance there, and he knew any wife of his would have to deal with his mother, which could not be easy. Admittedly he would not be the easiest husband either, with his strange brain fog and devotion to physical labor in Sussex. He'd never even last a season in London. She'd have to pack and move regularly to stay at his side.

He reached the door that led to the stairwell to the sales floor. A squeak sounded behind him and he saw two stout men pushing a wheeled rack loaded with the distinctive Redcake's boxes. They nodded at him, then turned to the right to take the rack onto the freight elevator, which was the latest hydraulic model.

Any man would be pleased to own a profitable business like this. He could count himself lucky that the Redcake family wanted to rusticate.

Alys found her coat, hat, and gloves and brought them with her upstairs, knowing her father would be sending her right out the door. Betsy would have to tidy the decorating room.

Ewan Hales appeared to be holding back a smirk as he ushered her into her father's presence and took her things before shutting the door behind him. Her father examined papers on his desk with a magnifying glass as she seated herself. After a pregnant pause, he set down the glass and looked at her.

Instinctively, Alys wanted to shrink back in her chair, but she stayed straight.

"I thought I made it clear you were no longer welcome here."

"I could not ignore the Marchioness of Hatbrook's order, sir," she said. "No one can do the work I can, and as she's seen my cakes, she'd have known if someone else decorated it. Also, I was unsure the order would be handled at all if I wasn't present. I left Redcake's so precipitously that I was unable to give instructions."

"You could have spoken to Ralph Popham last night."

"Work at the dinner table? You've expressly forbidden that for years."

"You cannot choose which of my rules to obey and which to not, Alys. I am your father. I will be obeyed."

She tried again. "I did not want to embarrass the family. We are attending the Hatbrook ball tonight. How could we hold our heads high if the firm did not supply the goods?"

"That would not be your decision to make. It would be mine." Her father's eyes narrowed. "You should have told me."

"I was angry."

Their stares locked for a moment, then, surprisingly, her father smiled. "It would have been better if you were a man, Alys, but you are not, and you must learn your place in this world. I will not have you damaging your sisters' chances."

Apparently, her father had not been warned that associating with Lady Lillian would damage them with no help from her. "I want them to be happy."

"Your behavior was appalling last night."

"Marrying me to your bakery manager would not endear my sisters on the marriage market."

"Ah, but he won't be my bakery manager then. I thought you were set on London? Your sisters will be in Sussex."

"You plan on separating me from them?" This was the last thing she had expected.

"No, I merely mean to place you with a husband."

"I'm not going to marry someone of such an advanced age. Why, he has a daughter old enough to work here."

"I thought Betsy was your friend."

"Friend, yes, but not daughter."

"Had you thought to marry better?"

His question struck her in a secret, prideful place. Her shoulders stiffened. "I had no thought to marry at all. I like having employment."

Her father picked up a fountain pen, then dropped it on the table. "You need to resign yourself to the elevation in your status."

"You still work. Gawain works. Seven days a week you come here."

"Not anymore, Alys. I've sold it, at least I think I have."

"What?"

"We're leaving, all of us. No more London. I hate it, Rose is ill."

"Mother likes it here. She loves the theater and other entertainments."

"She will be happy wherever I choose to be."

"And Matilda? Gawain? Lewis?"

"Matilda can find love in the country. Gawain will be miserable everywhere. Lewis stays here. I cannot believe neither of you informed me of his proposal."

"I did not take it very seriously." Though she should have, considering the Christmas gift. "I was never alone with him to discuss it."

"It should have been discussed with me. You do not behave as you should."

"I should have been a man," she said softly. "I could learn the business from you."

Her father waved a hand. "Oh, you have no head for business. You are happy with your cakes. Art and baking, female tasks. You have no idea what the rest of it is."

"You never offered me the chance to learn."

"Your sisters are far better educated than you are, and I can see they have nothing useful in their heads. I'm sure it would have been the same for you."

Alys's left hand shook. She tightened her fingers into a fist and pressed against the thick, black cloth of her dress. "I thought I was so valuable to you. I had so many ideas for the tea shop. My cakes made us popular at events of people with rank. And the Scotch trifle. I suggested we make it, and that brought you to the notice of the queen."

He stood slowly. His short stature did not reduce the awful majesty of his anger. "Do not ever think you are responsible for my success, young woman. You are a reflection of me, nothing more. Now leave here at once before I must consider further consequences to your disobedience and willfulness."

She stood at once, both hands in fists. With difficulty, she held her chin high, kept her booted feet from stomping. Slowly, she walked out and took her garments from Ewan. If he ever showed up at her dinner table, she'd slap the smirk from his revolting face.

She went into the street without even putting on her coat. Stinging snowflakes pelted her skin until she pulled on her hat and shrugged into her coat. She wished she had a muff so she didn't have to force her numbed fingers into gloves.

It took her much too long to walk home, but she couldn't find voice for even the most basic human interaction it would take for a conveyance.

When she reached the square, she discovered she couldn't enter her house and face her mother or sisters. Then, she saw her brother a few hundred yards away, in the middle of the square. She picked up her skirts and ran toward him, the cold air streaming from her mouth like smoke.

When she was a few feet away, she stopped and screamed at him.

"How can you not stop him? You could offer to buy it yourself with your army pay."

Gawain, expressionless, dropped his cheroot to the ground and ground it under his heel. "He did sell it then?"

"Or close enough."

"The tea shop means nothing to me."

Alys knew he must be lying. He must hurt like she did. "It has our family name on it."

He shrugged. "Arthur was the Redcake heir, not me."

She put her hand on his arm. "You are the heir now."

He tucked her hand more securely and began to walk again. "Father sent me into the army, to India. He didn't train me for the business, but discarded me."

Her brother's limping pace was as measured as his words, as if no emotion rested underneath. "He doesn't want Redcake's anymore. Shouldn't that make you want it all the more?"

"Oh, I've played at figures to keep the peace, but I can leave it now. No need for any more charades. I'm pleased with the start of my tea import business."

But not happy. She hadn't seen him happy since he joined the regiment at seventeen. "Gawain."

His mouth twisted. "While you were being a petted daughter, I was fighting villagers in the Black Mountains, losing my eye, damaging my hip."

Her heart thumped in outrage. "I wasn't petted! I worked. Things happened. Things I'll never tell you." Things she didn't care to remember herself.

"And there are things I'll never tell you."

She sniffed. Her nose must be flaming red from the cold now, and surely these tears clouding her vision were from the wind. "We were so close once."

"That was years ago. But don't worry, Twin. I still love you." He patted her hand and released her.

She found that he'd moved her in a circle that placed them in front of their house. "I don't know who I am without Redcake's. I'll die in the country."

"Then you'd better find a way to stay in London." He smiled tightly and walked away across the square.

Chapter Eight

She knew she couldn't stay here, not if staying meant marrying Ralph Popham. At least she didn't think her father was serious about him as a suitor. He wouldn't be so concerned with her new rank as the daughter of a knight if he was intent on the match.

She kicked at the remains of a snowman someone had built in the square, ignoring the damage to her boots as she ground the snow into grass. A scarf and disreputable top hat were soon all that remained. She picked them up, thinking they ought to go to the vicar's wife for her charities.

"Miss Redcake?" One of their matched pair of footmen approached. "Your mother would like to see you."

She sighed. "Yes, of course." One more lecture and then she'd need to get ready for the ball, assuming she hadn't been too disgraced to attend.

She hoped this wasn't the case. Other than the one wedding, she rarely had the opportunity to see her cakes in the setting for which they had been created. And, she must admit, she looked forward to seeing Hatbrook. Would he like the special chocolate cake his mother had planned for him and his cronies?

Even more deeply hidden was her desire to simply see him. If only the handsome man who'd entered her cake room this morning could have been a Redcake's employee, someone her social equal. If Ewan Hales or even Ralph Popham had his looks and manner she'd have been more inclined to favor them.

Once inside the house she went to her mother's dressing room. A large watercolor portrait of her father as a young man, painted by her mother, stared suspiciously at her, from next to a wardrobe.

"Alys," her mother said. "Your bath is ready in here, since Matilda is in your dressing room. Wash your hair, darling, you smell like the bakery."

"I'll never get it dry in time."

"Sit in front of the fire. I've had Lucy bring in your book so you can relax."

Alys narrowed her eyes. Her mother knew what she'd been doing this morning.

Edith cleared her throat and Alys allowed her mother's maid to help undress her, even though her cakie's uniform was easy to manage.

"Lewis packed his things," her mother said.

"You spoke to him?"

"Yes. He said you informed him that you do not plan to marry at all."

Her mother didn't know. She'd always wondered why they had never pressed her to wed. Her mother so clearly loved babies and surely wanted grandchildren while she was young enough to appreciate them.

"Personal choice, Mother," she said, as Edith unlaced her stays.

"I think there is more," her mother said slowly. "Won't you confide in me? You're lovely, never doubt it."

"You and Rose are positively beautiful," she said. "I'm passable at best. And not young."

"Fiddlesticks. Redheads can be lovely. We'll find someone for you. You simply cannot go on like you are, Father won't allow it."

"Surely there are other options."

"Like what? To live in Gawain's home, a spinster sister? You would be much happier running your own establishment."

Alys started to speak but her mother held up her hand. "Trust me as your mother, Alys. You would be happier wed."

"You've often spoken of your art and how you have no time to paint with so many children."

Her mother's hands lifted to her pale throat. "You think I regret my children?"

"You sound wistful when you say it."

"I wish to have more hours in the day, not fewer children," she said. "You must have children of your own to understand. Trust your father and me to know what is best."

"You are a very good painter. You could have been great, I expect, with more time."

"I'm happy, Alys, truly happy. I'd rather have joy than great art." She tapped her foot. "Enjoy your bath, darling. I know you don't like extravagance, but I did order you a new dress based on your measurements for the reception gown. Edith will help you dress when it's time."

Two housemaids entered with cans of steaming water and poured them into the tub, already half filled with cold water. Her mother tossed in a handful of lavender salts and then the maids left her to bathe.

"I have a little secret to share with you," her mother said.

"Yes?"

"While we are in the country, your father is going to have plumbing installed. Just cold water, since the heaters are so dangerous, but we'll have a permanent tub and sink with running water at the end of the hall!"

"He's keeping this house then?" Didn't her mother know about Redcake's? Maybe her father was only upgrading to make the house more valuable for sale.

"Of course. We'll need to come in for the Season until Gawain and your sisters wed."

Alys understood her meaning. She would be married off to someone very soon, probably before autumn. This house would never be her home again.

Michael couldn't resist sneaking into the second ballroom for a look at Alys's cake. The outside looked spectacular, of course, with its many, many threads of frosting and topping of numerals molded from paste, but he couldn't wait to taste it. The top layer smelled like chocolate, which would be a nice change of pace. He didn't eat it very often as it tended to make his tongue itch but a small slice would be something special for the taste buds.

As for the ball, he could do without it. A man in his position was expected to either dance with silly young debutantes if he was in search of a wife, or dance with whomever the hostess deemed necessary. Thankfully his mother didn't plan this type of event often. The best people never came to her parties, unless he was known to be attending. She blamed the poor attendance on Hatbrook House, which had not been redecorated in a quarter century due to lack of funds.

One of the doors opened and shut behind him. Expecting to hear a footman's boots, he was surprised by the *swish-click* of a lady's shoe. His mother, come after him? Surely she had better things to do. He turned.

The lady, dressed in a low-cut gown of draped blue-and-gray-striped silk that made her legs look impossibly long, was not his mother. She was a siren. Her hair looked like spun copper, smooth at the top then braided into a basketlike box at the back of her head. Gloves covered slim arms. The lady was a walking snare for gentlemen and he felt himself putting a foot into the trap. That small waist flared into hips made to cradle a man. His heart pumped furiously, sending blood south. He shifted, trying to think down a growing erection. Thank God for dim lighting.

She smiled tentatively. The slight movement had his focus moving from her hips to her face. That was when he realized this siren was Alys Redcake. The breath left his lungs so quickly that he coughed.

"Trying to sneak a slice, your lordship?" The accent was not aristocratic, but clear, bell-like. Pleasant and familiar.

He cleared his throat. "They haven't brought out the serving knives yet."

She stepped closer and he noticed her scent had changed slightly. Yes, he could smell orange flower water, but something sharper lurked there too. In her hair, perhaps? He leaned closer.

Her chest moved as she took a sharp breath. He realized he'd been about to sniff her.

He cleared his throat. "My apologies, Miss Redcake. You normally smell like cake but something is different tonight."

"And you like cake." The statement brought back a little laugh to her voice.

"Yes, yes of course." He put his hands on his hips, trying to restore some dignity. "Now you smell more like a woman than a cake, is all. Not a bad thing."

"You are the very font of flattery, my lord."

He gestured grandly. "I would venture to say you are more beautiful than this cake."

"Well, that would be saying something." She fluttered her arms as if not sure what to do with them.

"Do you remember that first day we met at Redcake's?" he asked.

"The Scotch trifle?"

"The very same. I recall wondering what you would look like in a ball gown. Now I don't have to wonder any longer." Had his voice actually cracked? How could he find her so lovely? She wasn't sweet or biddable.

"Do I meet expectations, my lord?" She stood still as he regarded her.

"I would not be surprised if someone carried you off before the night was through. You look positively edible." Another hot rush of blood moved south as his gaze found her breasts.

"A pity Ralph Popham is not here then." Her tone went sour.

He frowned. "Oh, you are not dressed to snare a Popham, Miss Redcake. Your lure is entirely above him."

"Not a bakery manager then, but perhaps some entirely superior sort, such as a butler?"

Her words caught him by surprise. He laughed, too hard, and put his hand to his chest. "Poor Alys. Do you not know you are fit for a prince?"

She stared at him. "Are you all right, sir? I was worried about you this morning."

He considered that declaration. "You never see me when I'm at my best."

"No?"

He thought. "You always see me when I'm hungry."

"Food can be very intimate." She cleared her throat.

He found himself fixated on her pale, powdered chest as it rose and fell, a bit too rapidly for a calm mind. "You have freckles, Miss Redcake."

Her hands moved to her breastbone. "It is not kind of you to mention them, sir."

"I like them," he decided. "You shouldn't try to cover them with powder. I'd rather see your skin glow naturally under the lights."

"This room isn't lit."

"Not by gas, perhaps. But candlelight is so flattering to a lady's skin."

She put her hand to her cheek. "Forgive me, but I've never spoken to a man like this before."

He touched one finger to her chin. "You need more flattery in your life, Miss Redcake. You surely deserve it."

Her large, nutmeg eyes stared into his. This was madness, but too much of his blood had found its way into a pulsating erection and there wasn't enough left in his brain to make sense of this conversation. Should he try for a kiss?

The double doors burst open. Booted feet and lady's heels sounded.

"Hatbrook!" exclaimed an irritable, high-pitched voice. "We have royal guests arriving. Come do your duty!"

Michael stepped back, before his mother could see he had his hands on a woman at her ball. He turned Alys slightly so she could not be recognized and moved toward his mother. When he reached her, he took her arm and guided her out.

Alys stayed in place for a moment. She wished she could sit here with her cake and try to figure things out, but obviously the room wasn't as private as it had seemed when Hatbrook had called her edible.

He said she needed more flattery. Did that mean his words were empty?

It didn't matter. The words of a marquess didn't matter to someone like her. The only way he'd be truly interested in her was if he needed her father's money, and he surely had his own fortune. Perhaps he simply liked her for herself?

It didn't matter. Thankfully, she didn't want to marry. She'd decided at fifteen that she didn't ever want a man to touch her. But Hatbrook had put his hand to her chin and she'd leaned closer. Her body wanted something her mind was certain it didn't.

She put both hands to her chin, turned in a circle. The room spun like her thoughts. Would she allow any man to touch her—or would only Hatbrook do? Could she let go of her past?

She rushed to the doors, opened one before her next thought. Hatbrook had left the immediate vicinity. She walked swiftly down the hall into the main ballroom, the light growing brighter as she reached the gaslit main ballroom. A succession of women was curtsying as Hatbrook walked by. As he came closer, she recognized the young man next to him—Prince Albert Victor, second in line to the throne. Swiftly, she dropped into a curtsy too. When she lifted her eyes, her gaze met Hatbrook's. Then his party passed by and entered the card room.

Any dreams she might just have begun to harbor must be dashed. This man was friendly with a future king! The music, the people, the heat and smells, all seemed too much to bear. She wanted to sit in a quiet corner by a fire.

"He's handsome, isn't he?" said the woman next to her. "The prince? I wonder who His Royal Highness will marry."

"Some foreign princess, no doubt," said her companion. "I admit I never thought to be in the same room with him."

"The marquess is said to be quite intimate with the royal family," said the first with a sigh. "I wonder who *he* will marry."

Alys looked more closely and thought the speaker was perhaps five years older than she was. In half mourning, for a husband perhaps, she might be on the lookout for another. But, she was too old for Hatbrook.

She heard a booming laugh, and recognized her father a few feet away. Turning, she went the opposite direction to look for her mother and sisters.

Ten minutes later she hadn't spotted any of the three, so she decided to look for Gawain. Knowing him, he'd be smoking somewhere, so when she found French doors leading to a patio, she braved the winter chill.

The dark shocked her vision and blinded her for a moment. No lit cigars pinpointed anyone outside, but as her eyes sharpened she thought she saw tall planters on one side that someone could hide behind. She stepped forward.

A thud resounded against a clay pot.

"Gawain?" she said softly.

Next came a moan, then a shuffle. The door opened behind her and loud booted steps moved in her direction.

"Florence?" said the man behind her.

More shuffles from behind the pot. A low curse.

"Florence!" shouted the man behind her.

Alys pressed herself against the stone wall of the house as a disheveled woman crept around the pot.

"Malcolm?" ventured the woman timidly. "Done with your card game so soon?"

"Get back into the house," the man said sharply.

She squealed, a thoroughly silly sound, and dashed back in.

Malcolm lit a cigar and puffed on it. Alys pressed back against the clay pot. She found a small opening, too tiny for a man, between the planter and the house. He dropped his match to the ground. As the match flared and died, she recognized Malcolm as Lord Mews, who held some government position.

"I know you're still there," Lord Mews said in a conversational tone.

Alys was about to step forward, but then she heard steps from the other side of the planter.

"What of it?" said a belligerent, slurred male voice.

"Do not presume to make sport of my wife and get away with it, sir."

The other man laughed. Alys could only see them as dark figures. The cigar illuminating Lord Mews's arm made him seem a bit demonic.

"Laugh, will you? I can stop that laugh, make you remember to stay away from us."

A rustle of clothing, a couple of running steps. The light from the cigar vanished momentarily. Then a man screamed.

"You bastard!"

"Fool!"

The light fell to the ground. The cigar must have dropped out of Lord Mews's hand. She smelled something burning, heard a slap, then the sound of a fist meeting flesh. A grunt. Then, both bodies were on the bricks, rolling around. The men barked at each other, throwing punches.

What should she do? Stay hidden? Try to break up the combatants? Surely, Lord Mews had been provoked, but if, as she thought, he'd burned the man with his cigar he was scarcely an innocent.

Hatbrook. She had to fetch him. It was his mother's party, after all. Swiftly, she crept along the house until she found the doors and opened them. A corridor stretched parallel to her. Where would Hatbrook be? She must be mindful of His Royal Highness. No scenes, no hysterics.

Swiftly, she went in the opposite direction of the ballroom, searching for the card room. After a couple of turns, she found herself in the main entryway. Sniffing, she hunted for cigar smoke, wasting precious moments.

"Can I help you, miss?" A footman came toward her from the direction of the ballroom. Tall, with sandy hair, his livery was impeccable.

"It is urgent that I speak to the marquess immediately."

"Miss?"

"I know it is highly unusual, but I'm trying to prevent scandal. Take me to him, please?"

The footman regarded her for a moment. "Scandal would be bad, miss."

"Yes. There's a fight."

He raised his eyebrows, then gestured to her. They walked toward the back of the entryway and he pushed a panel to the left of a grand staircase. It revealed a hidden opening and she followed him down a narrow passageway. Then, he pushed another panel and they were in a gaslit corridor.

"Wait here, miss. I'll fetch him."

She paced for a minute or two that felt like hours, then Hatbrook exited the room where the footman had entered. He held a glass of punch.

"Miss Redcake? James said something about a fight?" He took her elbow and pulled her close to a sconce. "Are you hurt?"

She felt a sizzle of heat where he touched her, and found it hard to think. "Not me. Lord Mews caught his wife with a man. I don't know who, it's so dark on the patio."

"Where?" He stared at her, then put his hand to her temple and smoothed her hair.

She leaned into his warm touch. "By those enormous planters? Out the French doors?"

He nodded and took her elbow again. "That could be two places. Show me?"

"You'd best take the footman. I'm completely lost."

"I can take you back to where I found you, miss. Will that do?"

She nodded, and they moved back to the grand hallway. When they reached it, she circled around then pointed. "That way."

"Lead on, Miss Redcake."

The footman found a candelabra on a table as they walked, helping her find her way.

She walked swiftly, because of the fight, but wished she could slow down, enjoy the press of Hatbrook's fingers on her glove. It was the work of a minute to find the doors. She heard a crash against one of them just as a party of ladies came into the corridor.

"Head them off," the marquess instructed James.

"Yes, my lord."

"Stay behind me," he said to Alys, then released her and opened the door. She took the three-pronged candelabra from James in case she needed a weapon.

The two men collided with Hatbrook as he stepped onto the flagstones. He stepped back and threw the contents of his glass into one of the men's faces—Alys wasn't sure which man—then punched the other.

She raised her candelabra to light the scene, shocked yet thrilled by Hatbrook's fighting prowess.

The man immediately went down on his backside. Hatbrook then grabbed the arm of Lord Mews, revealed to be a tall, bull-chested man of early middle years, and twisted it behind him, capturing him in a painful grip.

"You will stop this instant, Lord Mews," he said.

The man on the ground, really not much more than a boy despite being the adulterer, started coughing. His face appeared yellowish and bruised under the candlelight. Alys felt a sticky substance under her slipper when she took a step toward him. Blood?

"Who? What?" sputtered Lord Mews.

"It's Hatbrook. You are beating a man at the marchioness's ball, my lord."

"I-I was provoked."

"I can recall a similar scene at one of Countess Gerrick's parties last year," said Hatbrook, his voice turning to ice. "Do not attempt to persuade me that this is not a sick game between you and your wife."

Alys gripped the candelabra tighter. Could Hatbrook be serious?

"You," Hatbrook pointed to the man on the ground. "Manfred Cross, correct? I believe I was at school with your oldest brother."

The young man nodded, and winced, putting his hand to his mouth.

"I don't know if you are a usual part of this game or not, but I want you to leave. My footman is just inside this door and he will lead you out."

"Yes, my lord," slurred Manfred Cross, who was dressed in lower-quality evening wear. Alys could see where the stitching had pulled away on the arm seams of his half-open shirt.

She set down her candelabra and helped him to his feet. With her assistance, he stumbled back through the French doors. She was happy to see James had found another footman and he took charge of the drunk, who was unsteady on his feet, half dressed, and from the looks of him, had at least a few loose teeth after the night's exploits.

When she went back outside, Hatbrook had released Lord Mews and was remonstrating him in a low voice.

Lord Mews bowed when he saw her. "My apologies, miss."

Alys was sickened by the smells of fresh, coppery blood, rank sweat, and burned flesh. "Shall I ask the footman to fetch a doctor?"

Lord Mews grinned through bloodied teeth. "He got the best of it."

She wanted to put her hands over her eyes until he went away, but reminded herself she was made of sterner stuff than that.

"Collect your wife and leave quietly," Hatbrook instructed. "If any word of this gets out I'll report you to the prime minister."

Lord Mews gulped. "Now Hatbrook, no need to get overexcited. Why no one saw anything except this young lady, and I'm sure she won't tell."

"I'm sure I'd like to forget every part of this instantly," Alys snapped.

Hatbrook flexed his fingers. After one last glance at him, Lord Mews slunk out.

"Well done of you to have James come for me," Hatbrook said.

"You are welcome, your lordship," she ventured. "I wanted to be discreet. I know you have important guests."

"You behaved most appropriately, and for that I sincerely thank you. Let us go back inside. I expect we both need a bit of tidying."

She glanced at herself, noticed smears on her gloves. "Just my gloves, I think they are ruined."

"We'll find you a new pair," he said. "I'll take you to my sister, Lady Elizabeth. She isn't out yet, but she will be soon so she has all the garments we might require."

"You are too kind, sir, but don't you need to get back to His Royal Highness?"

"He is being looked after." The marquess smiled and held out his arm. "Come, we have earned a bit of time together after our exertion."

She felt the firm musculature of his arm as she took it. This was no ordinary man. He took her down a hall and up a staircase she'd never have found on her own. This place was a maze.

When they were surely far away from any guests, she asked, "Do fights happen often at balls? I've never been to a ball like this before."

"Do people sneak off for a bit of illicit fun? I expect that is common enough, but usually they are discreet and are not found."

So not too many fights then. "I am glad to hear it, my lord."

"You know, it's strange to have you here at my house after seeing you at Redcake's."

She flushed. "I can go back downstairs."

"No, not at all. You fit in here better than I'd hoped."

He'd had hopes about her? Alys felt an odd fluttering in her stomach. "Thank you, my lord. I have been in great houses before, on business for Redcake's." Though mostly in the kitchens.

"Yes, you are quite the artist with your cakes."

"Thank you. Tell me, did you feel better this morning, after eating the cake?"

"For a while. Ah, here we are." He opened a door and they entered the corridor of another wing. "Any sort of sweet makes me feel better for an hour or so, then it's back to feeling ill."

"Any food does that?"

"No, just sweets. If I ate a meal of meat and potatoes I'd feel fine for hours."

"It sounds as if sweet food isn't good for you."

He smiled. "But I love it so. I'm afraid I consume far too much of it."

When she looked at the way his evening clothes hugged his body, she found it hard to believe. He had the broad shoulders, wide chest, and strong legs of a sporting man. "Do you box, sir? You were quite effective in that fight."

"I've been known to spar with my stable hands at Hatbrook Farm, my estate in Sussex. When rain has kept us indoors."

"You do strike me as a man who likes to keep busy." Unable to resist, she gently squeezed his arm.

"Yes, I'm not one to sit on a sofa listening to music, or play cards for that matter. I'd rather ride or dance or do something else. I spend too much time in my chair doing paperwork."

They stopped at a fine, paneled door and Hatbrook knocked. After a moment, the door opened and a slim girl with his sun-kissed hair peered out.

"Michael? What are you doing up here? It's so early." She tilted her head when she noticed Alys.

She took her hand from his arm.

"Beth, may I present Miss Alys Redcake? Alys, this is my sister, Lady Elizabeth Shield."

Chapter Nine

Until now, Alys hadn't realized she'd never known Hatbrook's full name—Michael Shield. Quite nice.

"Call me Beth," his sister said. "If you're a friend of Michael's."

Alys glanced at Hatbrook and he smiled encouragingly, so she stuck out her hand. "Nice to meet you, Beth."

Beth reached for her, then pulled back. "Oh? What happened to your glove? Did you have a bloody nose? I get those in the winter sometimes."

"No, she helped me break up a fight," Hatbrook said.

"How scandalous!" Beth's eyes widened. "You must come in, Alys, and tell me everything. Go away, Michael, and don't come back for half an hour or so. We shall be tidying."

Hatbrook winked at Alys and patted his sister on the shoulder. "Be good."

Beth drew Alys into a comfortable sitting room and reached for the bell pull. "Strip off those gloves and I'll have some soap and water brought."

"Thank you."

"Are you part of Michael's set?" Beth asked.

"No, I'm new to this world." She wanted to laugh. Alys Redcake, part of a set that played cards with a prince?

"Oh, come up from the country?"

Alys fought with the tiny buttons on her gloves.

"I'll help you." Beth pushed her gently onto a sofa and sat next to her so she could undo the buttons.

"No, I've lived in London for a couple of years now. We came from Bristol."

"Where did you meet Hatbrook?"

"At Redcake's Tea Shop and Emporium."

"I do love it there. My mother has taken me there twice. You must be a member of that family?"

"Yes, I worked there until recently."

"Worked there?" Beth looked shocked, but not censorious.

"Yes, I made the special occasion cakes. It is a passion of mine."

"Why did you stop?"

"My parents want me to marry."

"Ah. That is my fear, that my mother will try to marry me off my first Season. But I don't want the fun to stop so soon."

"I'm quite a bit older than you," Alys confessed.

"Have your parents chosen a husband?"

"I had a proposal from a cousin that they frowned on, and I'm not thrilled with my father's choice. He's forty."

"My goodness, that's entirely too elderly," Beth agreed. "Is he terribly rich?"

"Not at all, he works for my father. But my parents want me married quickly, so they can focus on my younger sisters. Rose is just a year older than you, and Matilda is twenty-one."

"Are they as nice as you are? Does Michael know them?"

"They were introduced at a musicale recently. We were raised rather differently, with them attending finishing school."

"And you worked." The shrewd expression was jarring on a young girl.

"Yes, my family didn't have much money when I was young. My grandfather died in terrible debt and my father had to rebuild."

"Just like Michael! He's worked terribly hard to restore the family fortune. To think, my mother suggested he ought to marry an American heiress only a year ago."

She would rate even lower than an American trade or manufacturing heiress. No mystique. Besides, Lady Hatbrook didn't like her. "My sisters are friendly with Lady Lillian Cander, from finishing school. Are you acquainted?"

Beth shook her head. "Even if I was out, she runs with a fast crowd."

"That is my understanding. But I'm afraid I don't know anyone else in the social whirl."

"You know me, now. After I've debuted in May we'll see each other frequently."

Alys smiled, touched beyond words that this young girl wanted to be friendly with her. "It will do my sisters a world of good to have such a friend as you."

A maid entered, and Beth instructed her to bring warm water, towels, and fresh gloves.

"We went to Paris a couple of months ago, and ordered the most horribly expensive new wardrobe, but Mother wanted to shop before the Americans descended. Can you imagine a wardrobe costing twenty thousand pounds? I know it's vulgar to discuss money, but my heavens."

"That does seem excessive," Alys agreed as she cleaned her arms and dried them.

"We'll button you into the new gloves and you'll be good as new if your charming gown is clean. Stand up and we'll inspect you."

Beth circled Alys as she stood in the center of the rug. "No, I don't see any stains. My, but you have lovely curves."

Alys blushed. Beth and her maid had scarcely finished buttoning her into the even tighter gloves before a discreet knock came on the door.

"That will be Michael come to fetch you. Have a lovely time and I hope you'll call on me soon."

"I'd like that."

Beth answered the door, then ushered her out with a smile.

"Good as new?" Hatbrook asked as the door closed behind them.

"Yes. My dress didn't need sponging and Beth offered me these gloves. I hadn't realized how muscled my arms were until she tried to button me into them. We are the same size otherwise, I think." She blushed again when she realized how improper her conversation must be.

"If you may permit, my thought when I first saw you was how slim you were. I should not have expected a full-grown woman to fit into a girl's gloves."

"You are full of flattery, sir."

"Do you know, it was your ankles that attracted me when we first met."

Alys found it hard to take a breath. "My ankles?"

"Yes. And your fiery dark eyes. You have a magnificent spirit."

She swallowed hard, fisted her hands in the too-tight gloves. "I like your hair."

He leaned casually against the wall. "You do?"

"Yes. I always think of it as sun-kissed."

"I spend a lot of time outdoors. But the color usually darkens in the winter."

"A pity. It's quite nice as it is." She spoke the next words in a rush. "You have hungry eyes, I think."

The corners of his eyes crinkled. "I do?"

"That was my first impression of you. An austere, almost haughty demeanor, but hungry eyes."

"Austere. I never thought of myself that way."

"You seem to set yourself apart a little. No one would think you were the average man."

"I could say the same about you."

She took a step forward. "But I am not a man."

He lifted her hand, touched her cheek with one finger. "I know that."

Time seemed to have stopped. Her lips parted instinctively, even as her brain screamed, "This is a marquess! What are you thinking?"

"I'm a woman," she whispered.

One finger became a palm against her cheek. It slid down along her jaw, then caressed the back of her neck. He drew her toward him. The side of her arm touched the wall, underneath a painting of Jupiter seducing a maiden.

"Alys, you are lovely."

Her breath caught. His fingers had found her back now, made circles on her skin. His other hand reached out to her free arm. It moved down her arm and found her gloved fingers. He tugged until her hand was on his chest.

"Are you real?"

His mouth quirked. "Oh yes, Alys."

He tilted toward her, until she could feel his warm breath on her cheek. She kept her eyes open, saw the way his eyebrows fanned out at the edges, how the tip of his nose was just a little crooked. He had a tiny mole high on his left cheek. His upper lip, slightly shorter than the lower, had a prominent bow. He smelled like gingerbread.

She felt the tips of her breasts harden. The unfamiliar sensation made her want to press herself against him. He seemed to feel the same way, because his hands linked behind her, pulled her forward.

"You're very warm."

"You're very pretty."

Then, they were much too close not to kiss, even she knew that, who had not been kissed in more than a decade. Her lips moved toward his, his head dipped to her. Breath met, then soft skin. Her hand crept to his neck and her fingers clasped him, clung.

She felt the moist tickle of his tongue at the corner of her mouth. Surprise opened her lips and he swept in, bringing ginger and cake and something unfamiliar, so male, so foreign, yet so enticing she felt her legs quiver.

Her other hand moved inside his coat, inside his waistcoat, until all that was between her and his warm flesh was a thin shirt and her glove. How he radiated heat. The muscles of his shoulders moved under her other fingers as he toyed with her mouth.

Then, suddenly, he was no longer inside her mouth, against her. He moved her hand from his neck. Had she done something wrong?

"Yes?" Hatbrook asked.

Fingers of shock danced down her back when she realized someone else had come into the corridor. She dared not extricate herself and reveal her face.

"Your mother sent me to ask after you?"

She recognized the footman's voice and sagged with relief.

"I'll be right down, James. Thank you."

She kept her face to Hatbrook's shoulder until the footsteps died away. A moment later, she felt his finger under her chin, lifting. His gaze found hers.

"We should have expected that."

"It's the middle of a ball."

His lips brushed the tip of her nose. "Thank you for everything tonight, Alys."

She nodded, robbed of speech.

"You're all put to rights? Your hair is pinned securely."

She touched it. "Yes, I don't think I'm mussed."

"Then I must offer you my arm. I'll take you to your family."

"I think I'll go alone, once we're downstairs. You should get back to your responsibilities."

His sea-glass gaze didn't falter. "Very well."

They went back down in silence. She had no idea what to say to him and was afraid if she opened her mouth, she'd beg him to take her back, kiss her again, and she couldn't ask for that. So instead, she curtsied very slightly when they reached the front hallway. She went into the ballroom and he headed for the prince.

"Did you bolt into a corner like a mouse?" Matilda asked the next day as they were seated in the back parlor, sipping tea with Lady Lillian.

Alys could hear wind in the chimney, though she still felt unaccountably warm, as if Hatbrook's kiss had the effect of an invisible fur blanket wrapped around her.

"Miss Redcake?" Lady Lillian asked.

She blinked. "Sorry, no, woolgathering. Actually, I had a most eventful evening."

"I don't see how that is possible. Father brought some man to meet you and you weren't even in the ballroom!"

"I couldn't find you and so I went to look for Gawain."

"So you spent the evening with our brother?" Rose asked. "When you might have been dancing?"

"I went outside during my hunt and things became complicated after that."

Matilda's eyes narrowed. "I was right. I knew something had happened. You seemed so flustered."

Alys's mind went to the kiss. But no, surely she had composed herself sufficiently to hide her emotions after such an experience. She'd schooled herself in front of customers regardless of her mood for years. "I had to replace my gloves. Lady Elizabeth, the marchioness's daughter, lent me a pair. I suppose I should return them. Or purchase her another pair?" She looked to Lady Lillian for guidance. "Oh, but they are French. I couldn't replace them."

"Simply have them cleaned," said the earl's daughter.

"Thank you. I'm so relieved that will be sufficient."

Lady Lillian reached for a third biscuit. "How did you meet her? She isn't out yet."

Alys recounted witnessing the fight and getting blood on her hands. She let the girls believe a footman took her to the daughter of the house. Her time with Hatbrook felt too intimate to share. With difficulty, she kept her fingers from creeping to her lips as she remembered. Indeed, she had barely slept all night for remembering the feel of his mouth against, inside, hers.

"You really do need to become engaged to someone," Lady Lillian told her. "You need not marry to open the field for your sisters. Just give your parents hope so they will stop focusing all their attentions on you and give your sisters a chance."

"That is why I was upset with you," Matilda agreed. "When you hide away, you ruin things for us."

"Perhaps Lewis?" Rose asked.

Alys shook her head. "I couldn't pretend to love him properly."

"Father would go insane," Matilda said. "Besides, I happen to know he's bringing another possible suitor to dinner tomorrow night. That was agreed when he couldn't be introduced to you at the ball."

"Excellent." Lady Lillian clasped her hands together. "You just need to have him propose, then if you don't suit, you can break it off in the summer after the Season has ended."

"Do you think we can find husbands in one Season?" Rose coughed daintily into her handkerchief.

"With your looks and money? Of course."

Alys expected her father to demand they pack for the country, but instead, the next night, he came home with another bachelor dinner guest as Matilda had claimed he would. Were they going to stay in London until she'd made a match?

Rose had stayed in bed much of the day, pale and racked with coughs. She waved away cigar smoke, saying the treatment made her dizzy, but the lobelia tincture helped enough that she was able to dress for dinner after a cup of coffee.

Alys walked in front of Rose down the stairs, so she could break her fall if her unsteady sister lost her balance. Matilda walked behind. They were both wearing new dresses, wheedled out of their mother the day their reception gowns were ordered. Alys wore her old green sateen, which she'd thought very nice until she saw her sisters' new gowns. Since sateen was more durable than satin, the dress had been in her wardrobe since 1884 and was not in the newest style. It had a short, draped apron front that no longer looked fashionable next to Rose's sashes and Matilda's flat panel of rose-bedecked satin.

"You really should have something new," Matilda said, echoing her thoughts. "You are the one on display tonight."

"Who is the gentleman?" Alys asked when they reached the bottom of the stairs.

As they walked into the drawing room, Matilda said, "Theodore Bliven."

Alys also said, "Theodore Bliven," recognizing the wavy, almost curly chestnut-brown hair and dimpled grin, currently being used on their mother.

"You remember meeting him at the musicale?" Rose whispered.

"We met at Redcake's." She remembered him as a tease.

"They say he is dependent on an uncle for his allowance," reported Matilda. "So a rich wife might be just the thing."

"How does he spend his time?"

"You'll have to speak to him." Rose gave her a little push.

"Ah, my daughters," Sir Bartley said, gesturing them over.

Mr. Bliven bowed slightly as they walked forward. "Yes, I had the pleasure of meeting the young ladies shortly before Christmas."

"We met in November at Redcake's," Alys said.

He nodded. "Of course."

She couldn't stop herself from continuing, despite Matilda's horrified stare at her. "You were with the Marquess of Hatbrook."

"Indeed, one of my oldest friends. Your father brought me to your delightful sisters last night at the ball, but I missed you."

She nodded. "Perhaps the marquess explained what happened."

"I did call today," he admitted.

At least he didn't smile at that. Surely Hatbrook hadn't told him about their kiss, just about the fight.

"Dinner is served," Pounds said, coming into the room.

Mr. Bliven offered Alys his arm and they walked into the dining room together behind her parents. Her mother managed to seat him next to her, across from Matilda.

"You thought quickly," he said, after the mock turtle soup had been served. "I believe most women would have run screaming, rather than possess the self-control to get help, but I suppose you are used to drama in the tearoom."

Alys dropped her spoon into her soup. It clattered loudly, spraying the broth across the white linen tablecloth. She checked her dress but thankfully it hadn't been stained.

Mr. Bliven cleared his throat. "Or perhaps you like drama in general."

Matilda tittered. "You are such a rogue, Mr. Bliven, I do declare."

He nodded modestly, his mouth twisted up on one side.

Alys found she quite disliked this friend of Hatbrook's. "You said you are an old friend of the marquess?"

"Yes, at Oxford together. He never came to London before that and I've always lived here, but we see each other frequently now."

"Belong to the same clubs and all that?"

"No, actually. We have different political leanings and our clubs are slanted along those lines. I belong to White's and he belongs to Brook's."

Alys thought that meant he was a Tory, a conservative, which meant Hatbrook had liberal leanings, but her newspaper reading tended to focus on personalities more than politics. "I see, so it is the past that binds you together?"

"I like to think we share a sense of humor," he said blandly.

She realized she was spending far too much time discussing Hatbrook and not enough time discussing Mr. Bliven. The fact that she'd rather discuss Hatbrook was beside the point.

"A sense of humor is so important, I find," Matilda said.

Alys thought her sister had developed a rather stuffy manner of speech all of a sudden. Her cheeks were pink as well. Did she find Theodore Bliven charming? "I believe gentlemen make the most amusing bets at clubs. Do you like to make bets?"

She heard a squeak and glanced at Rose, afraid it had really been a wheeze, the start of an attack, but realized the noise had been a horrified one and came from her mother. "Not that I mean to imply you are a gambler, sir."

His dimples showed. "Once again I am the source of your discomposure, Miss Redcake."

"I was merely attempting to ascertain your type of humor, sir. Everyone at this table enjoys a good laugh." Except Gawain, perhaps, though that wasn't always true.

"I did witness a three-thousand-pound bet once, between two young gentlemen."

"Good heavens," Rose said, "it must have been very important."

"Only in the financial sense. The bet was over which of their sisters' cats had the most whiskers. Emissaries were sent to do the counting. I remember it most particularly because one of the sisters in question ended up marrying the man who counted."

"Oh dear," said their mother faintly.

Sir Bartley chuckled loudly. "Capital fun! I cannot say my club gets up to such hijinks."

"Not every day is such fun, I admit. I prefer a greater variety in my dining options, for one thing."

"Alys is a wonderful cook," her mother said.

"I don't cook at all, actually," Alys said. "I bake."

"But when you were younger—" her mother said, then stopped, perhaps because her father narrowed his eyes.

Alys supposed wealthy young ladies never saw a kitchen, much less learned to cook.

"I did know you baked," said Mr. Bliven in an ostentatious tone that made clear he knew he was being gracious. "I've had the honor of tasting your cakes a time or two. That chocolate cake last night was quite deliciously rich."

"Are you a fan of chocolate, Mr. Bliven?" Matilda set her spoon to the side of her bowl. "I find many gentlemen are not."

"I like it excessively," he said, patting his waistcoat.

"What other enjoyments have you?" Alys asked, then realized that could be a very improper question.

He dimpled, but took the high road. "I enjoy riding and a variety of outdoor pursuits as well as reading and talking politics. Hatbrook would call me a gossip, but that's a rather womanish term, I think."

"I expect I like gossip too," she said, "but not so much about people I know, as people who are in the news, that kind of thing."

"I like both," he said decidedly, as the fish course was brought in. "Ah, sole. I do love a good fish."

"You enjoy food," Matilda said.

"Why wouldn't I? Though not so much as Hatbrook. He leans to the pastry line, but he's quite an aficionado." He winked at Alys.

After that, she gave up and left the floor to Matilda. Mr. Bliven clearly knew, or thought he knew, that she was more interested in his friend. Sadly, Mr. Bliven was apparently within her marital prospects while the marquess was not. And Lady Lillian had said she should at least become engaged to smooth her sisters' paths, even if she broke the engagement off later. Theodore Bliven would probably not have minded a broken engagement very much, but she could see Matilda was genuinely intrigued by him.

So when Mr. Theodore Bliven was announced at three in the afternoon the next day, she was not surprised that he called for Matilda, not for her. Perhaps Matilda would find a husband and she would not even have to become engaged. This suited her very well.

She decided to sneak out for a walk, since her conversational skills were not required. Not surprisingly, she found herself on the well-worn path to Redcake's. Would the façade look any different to her now that she'd been away for a few days?

As the bitter, coal-soaked air coated the back of her throat, she wondered what she would do with herself in the country. Even a walk would be so different. There'd be no urban sounds, no one to jostle her. She'd probably hear more birdsong than voices. There might be days with no companions other than her sisters. She loved them, but their constant company would drive her mad. Even their concerns would have to change. Who would know if they dressed in the latest fashions deep in the country? It would be a rare thing to have a handsome gentleman cross their path. She foresaw some type of Jane Austen life, and she couldn't stand that lady's novels. So utterly dull, to think of nothing but husbands all the time.

Because it was cold and foggy, not because she needed to visit, she decided to pop in for a cup of tea. The tea shop was quite empty for that time of day and she found herself thinking of ways to boost street traffic before she remembered it wasn't her business anymore. The entire enterprise was probably a very small part of her father's holdings, despite the importance it held to her.

"Miss Redcake!"

Alys turned, expecting to find Popham or Hellman or Hales, since the voice was familiar, but when she looked to the right she discovered Hatbrook at a table. She wondered how she could possibly have thought her name came from the lips of anyone else. Perhaps because he'd spoken in a loud whisper, rather than in his usual bass tones. He looked a bit pale and perhaps his hair had begun to dull a bit. Had he spent too much time indoors?

She noticed the telltale remains of raspberry jam in his empty dish. "Enjoying the trifle before it goes off the menu again, my lord?" The sheen on his lips reminded her of his kiss. Suddenly, her body felt so warm it was as if she'd never been outside.

"Couldn't resist." He stacked a sheath of papers and tucked it into a leather case, then stood. "Join me?"

"I just came in for a moment to get warm," she lied, not wanting to tempt him into seconds of his treat. Unless she was mistaken, his collar seemed tight. Either he'd put on someone else's clothing this morning or he'd put on a bit of holiday weight. "Would you care to join me on my walk?"

"I would like that," he said. "I sat next to the lamp to get good light, but the hissing and clanking does get to one after a time."

"Indeed, my lord." That must be it. He looked pinched because of a headache. "I cannot promise fresh air, precisely, but a change."

"A change is an excellent thing. Business keeps me in London for now, but I must escape soon." He took his coat from the chair next to him and put it on, then found his hat and tucked his case under his arm.

She waved to Betsy Popham as they walked out. Did she know of her father's romantic intentions? Of course, after the scene with Lewis, she hadn't seen Popham again. He'd probably been scared off by it. All for the best. And now, she tempted herself with a most unsuitable man, though perfectly wonderful in her eyes.

"What plans do you have for the new year, Miss Redcake?"

She made a general sort of noise.

He straightened his coat collar. "The Jubilee celebrations should be a good bit of fun. Her Majesty and the other royalties will be making all kinds of appearances."

She'd see them only from afar, while he'd be at all the best events. "I expect there will be a lot of parties and things, even in Sussex?"

"I expect so."

The differences between them made her change the subject. "What kind of hobbies do you take up in the country, sir, other than boxing with stable hands?"

"I make wine." He took her arm as they crossed a busy street. "Would you like some roasted chestnuts?"

"Certainly." They'd feel lovely in her hands, almost as lovely as the feel of his hand on her mantle.

He made a purchase from a street vendor and gave her the paper cone.

"Thank you. Do you think I could make wine?" She offered him a chestnut but he waved it away.

"It takes a vineyard. Did your father buy land?"

"Lots of it, I believe, but I think there are tenant farms."

"You might pursue charity. These farm families often have so many children. I can't imagine how the women manage."

"Yes, I expect I'll do that." She remembered poverty, though nothing like farm poverty.

"Do you like children?"

What an odd question from a man. "I suppose I don't spend much time with them. I do not have any nieces or nephews as of yet."

"Nor I."

"Theodore Bliven is calling on my sister this afternoon." She peeled the shell off a warm chestnut, then removed the papery skin.

"He said he was having dinner with your family last night." His statement sounded like a question.

She sighed. "We mixed as well as oil and water, just like the day we met at Redcake's. He's not serious enough for me."

"I am sorry. He does like his fun. We see each other quite a bit in town. But he has never been to Sussex."

"I'm not sorry. Maybe he and Matilda will suit. She seemed amenable."

"He does have prospects. And your other sister, does she have suitors?"

"Not as of yet. She's just a year older than Lady Elizabeth."

"We'll have to ensure their acquaintance."

He really did seem to accept her family. Were they to be part of his set now? Her heart fluttered. Could she stand to be close to him? "Indeed. Rose will be in raptures over your sister's Paris wardrobe. Oh, I need to return Lady Elizabeth's gloves. I'm having them washed today."

"I'm sure she wouldn't mind if you kept them, or even gave them to Miss Rose Redcake if they don't suit you."

"They might fit her better," Alys agreed.

"And you, Miss Redcake? Do you have suitors?"

Chapter Ten

Suitors? Did she have suitors? Was Hatbrook a suitor? "I didn't look to marry," Alys said.

He smiled. "That doesn't mean you have no suitors. Though I suppose it may mean you have none who interest you."

She remembered his kiss. That moment had suited her very well. She couldn't imagine such a kiss from Lewis, or Ralph Popham, or even handsome Theodore Bliven. But if Hatbrook was her suitor, she could imagine being swept up in a courtship. "That may be the case."

"I expect your father will find another. Theo said he seemed quite determined."

The chestnuts no longer looked appealing. "How humiliating."

"Not at all. No one who met you would think for a moment they needed to be forced to offer you their regard. You are a most attractive girl, Miss Redcake."

"I'm twenty-six, definitely a spinster."

"A lot of people have delayed marriage in these difficult financial times. Men need to build their fortunes. It takes time."

"Is that why you have not married?"

"I would have needed a delay two years ago when my father died, if I'd had a prospective bride at the time. But I've been in no hurry, since I have a suitable heir."

"No pressure from your mother?"

"I doubt she is in any rush to move into the Dower Cottage."

"Especially with your sister to bring out."

"Quite. Who could blame her? I do expect she'd clash with a saint, so I need to choose my bride most carefully."

It would be the height of ill manners to agree with him regarding his mother, so Alys kept her mouth closed. She'd rather return to the part of the conversation about her attractiveness. Flattery had never interested her until it came from those lips.

"Would you like to come back to the house to see Mr. Bliven?" Alys asked.

"I'd rather stay out here. Come." He took her arm and drew her up the steps of a shuttered storefront. The sign in the window said the owner was visiting family and would return Tuesday.

A little alcove to the left held just enough space for them both, partially protected from the world of the street.

"This is very nice, don't you think?" he asked.

Alys felt very warm, despite the chill air. She tucked the rest of her chestnuts into her muff, withholding one. After peeling it, she lifted it to his mouth. "Chestnut?"

He parted his lips. She could smell the Drambuie on his breath as she fed it to him.

"Better for you than pastry, I expect, sir. I understand some eat chestnuts instead of potatoes."

His lips closed around the nut and he chewed it slowly. "Delicious. You do enjoy feeding people."

The color had come back to his cheeks, the high color of winter cold and his nose had reddened a bit, but she could see his eyes clearly for the first time. A true sea blue with a dark ring around the edge of the iris, just a hint of gray in the color.

"You have handsome eyes," she said without thinking.

He swallowed hard, spluttered a bit. "I think I'm the one to say that."

She laughed, and to cover her nerves peeled another chestnut and fed it to him, then prepared one for herself. In companionable fashion they finished the cone.

"You seemed to eat them with as much enthusiasm as you do pastry."

"Being fed by hand does add a certain spice that makes up for the lack of butter and cream," he said, twinkling. "Alys, what is it that we are doing here?"

She hesitated for a moment. What could she say? He felt like a friend, though she had little experience with friendship. She found him very attractive. Perhaps this was the kind of relationship that led to one's becoming a mistress, but she had no experience with such things, nor understanding of men of his rank. Or did her father's money command a different approach from him? "I—I'm not sure, my lord. Have we been terribly improper?"

"What do you think?"

"We've been alone together, but not behind closed doors. We've walked together but not touching as would be inappropriate."

"Yes?"

She touched her lips. "You kissed me."

"What did you think about that?"

His sea gaze seemed to swallow her up. "It was lovely. Quite the loveliest thing I could imagine."

"Alys," he said, his voice gone hoarse. "I had not expected you."

He reached for her and she found her hands pressed against his coat. Her muff hit the pavement. When his lips came down to meet hers, she touched him with a gasp of surprise and a melting feeling of submission. If this was how one became a mistress, then she was doomed to fall. How could she resist him?

His lips were cold but inside he emanated a warm, spicy heat. She flung her arms around his neck and pressed herself closer, drowning in his masculine warmth. Oh, but she could feel so little with all this winter fabric between them! He turned her so she rested against the wall, let his lips slip to her cheek, then to her neck. Her muffler loosened as his warmed lips danced there. She felt his tongue slide along the underside of her jaw.

"Hatbrook," she whispered.

"Call me Michael." He found her lips again, dipped in, plundered.

Pounding feet rang on the street outside the doorstep. A policeman's whistle sounded and a woman screamed. Alys heard all this distantly, but then Michael lifted his lips from her mouth. She made a sound of protest but he stepped back.

"I believe we've lost our privacy." He snuggled her muffler against her neck. "I'm afraid I do have somewhere to be soon besides."

Alys glanced at the sky through the doorway and saw dark approaching. "I need to get home too."

"May I call on you tomorrow?"

Alys's stomach, and heart too, took wing. He wanted to call on her? That indicated a respectable interest, not a tawdry one. Or so she thought. She'd missed the kind of education young ladies had in finishing school. The gossip she'd heard in the workplace was an earthier brew. She hoped she didn't make any egregious misstep.

What if he proposed? Her parents could find no fault in her, or her sisters. She would have months of peace.

"We will be at home at the usual hour," she said primly, touching her hat.

"You look fine, Miss Redcake. Quite a picture."

"Thank you, my lord." She grinned at him.

"Let me escort you to the square."

She rewrapped her muff. "If it is not out of your way."

"It is not."

He offered her his arm as she stepped into the damp street, then she let go as propriety demanded. Ironic, since her lips, her neck, her very skin still tingled from his touch. She'd never felt so warm, so liquid, so alive. The sensation made her giddy, made her want to skip like a child.

A marquess wanted to call on her, she, Alys Redcake. Far more importantly, Michael did. Her father would not plan more uncomfortable dinners for her if a marquess called.

"Starting to rain," Michael said, looking up.

"I suppose we should walk faster," Alys said, wishing she could take tiny, slow steps to prolong the excursion. But, she soon thought differently as the rain turned to hail.

They ran down the slippery pavement, Michael's hand at her elbow.

"Maybe we should stop until it passes."

"You'll be late," she gasped. "It's not much farther." She did not want to irritate him.

They ran again, the hail turned to snow, then rain again, all in the space of fifteen minutes. Soon, they were at the edge of the square.

"I feel quite exercised," Michael said, reminding Alys that she thought he'd gained weight.

"I am glad we both have good lungs," Alys huffed. "Thank you."

Michael bowed his head slightly to her, then crossed the street. She stood despite the weather, watching his top hat until she couldn't tell the difference between him and half a dozen more male passers-by, warmed by his kiss and his promise. Then, she pushed dripping wet hair out of her eyes and went to her front door.

"Miss!" Pounds said, alarm in his voice when he regarded her. "You'll catch your death."

"On the contrary, I've never felt more alive," she said, still a bit out of breath. "But I must get out of these wet things."

"Your father has come home and needs to see you in the study."

"Oh, miss!" Lucy said, walking across the hall. "I'll have a bath sent for immediately."

Lucy helped her off with her outer layer, then Alys tucked her hair behind her ears and squelched to her father's study. He could find no fault with her now. She had a marquess to call on her.

Feeling lighter than air, she drifted into a chair in front of his desk. "You wanted me, Father?"

She glanced at what he was studying and noted it was a railway timetable. "Do you have to visit the mills?"

"Not just now. Alys, have you any thoughts about your sister's condition?"

"About Rose?"

"Yes." He set down his magnifying glass. He refused to wear pince-nez, though he needed them.

Alys considered. "She's worse in the winter."

"Do you think she's been more ill since we came to London?"

"I believe so, though I cannot say why. There might be any number of factors."

"You would agree though, that it would be best for her to visit some other clime to ascertain if it would help."

"If a doctor gave that opinion."

"Rose suffered an acute attack while chaperoning Matilda and Mr. Bliven this afternoon."

"Oh dear. Has the doctor been sent for? Has she recovered?"

"Your mother feels her remedies have been more successful than those of any doctor we have tried, and she is feeling better, but I wish for her to go to the new house tomorrow. Even as we speak, your maid is packing."

"I see." All of Alys's lightness left her and she felt anchored to the chair by her wet skirts.

"Matilda cannot leave, with Mr. Bliven on the leash."

She wondered if she should tell her father about Hatbrook, but Rose needed a sensible travelling companion. For once though, she wished she could be selfish. She wanted another kiss. "Is Mother going to Sussex?"

"No, she'll be needed to chaperone. If Rose continues to be ill, we'll have to have Grandmother Noble stay here and send your mother south, but I'd rather not go to that extreme."

Of course not. Her father did not get along with her.

"Your mother has stated that you are competent to give Rose her remedies. Lucy knows what to do and your mother will speak to both of you this evening. Gawain will take the three of you to Victoria Station tomorrow morning."

She bowed her head. She'd leave a note for Hatbrook with Pounds. He would understand. After all, she didn't plan to marry him or anyone else, she merely wanted the status his visit might bring. She ignored the tight sensation in her chest. That was not a reason to discomfort an ill sister. "Very well, I shall be prepared."

He nodded. "You are a good sister. I'm sure she will be better with a little sun and country air."

"Yes, Father."

"You'll have her in tiptop shape by April and can both come back for the Season."

Was he trying to comfort her? What interest had she in the Season? Although, she had to admit to having a good time at Hatbrook's ball. Maybe there was something to parties after all.

"Does it seem that Mr. Bliven will propose?"

"I know he is looking for a girl with money," he said bluntly. "His father told me as much. And while of good family, he may never see a title. His cousin has just become engaged despite being over forty-five and if he has an heir, well, Mr. Bliven's prospects are dashed."

"I see." So the Redcake girls were not suited to men likely to receive titles, much less those who held them.

Her father rubbed his chin. "He wasn't very nice to you. Do you object to him?"

"He may object to me," she said. "But I think he meant to be droll."

"Better to have you out of the house at any rate," her father said. "Matilda will shine best on her own, without your tongue to amuse or Rose's beauty to distract. We shall resolve the situation. You may go."

Alys pushed herself out of the chair, leaving a dark line of wet on the rug as she left the study. Her father treated Mr. Bliven like any other business problem. An interesting approach to matrimony. She was very glad to see the tin tub being filled when she entered her dressing room.

Her privacy was protected by a screen as she warmed herself in front of the fire but she could hear Lucy rushing around behind it, and even Edith once or twice. She fell into a daze in the tub, reliving both kisses with Michael over and over again. If there had been more privacy, she'd have touched her lips like he had, her neck, but when she heard her mother, she knew she needed to rouse herself.

She found a towel, then her wrapper, and sat next to the fire to unpin her hair. The train ride would make her so filthy there wasn't any point to washing it now.

"Warmer now?" her mother asked, peering around the screen. "This room is freezing."

"Sorry, we can move the screen. How is Rose?"

"She is sleeping, but I'm afraid her attack upset Mr. Bliven. Poor Matilda was torn between caring for her sister and making it clear she doesn't share the affliction."

"I'm sorry I wasn't here." She helped her mother fold the screen and drag it to the corner.

Lucy had dresses spread across the chaise longue and stared at them with her hands akimbo, clucking her tongue.

"No darling, you weren't asked to be. I know it's a blow that he called for Matilda and not you."

Alys picked up her brush, wondering what had given her mother that idea. "Not at all. He makes me uncomfortable."

"Too uncomfortable to become your brother someday?"

"No, that sort of teasing relationship seems perfect in a brother."

"You must miss that camaraderie with Gawain."

"And with Lewis."

"Things have changed a great deal recently, have they not?"

Lucy brought Alys her corset and petticoats. "I think they have been changing for more than a year and it was only now that I've noticed. Gawain came home, Father bought Redcake Manor and started making decisions he didn't announce for a time. Rose turned eighteen in the late summer."

"That is true. I have no more in the schoolroom."

She wrapped her arms around her mother. "Has it been hard for you?"

"All change is hard, but these are mostly good changes. I wish Gawain hadn't been hurt, but at least he's home with us."

"I have your dinner dress, miss," Lucy said.

"I'll have a tray up here instead," Alys told her. "So I can help you and keep an eye on Rose. Mother, you go down."

Her mother hesitated.

"A number of small repairs need to be made to the gowns," Lucy said. "More than I can do myself."

"Alys doesn't like to sew."

"I need the practice, Mother," Alys said. "After all, you aren't coming with us to Sussex."

"Very well, but I'll be back after dinner to speak to you about Rose's medicine."

Alys nodded, glad to lose herself in menial tasks. They gave her time to daydream.

They first took the train to Eastbourne, then transferred north to travel the few miles to Polegate.

"This is larger than I expected," Rose said, noting the three platforms.

"It's quite the historic area," Alys observed. "We are near Hastings, after all."

Rose coughed, bending forward to catch herself. As soon as she was under control, Alys guided her inside to find the driver who was supposed to be awaiting them. Lucy brought up the rear. A porter directed them to the man and they were soon ensconced in a rented carriage, their boxes tied on top.

"Where is Redcake Manor?" Alys asked.

"Bit south of here, maybe two miles," the driver said, climbing into the box. "Get inside now, miss."

Alys kept her eyes on Rose during the drive. Though her lips weren't blue, she had a pale cast to her face and often applied smelling salts to her nose, which seemed to help her breathing.

When the carriage stopped and the driver opened the door, Alys was shocked to find herself in the courtyard of a dilapidated Elizabethan manor of stone, built in the H-plan.

He spoke. "An abbey was here first, and there's a ruined Norman shell keep on a mound a few acres away. A nice walk, but watch out for falling stones. And for the ghosts of Roman soldiers, who are said to walk the mound in twilight."

Rose giggled as the driver helped her down, then coughed. "No lady ghosts?"

"I'm sure it's possible, miss. This house was built in fifteen-seventy-seven, after all. My grandfather is by way of being the local historian. He loves to tell stories."

"We'll have to pay a visit to him," Alys said.

"Oh, he'd like that, miss."

"Did my father hire any staff for the house?"

Lucy looked alarmed at the idea of their being alone here.

"I know Bertha and George Pelham are still here. She's the housekeeper and he keeps an eye on the gardens. I'd imagine she's brought on a few of the local girls."

The front doors opened and a woman dressed in black stepped out.

"Oh, and I forgot, miss. The Pelhams had a daughter. They are in mourning. Poor girl was sixteen when she died last spring."

"In the house?" Lucy asked faintly.

"Yes, in the servants' quarters."

Rose tittered, a nervous sound.

The woman walked down the front stairs and Alys greeted her. "Thank you for welcoming us, Mrs. Pelham."

"I'm happy you've arrived in one piece. We only just had the letter to announce you were coming."

"We'll need a lovely warm room for my sister. She's been ill."

"I doubt there's an inch of the old place that isn't drafty," said the thin, middle-aged woman. "But we'll do our best for you."

A man walked around the side of the house. "Here, Robbie. I'll help you with the trunks."

The driver touched his cap and the sisters and Lucy followed the housekeeper into the house. The first thing Alys noticed in the great hall were cobwebs, high in every corner and window. She had no idea how one cleaned such spaces, but they desperately needed an application of vinegar and water. Interspersed were crumbling tapestries and ancient weapons, rusty and disused.

"Well, I never," Lucy said under her breath.

"We'll be hiring footmen," Mrs. Pelham said. "I understand your butler will eventually come down from London."

"Yes, Pounds is his name."

"Very good. Perhaps you would like to interview the final candidates, Miss Redcake? I have initial interviews tomorrow with five young men."

"How many are you hiring? Two?"

"Yes, miss."

"Yes, I'd like to meet the final three," Alys said. "And housemaids?"

"We've just brought on a tweenie to light the fires and help me in the kitchen."

"A cook?" Rose asked. "I require a great deal of hot broth throughout the day to help my lungs. And pots of coffee."

"I'll send Mr. Pelham for supplies. We weren't told to hire a cook. Besides we only have the original kitchen to work with, nothing modern."

"I'll write Mother immediately," Alys promised. "But for now, I'd like to have my sister settled in a very clean room."

"We've been trying to clear out the East Wing, that's in the best repair."

"Are the staircases safe?"

Mrs. Pelham shrugged. "Never been any accidents."

"Very well." What mischief had their father wrought now?

Alys took Rose's arm, in case she needed help on the staircase. Thankfully, the first room available was close to the staircase, which seemed secure enough.

"The long gallery is just through that door there. If you like paintings of dead people it's quite a treat."

"Lovely," Alys said.

"I like to paint watercolors," Rose said.

"You'll find the light is good. The solar is at the end of the hall, you'll probably want to set up there." She opened the door.

"Does the fireplace draw properly?" Alys asked as they entered the cavernous space. The wood floor was spotless and the bed hangings looked clean enough, though they were of tattered orange velvet.

"Yes, it's been cleaned and the mattress is new. All the linens are clean and the clothing press is empty."

"No mouse droppings?"

"No, miss, we found only spiderwebs and dust."

"Chilly," Rose commented.

"It is January, miss. I expect it is cold everywhere." Mrs. Pelham drew back the curtains, exposing a thin white light.

Alys was satisfied that the windows faced south, which would keep the room bright and as warm as possible during the day. She was torn between wanting to keep an eye on her sister and checking the kitchens, but when her sister requested coffee and broth she decided to go with Mrs. Pelham while Lucy organized.

The kitchen was in an outbuilding, connected by a breezeway. Alys hugged herself to stay warm.

"Smokehouse is over there, and the stillroom is off the kitchen. We've plenty of space at least and have designated a cold larder."

"What about a pastry room?"

"There's space if you can get the equipment." The housekeeper opened the heavy wooden door and ushered her in.

Alys saw a large, high-ceilinged room with a stone floor. That much was suitable. At one end was an enormous fireplace with a built-in brick oven to the right. Various tables served for work spaces, along with a waist-high mortar and pestle.

"The dairy is separate," Mrs. Pelham announced.

"You'll need a full staff to manage this," Alys said.

"Yes, miss. I'd better send for coffee, but it won't be available until tomorrow. We're a mile from the village, as you saw, and it is getting late."

"Can you make broth?"

"I have stew prepared."

"That's very heavy for Rose. Can you strain out the meat and make her a pot of strong tea?"

"Yes, I'll do that."

"Very well. I think I shall go back upstairs and write Mother. There's a great deal that needs doing."

"Did you bring any kind of kitchen supplies?"

The Marquess of Cake • 129

"Nothing. We only knew we were coming last night, though my father had been planning the trip."

"He's never been here," Mrs. Pelham said.

"How did he buy the house then?"

"Through an agent."

"Had it been vacant long?"

"At least since I was a girl."

"What was it called before he renamed it?"

"Pelham Manor. A cadet branch of those who lived in Pevensey Castle, I believe, built the house."

"And Pelham is your name too."

"Yes, miss, but I have no idea what the connection is. My husband's mother died when he was young and all that sort of knowledge was lost with her."

"Perhaps Robbie's father will know something more." A stray thought she'd had on the train coalesced. She needed an occupation. Learning about the house's history might be interesting. Certainly overseeing the modernization of the kitchen would keep her busy but her father might have that in hand. "Which room is mine? The one next to Rose?"

"We only cleaned the one, miss. We can start on the next one tomorrow if you wish."

"I think that would be advisable. It's possible more of my family will come soon and we can't all stay in one room."

Mrs. Pelham's lips pursed in an unattractive manner. Really, one wondered if she was suited for this position or perhaps she'd have done better as a mere caretaker, though from the look of the place, not much care had been taken.

"I'll have my letter ready for you to post by the time you bring up our food." There'd be no point in asking for a bath, filthy though both of them were. The dirt wouldn't be good for Rose's lungs. Maybe she could heat some water by the fire and at least wipe away the coal marks. She'd send Lucy for a cauldron and water when she arrived upstairs.

At least she'd not be bored.

"Is it true you're courting the middle Redcake daughter?" Michael asked Theodore Bliven as they sat at Hatbrook House with brandy and cigars after dinner on Thursday.

"Sir Bartley hoped for a match with his oldest daughter, but she's not to my taste."

Michael had noticed Theo hadn't taken an instant liking to Alys like he had back when they had first met at the tea shop, but beyond her personality, he much preferred Alys's active intelligence and body to the younger, softer sister. Matilda Redcake seemed a dreamy sort.

"I don't think the eldest Miss Redcake minded. Perhaps she has a secret lover."

Michael took a sip of brandy. He preferred to keep his own counsel about the state of Alys's love life. In fact, he hadn't been able to call on her as he'd told her he would, deciding he needed to complete the purchase of her father's property before he could decide how he felt about her. He'd received a message from Mumford first thing that morning, necessitating a visit to his office that took up the entire day. He would be very happy when his new man of business understood all his affairs and he didn't have to manage both his business and the firm's. All he'd had time to do was leave his card at the door with the Redcake butler late in the day.

"So you turned your affections to Matilda Redcake?"

"I don't know if I would term it as affection, though I did call on her the next day. She's a bit dreamy, but very eager to wed, I think. Her mother chaperoned us and did much of the talking."

"Mothers." They shared a rueful smile.

"Yes, maids are much better chaperones. They don't care what goes on as long as they are allowed to sit quietly."

"Will you call on her again?"

"I don't want to rush into anything, but my father is pressing me. The pockets are a bit empty and Matilda comes with a good dowry."

"They seem like a nice family, despite the tradesman aspect of things."

"You are taking the London face of the business off their hands," Theo said. "That will dull the tradesman sheen."

"They bought a house near Hatbrook Farm. You wouldn't have to go too far afield to visit your bride's family."

"Yes, better than if I married Courtnay's daughter."

Courtnay was a dye magnate who had a suitable daughter who'd been a considerable presence during the autumn Season. But he'd made it clear the family was based in Liverpool and his daughter would have to visit her mother frequently. Theo hadn't quite been able to bring himself to propose.

"Is she still on the market?"

"I believe so. Her father headed off a fortune hunter or two."

"Good that you're more subtle about the thing."

"I may not have the luxury if my father's losses are as steep as he claims. And now my cousin is marrying. Really, the news couldn't be worse."

"You could manage Redcake's for me when the deal is done."

Theo laughed heartily. "I'm not suited for the tradesman life. If I had to take a job I'd rather go out to India, get rich."

"Have the money for the fare?"

Theo grinned ruefully. "Don't suppose you'd let me have Beth?"

"She's not even out yet, my friend. Too young for you anyway, and much too innocent."

"Probably best to propose to Matilda, if I must. You don't think her father expects me to work?"

"No, I think he wants to have a country gentry family. That is what Miss Redcake indicated."

Theo took a sip of brandy, then leaned back and sucked his cigar. "She's already in the country, with the pale sister."

Michael wondered how rare these luxuries had become for his friend. Only two months ago he'd been in entirely different spirits. As Theo blew a smoke ring, his brain fixed on what Theo had just said.

"She is?" Alys had left London? How could he not know? She might have sent a note to Beth, at least. His sister had indicated they had built quite a rapport in one short meeting.

"Yes, left Tuesday. Rose was chaperoning us when I called Monday but she became ill and went upstairs."

So Alys hadn't been in London when he'd missed his call on her. Good. He'd appear less than a cad. But still, he did like her, liked the idea of meeting her on the street or at the tea shop. "How ill? Something serious?"

"A common lung complaint of hers, I believe. Nothing out of the ordinary. Too bad. She's a dashed pretty thing, a veritable china doll."

Unlike her older sister who was blooming and robust. Perhaps it was time to take a trip down to his farm. He could visit the sisters on the way. He'd felt it increasingly difficult to button his waistcoat this past week. Nothing to do on the Farm of course, at this time of year, but maybe he could help the blacksmith with repairs or some such physical labor. Make Mumford earn his pay. Not the fashionable time of year to be in London anyway. He could persuade his mother to bring Beth home for a few weeks.

"I'll offer you my congratulations, then. Think Redcake will let you marry Matilda this year?"

"I haven't asked, but he's friendly with my father, so I expect they'll work out the details if I must."

"Shall we join the ladies?" Michael asked. "I think we've kept them waiting long enough."

Chapter Eleven

Michael knew where Redcake Manor was, since Sir Bartley had mentioned it during their business dealings over the tea shop and emporium. Resolving to visit, he arrived in Polegate the next day, getting off there instead of taking the six-year-old Cuckoo Line up to Heathfield, near his farm. He swayed on his feet as he exited the train. Far too muzzy-feeling to descend on the sisters right now. He went to find a pub so he could have something to eat.

His mother had refused to come down to the Farm, or to allow Beth to come with him. She'd have remembered to bring a hamper and force a sandwich into his hand, but quite a bit of society was still in town, thanks to the filthy weather, and parties were abundant, though not with the best people. Poor Beth would be left to her own devices, not being out. Quite selfish of Mother, but no surprise on that account. At any rate, he'd told her he just meant to pop down for a few days then come back again. A week of visits and labor and he'd be fit for London again.

At least this meant he didn't have to go all the way to his farm first. He might have managed a womanish faint if he'd had to stay on the train any longer.

He checked through blurred vision for the sight of a pub on the street. Churches, a grocer, but no pub. Not a tea shop in sight, of course. He stumbled on a rock and would have gone down if he hadn't been caught under the arm by a firm hand.

"My lord! Are you drunk?" A familiar pair of nutmeg eyes peered under his hat.

Of all the people to meet on the street.

"No, ill," she mused, squeezing his arm. "But you don't look feverish."

"Haven't eaten since breakfast. I was coming to see you, Alys," he said thickly, hoping he wasn't hallucinating her.

"Robbie!" she called.

A man jumped down from a rundown hired carriage. "Yes, miss?"

"My excursion has been cancelled. Please help his lordship into the carriage. I'll be back in just a minute."

Michael watched Alys dash into the greengrocer's while a large man dressed in coarse brown took his elbow as if he were an elderly aunt.

"Were we expecting you, my lord?"

He shook off the hand gently. "No, friend of the family."

Robbie shook his head. "Don't know where they'll put you. That house isn't fit for Quality. Don't know what Morris was thinking. He's a bloody pirate, taking money for that place."

"Morris?"

"The purveyor of property what sold that tumbledown house to Sir Bartley. That land is fine, sure, but to claim the house was hospitable? Just not right."

Michael closed his eyes as he stepped into the swaying carriage. Robbie stuck his head in, bringing with him the odor of onions.

"Do you have a bit of bread and cheese about your person, my lad?" He reached into his pocket and inspected what dropped onto his palm. "I'll give you three shillings for it."

Robbie raised his eyebrows. "Back in a tick."

A minute later, a greasy packet of soft cheese and rye bread was thrust into Michael's hand. It might have been Scotch trifle for all the pleasure he took in the sight and smell of the bread. He flipped the driver his shillings. "You are a prince among men."

The driver put a finger to his forehead. "Pleasure doing business, my lord."

Michael still shook two minutes later, but thanks to the food he'd wolfed down he knew he'd feel better soon. By the time Alys climbed back into the carriage, a wave of exhaustion had made him ready for a nap. She held up a withered apple and offered it to him.

He took it. "Thank you, and I took the driver's lunch off him."

"Very resourceful."

"I don't like the sound of that house of yours. Everything all right?"

Alys's full lips curved. "No pastry room."

"No!" Michael said with a grimace. "I am serious. The place has a roof?"

"No leaking in the room Rose and I slept in last night."

"What was it called before your father renamed it?"

"Pelham Manor."

The carriage jerked as the driver called to the horses. Michael took a bite of the sour apple, relishing the tartness if not the mealy texture of the fruit.

"I have a vague sense of the place. Seems like some work was done there about the time I went to Oxford, but I don't recall hearing anyone had moved in."

"The housekeeper and one maid managed to do their duty by one bedroom. The kitchen was clean enough, if terribly old-fashioned. I came into town to post a letter to Father as well as to pick up a few special items for Rose."

"How is she feeling? Bliven said she'd had a lung attack."

"Yes, she has asthma quite badly in the winter. Already I think she has improved, being out of London."

"I'm glad to hear it."

"I am so sorry to have missed your call, but because of Rose I had to leave London so suddenly."

Her fingers brushed his. A bolt of heat shot south. "I consider myself to be at fault. I didn't know you had left because I only left a card at your door that day."

"Oh?"

She looked bewildered. Michael opened a window and tossed his apple core out.

"I had unexpected meetings. New man of business is complicating my life. Too late to pay a decent call, but I didn't want you to think I'd forgotten my promise."

"Surely you don't think I expect anything from you, my lord."

He patted her hand, noted she didn't draw away. "I expect courtesy from myself. I wouldn't want to behave as less than a gentleman."

"I don't expect you could," she said, staring forward as he played with her glove.

She didn't speak again until the carriage stopped in front of the house, though the silence was companionable. Scraggly bushes lined the drive, but the main path was clean of weeds. He saw a cat slink around the side. At least they had a line of defense against mice.

His heart sank when they stepped inside and he saw the dingy condition of the great hall. "You are going to need an army of servants to make this place right."

"We are interviewing footmen today."

"What about housemaids?"

"I'm not sure. The housekeeper wasn't prepared for us."

"I cannot believe your father sent a sick girl here. You cannot manage everything, Alys."

Robbie came in behind them and deposited two large market baskets at Alys's feet.

"Pack them up again," Michael said. "I'm taking the Misses Redcake to Hatbrook Farm. Water the horses if you need to, and call whoever is about to bring down the ladies' boxes."

Robbie touched his cap. "Excellent notion, your lordship."

"It isn't proper!" Alys gasped. "A bachelor? I cannot subject my sister—"

"My great-aunt is in residence," he interrupted. "She is no chaperone in truth, being confined to her room due to ill health, but it's enough for proprieties. I imagine Miss Rose is best confined to her room for the time being as well. I shall write my mother, and Beth too. I'm sure they can come down in a few days."

Alys blinked, her eyes bright. "I am concerned about Rose receiving nourishing, hot food. The kitchens are so far from the room we've been placed in and there's no cook."

He wanted to hug her. "You'll send Sir Bartley a note from the Farm," he said, "but for now, make your sister ready. Do you think she needs to be carried?"

"She made it up the steps. I'm sure she can come down them."

Michael judged his own legs. The carriage ride had given his body time to strengthen. "I'll come up with you and wait outside the room. If you need me, call, and I'll carry her."

Uncharacteristically, Alys's eyes brimmed with tears. He'd never seen any emotion in her other than passion before. She took a step toward him and kissed him softly on the cheek. "Thank you, for Rose's sake."

Lightly, she ran across the hall and back into the entry, then up the staircase. Michael followed more slowly, wanting to conserve his strength. He stomped on the steps as he went up, but found nothing more than a few squeaks with some of the treads. The hallway was clean enough, but no rugs. One door was open past the one Alys had entered, and he peeked in.

Years of being shut up had made the air close and palpably dusty. At least sheets still covered the furniture. A bed, a couple of chairs and a table, a washstand. The walls were faded and he expected a shadow near the floor was a mouse hole. Thankfully Hatbrook Farm had been well cared for, not to mention it was about two hundred years newer construction. Sir Bartley had a lot to answer for. His business was minded better than his daughters.

"My lord?" Alys appeared at the door.

He turned.

"I will have to help Rose get dressed." Creases appeared between her eyebrows. "She's terribly cold. The fire died down while I was gone and no one checked on her."

"We'll get to the bottom of this ill-use later. Why don't you wrap her in a heavy cloak and I'll take her down?" He heard coughing in the next room.

"It's so improper."

He ignored the pro forma complaint. "Do you have medicines for her?"

"Yes, it will be just the work of a moment to sweep it all into a bag."

She went back into the room and he waited a couple of minutes until she called for him, then he came in.

Rose looked very pale indeed, though her bonnet obscured much of her face, and her breathing rasped. She sat in a chair and her mouth fell open when she saw him. "Your lordship?"

"It's only about a twelve-mile drive, Miss Redcake," he said. "You'll be so much more comfortable at the end of the journey."

"I expect so, sir," she said faintly. "Father could not have known what this place was like."

"We are lucky that I am your neighbor and that I met your sister in Polegate," he said.

The air was bitterly chill for indoors. He heard footsteps outside as he swung Rose into his arms. A middle-aged woman in black came into the room.

"We're going to Hatbrook Farm," Alys said, picking up the satchel of medicines. "You'll have to pack for us and send our boxes along tomorrow."

"What about the footmen?"

"Hire the best candidates you find. You have a dreadful amount of work that needs doing here. If Robbie will take a job with us, please hire him on as well. A top wage, if you please, double what you offer the footmen, and new livery."

"What livery?"

"Have him measured for a black suit with a red waistcoat. For the footmen you hire as well."

"Will your family approve all this? With you not even in residence?"

"Of course," Alys said. "The house needs to be made fit for our return. Write my father for the funds. Also hire two housemaids, a laundry maid, and then when you have them working, two kitchen maids."

Rose coughed convulsively, then rested her head on Michael's shoulder.

"I'm taking her down."

Alys nodded to Mrs. Pelham, grabbed a second satchel from the table, and followed him down the stairs.

"I don't think she's up to the task," Michael said when they were rattling along in the carriage.

Rose had been wrapped in furs, but still seemed chilled. She rested against his shoulder, like a boneless child. He had to keep his arm around her to keep her from being jostled. Alys sat across from them, her eyes flickering between them both.

She couldn't be jealous, could she? He had no interest in her sister. But what did that mean? What was his interest in Alys? She had too much fire for him. He knew her to be borderline caustic. She took decisions she didn't approve of with ill grace. In her favor, she had some skill in handling his mother, but only in servant lines. His mother would eat her, a tradesman's daughter, alive, skin her, and have her cook roast Alys on a spit.

Then feed her to him under béchamel sauce with asparagus.

Yet here he was, bringing her under his roof. As Rose rubbed her cheek on his shoulder, he composed a letter to Sir Bartley in his head. The deal was nearly ready to be signed. Surely his actions were to his profit. If Sir Bartley had to rush down to Sussex to take charge of an ill daughter, their deal would be delayed.

Michael rubbed a chilly glove across his face and wished for a bun. That was the problem. His brain was going muzzy from lack of a solid meal.

On one level, Alys knew it was all Rose's fault. She'd been the one curled into Hatbrook like a cat. She'd been the one cradled in his arms while he rushed her into a room at the Farm fit for a queen, while Alys chose a bed in the dressing room so she'd be nearby. Rose had kissed Hatbrook's cheek in thanks and received beef tea from a cup held in his hands because her dainty paws shook when she tried to lift it.

Hatbrook had merely been kind. But oh, she wanted to be in his arms, in his best guest room, drinking from his hands.

Now, Rose was asleep, medicines having had good effect along with hot food and a warm room, and Alys had been offered a bath in a chamber designed for that purpose complete with a hot-water boiler.

Clean and dressed in her freshly brushed, green wool gown with black velvet accents and a sateen underskirt, she regarded herself with pleasure. It fit her shape to perfection, even if the design was a year old. Since she didn't want to go far from Rose, a housemaid led her into a pretty, feminine sitting room with rose-patterned wallpaper that was only across the hall. She brought a tea tray set for two but Alys went to the writing table in the corner and began to compose a letter to her father. She'd also need to write her mother separately and update her on Rose.

When she was but two lines into her first composition, she heard a knock on the door and someone entered. A whiff of soap and sandalwood drifted to her and she turned to see Hatbrook, also considerably refreshed.

"Shall I pour?" she asked.

"Please. How is Rose?"

"Resting comfortably. Thank you for your many kindnesses."

He nodded. "I stopped in to speak to my aunt. She said she would have you to tea in her room tomorrow."

"Very kind of her. Milk, sugar, or lemon?"

"Milk and sugar. As long as you visit a short time it shouldn't tire her too much. She is good for perhaps one long conversation a day."

She handed him the tea and a plate of shortbread. "Your aunt is a very elderly person?"

"She is nearly eighty, I believe. Must be." He frowned. "She is my late grandfather's older sister. Never married because her fiancé died of a fever three weeks before the wedding and it made her a bit peculiar for a time. Stole the bloom from her, I'm told."

"How very tragic."

His hand shook slightly as he lifted the fragile teacup to his lips. "It happens that way, people who are only capable of loving once."

"Have you ever loved anyone?"

He spluttered a bit. "A girl, you mean? No, I suppose not."

She took a bite of shortbread, wondering what his lack of love at his age meant for his character. "Should we ring for something more substantial?"

"No, it's late for teatime. We'll have dinner at eight. I'll be fine until then." He set down his cup and took a large bite of shortbread, which he had smeared with blackberry jam.

She wanted to mention the shaking but didn't want to be rude. "You were quite heroic with my sister."

He smiled faintly.

She leaned forward and put a finger to the side of his mouth. "You have a crumb."

He allowed her to dust it away.

"Do you really mean you have never been in love, or only that you have never been in love with someone suitable?"

"A gentleman never expects to answer a question like that."

"I suppose a lady wouldn't ask it. But I'm not some aristocratic virgin who has never seen the other side of life, you know."

"You aren't?"

"No, not at all." She pressed her lips together, then decided he might as well know. "I'm not only working class, I'm not a virgin at all."

He smiled tightly. "You'd be surprised how many aristocratic virgins aren't virgins either, Alys."

She felt deflated. "Oh."

He drained his cup, then set it down hard enough to clatter against the tray. "Were you in love?"

She shook her head. "No, I was just a silly factory girl. He'd been making eyes at me for close to a year and at fifteen I was simple enough to be flattered. When he caught me behind an outbuilding one day, I couldn't stop him, but I managed to avoid him after that. I stopped going anywhere alone."

"You mean you were raped."

She shook her head. She didn't like to think of it. She'd relived the experience in bad dreams for years, until they'd left Bristol. "No, I just mean it wasn't nice."

"That sounds like rape to me."

"It doesn't matter."

"I think it does. Didn't you tell anyone?"

"No. Once I saw there wasn't a child, I tried to forget."

"That is appalling."

"But you see why I can't marry. I'm not fit for the kind of man my father thinks I'm suitable for, the Theodore Blivens, if not the Ralph Pophams, of course."

"I don't see why. This was forced upon you. You aren't loose."

She begged to differ. "I've kissed you a time or two."

"But you like me."

"I do, very much." She stared at her hands.

"I like you as well. Have you kissed anyone else?"

"Never in my life," she admitted. "You make me feel different."

"Like how?"

She blushed. "I don't know. All tingly inside. Like I can't quite breathe."

"I'd like to kiss you now."

She perched forward on her chair, then was alarmed by how her body had responded, even before her thoughts had time to form.

He chuckled. "You look like a country miss about to receive her first kiss."

But despite his tease, she felt the soft brush of his mouth against hers. The teacup in her hand rattled in her lap as his tongue brushed the seam of her mouth. She opened to him, felt his tongue dance over the underside of her lip. This was heaven.

Then he cursed, left her mouth, stood.

She opened her eyes, shocked by his sudden change of mood, and found her tea was spreading down his trousers. She leapt up, spilling the cup to the floor, and grabbed her napkin. She scrubbed at his leg while he swore at the burn.

"I am so sorry."

"No, no." He grinned ruefully. "Entirely my fault."

A knock came on the door and before either of them could do more than look toward it, the door opened.

The housemaid's eyes widened at the sight before she schooled her expression. "Miss Rose is asking for Miss Redcake."

Michael cleared his throat. "Thank you, Marian."

After she shut the door, Michael lowered his hand and helped Alys to her feet.

"I'm afraid I've embarrassed you," she said. "Both my conversation and my actions."

"No, Alys," he said. "Both intrigue me greatly. And to answer your question, no, I really have never been in love, despite a liaison or two with less than respectable women, though I now find myself curious." He slapped at his leg.

"Curious?"

"Yes. Could I feel love the way the poets describe it?" He struck a pose, making her smile, and declaimed, "'Twas a new feeling— something more/Than we had dared to own before/Which then we hid not;/We saw it in each other's eye."

Alys hugged herself as he dropped his pose, feeling transported by the romance of the moment. No one had ever recited to her before. He was splendid.

"Well, that poem by Thomas Moore ends with the lovers not having what they wished," he said. "You'd best go to Miss Rose. I'll call for a doctor if you think I should."

Was he telling her he couldn't have what he wanted? Was that something her? He shifted and she saw he must be uncomfortable in his wet, stained trousers. "I hope you aren't burned."

"I shall be fine. I take worse punishment from my stable hands."

"I did not intend punishment."

"I know. An untimely accident." He shifted again.

"I'll ring if it is necessary to have a doctor for Rose," she promised, reluctant to move. "I've never found myself so full of regret to leave another person as I do now."

He took her hand from her waist and kissed the back of it. "If I were a poet I could come up with a very nice verse from that thought alone."

She nodded, confused by this marquess who seemed to be courting her so very unsuitable self, and trotted out of the room, feeling like she ran on air. Any woman, even the highest, would be lucky to have him. Why was he focused on her? How could she resist poetry and boxing and kindness? And those kisses too. It was enough to turn a spinster into a wanton.

In the end, the doctor did have to be called. Rose developed a fever along with her lung issues. Alys and Rose had spent three nights under Hatbrook's roof before Rose rallied. When Alys was finally sure her sister slept deeply and comfortably early Monday morning, she crept out of the bedchamber and into the bathroom. After having helped Rose with baths she knew how to work the boiler and she sat wearily on a stool as the steam rose, watching weak rays of sunlight stream through the window. Thankfully, she'd brought an old work dress made of stout Oxford shirting in her boxes. She'd never have survived the past few days if she'd been restricted by lady's finery. But after three days of the sickroom the dress needed a good wash.

Hatbrook had rallied his staff to assist and he had visited each day at teatime to read to Rose from magazines. His aunt had sent soothing messages as well as one of her afghans. Still, Alys had insisted on doing most of the work herself, feeling guilty for ever putting thoughts of her cakes over her sister's fragile health.

Eyes closed, she undid the buttons from neck to waist and let it fall off her shoulders. Then she reached behind and undid the laces of her stays. Even that seemed too much work, but eventually she was down to her combinations. Yawning, she reached for the taps.

The door squeaked open. Expecting a housemaid, or even Great-aunt Mary's maid, she didn't look up, but turned on the cold water, then the hot.

"I'm sorry."

The male voice had her rearing back, hands over her breasts. Hatbrook held up his hands and apologized again.

"The door wasn't locked." His gaze drifted to her bosom, then back to her face.

She blushed. "I didn't think it needed to be." She couldn't bring herself to order him out, like a proper maiden would.

Instead, she noticed Hatbrook wore a dressing gown over some kind of loose, silky trouser. His feet were bare. She liked the look of them, long and wide with narrow toes, the masculinity enhanced by the tuft of hair on each big toe.

He put a hand to his hair, scratched his ear, and shifted his stance. "You look exhausted. But Rose is better?"

"Yes. Marian said she'd sit with her while she slept. Do you always wake so early?"

"Earlier, very often." His toes dug into the carpet.

She turned to check the water and heard an audible pop in her neck. "Ouch." She rubbed the kinked spot.

"Here, let me."

Michael moved closer and sat on the stool, then pulled her onto his knee. She wanted to protest, but then his warm hands molded to her neck and he began to knead her flesh. It felt so good, she could have let her head drop to his shoulder.

She could have fallen asleep like that, warm from the steamy water, relaxed from his hands and the scent of sandalwood and scones. Her sense of propriety had become dangerously relaxed, from seeing him in Rose's bedroom every day.

"You don't smell like cake," he murmured against her ear.

"More like chest rub and spilled tea. But you smell like scones." She looked up at him.

He licked the corner of his mouth. "I think I left a speck of honey. Want to taste?"

She did, and felt a little less tired when she touched his mouth with her fingertip, then licked it. "No, you got it all."

"Where is that orange flower soap you use?"

"You know my soap?"

"I love how you smell," he said simply. "I'll wash your hair for you."

"Hatbrook! How indecent." She faltered when she saw how he stared.

That hungry look she'd seen in his eyes before was back. "I have a beautiful woman in my arms. I feel very indecent."

Swirls of sandy hair decorated his chest between the lapels of his robe. She let her fingers sample the textures there. The wiry hair, the hard, warm chest, the soft wool. His lips found her temple, her cheek, her neck.

"Do you want to undo my buttons?" she whispered. Was the heat from the boiler the reason her inner thighs had moistened, for the languorous feeling in her limbs?

"Do you want me to?" His voice had developed a rasp she found endearing. "I'd better lock the door."

When she didn't protest, he picked her up and stepped to the door, then turned the key. She put her arms around his neck and he let her slide down his body. Then, he undid the buttons of her combinations to the tops of her hip bones. She gasped, a tiny sound magnified by the high ceiling, but didn't protest.

His fingers danced down her breastbone. "You have beautiful curves."

"I do?"

"Yes, your breasts are high and perfect, and your hips have such a delicate flare." He shrugged out of his robe and let it pool on the floor.

She sat back on the stool, drinking in the virile stretch of his chest and back muscles, as he turned off the taps and found her soap.

"Come and lean your head over the tub."

She slid off the stool and allowed him to lean her back so her head rested on the lip. Gently, his fingers found her pins and dismantled her braid. She'd never thought washing had such allure.

"Now I can smell flowers," he said, running his nose along the outside of her ear.

He let her hair sink into the water, then dipped a pitcher into the tub and poured the warm water over her scalp. She moaned with pleasure as it trickled over sore spots caused by having pins in for too long. When it was damp enough for his purposes, his deft fingers began to work in the soap.

"You've done this before," she ventured.

"I've washed horses," he said.

She closed her eyes. "I'm no horse."

"No, I wouldn't do this to a horse."

She felt a damp hand on her thigh, then, shockingly, he was spreading the fabric open between her legs. "You're going to wash the hair there too?"

"In a bit." Instead, his fingers moistened the seam between her legs, then spread her lips and dipped in.

Her thighs jerked. She was hot there, and damper than she realized. His fingers slipped easily, rubbing, creating little fires under her skin. Her eyes widened when he found her channel and pressed his finger in. Why wasn't she stopping him? She couldn't. She was so tired and it felt so nice, and he smelled so good.

"Do you like that?"

She couldn't answer, just moved restlessly.

"Keep your head back. It's covered with soap."

Her fingers found his silk-covered thigh and her nails bit into the fabric when he caressed her again, higher this time. He found a little hood of flesh and pressed there. She squirmed.

"I could tell you liked that."

She panted. "What are you doing?"

"Haven't you ever done this to yourself before?"

"No." She was positive that if she touched herself like this, it would not have the same effect.

"Then there is much I can teach you."

But would she survive the teaching? She felt as coiled as a snake, and just as ready to strike, but at what?

Chapter Twelve

Alys desperately wanted to be a fast learner, to move ahead of Michael's insistent touch, to understand. His fingers plucked at the small pearl of flesh at the juncture of her thighs, then dipped back between her legs. Her breasts felt full and tight and she wanted to touch herself there, but felt like if she let go of his leg she'd spiral into the heavens with nothing to anchor her to earth.

Gently, he increased the tempo, spreading the moisture that her body created in response to his sensuous movements. Her hips bucked against his hand.

"You're so responsive," he whispered.

A noise of protest came from her lips. She moved her head and soap dripped onto her shoulder. How could she be anything else with his touch against her body? She heard a loud click behind her and tried to turn, but his fingers did something miraculous that made her reach, just a little bit higher, but how?

"Shhh, let it come."

She didn't know what he meant exactly, just that his fingers were creating a tight, hot need for her to break free from her own skin. She felt her chest bloom with heated blotches when his lips found her neck, then drifted lower. His breath enflamed the tips of her breasts and she lost her grip on reality.

She arched backward, riding the hardness of his finger inside her tight sheath. Stars burst behind her closed eyelids and she finally took a gasping breath. He kept rubbing her slowly, until she found another breath.

"Beautiful," he murmured, soothing her with soft pats.

"I've never felt like that before," she whispered.

"I hope it is far from the last time." He kissed her temple. "Stay in the moment."

She could feel her pulse beating under his lips. Her entire body felt alive but languorous at the same time. He moved away, then she heard something in the tub and warm water caressed her scalp again, taking away the fragrant soap.

He turned the pitcher over her head twice more, then rubbed strands of her hair between his fingers. "I removed it all, I think."

"I've never been so relaxed in all my life," she murmured.

He dabbed her face with the towel. "Let's get you into the tub."

She didn't protest as he took her arms out of her combinations and pulled the fabric down her legs. Her eyes were closed so she heard, rather than saw, him take off his trousers. Then he bent, picked her up, and stepped into the tub, lowering them both.

Feeling boneless, she sagged against his chest, as though she'd never have energy to move again. His chest hair gently abraded her back, constantly reminding her of his presence.

He proved her idea wrong, however, when he began to wash her with the cake of soap. He slid it along her collarbone, raising tiny bubbles, then swirled it between her breasts. When it moved over her feminine patch of hair she still felt languid, but when it slid between her thighs, she recharged as if a bolt of lightning had struck there.

She turned to him, meaning to say something, but then he dropped the soap and took her hips between slippery fingers and pulled her to him, belly to belly.

How could they be so similar yet so different? Even his skin was shaded differently, with his darkened patch at throat and lower arms, a tan that must be permanently burned in from working outdoors. She might have breasts, but he had firm rectangles of muscle surrounding nipples that tightened into tiny peaks when she touched them. He was beautiful and alien and breathtaking and frightening all at once.

"Sensitive?" she whispered.

"Oh, yes."

A line of hair began below his breastbone, widening into a thatch like hers, only chocolate brown instead of her fire red. And fire described her perfectly, the way she felt when he caressed her breasts and hips. He burst her into flame. Without thinking, she let her thighs slip over his. She was completely open to him, completely desiring.

His erection bobbed in the water, pointing toward her belly. She only needed to move a little closer, a little upward, to take him into herself. Could she steal this moment of pleasure from the world, discover what the novels claimed lovemaking could be like?

"This isn't how a virgin should be taken," he said, gripping her thighs.

"I'm not a virgin." She touched the tip of his penis, then slid her fingers over the flared head. She heard his harsh swallow and took him in both hands.

"Nearly so."

"I'm not some tender aristocratic miss. I'm twenty-six." She touched him as if she was kneading scone dough, though of course this experience was nothing like that. Instead of becoming more pliant, his penis became harder, thicker, hotter, with each stroke of her fists.

"You're still a special woman and I want to treat you as such."

She rotated her shoulders. "You are thinking too much. I must not be doing this right."

"Do you want this to be over quickly?"

"Yes," she said, surprised. "This is a stolen moment from our responsibilities. We don't have long."

"If you can think of responsibility I'm not seducing you effectively." He tilted his head and found her lips with his, and pushed his fingers into her hair, twisting it into a thick plait.

Her rhythm faltered and her hands fell to his thighs. "Is this a seduction?"

With a grunt of domination, he took his hands from her hair and reached for her hips. She felt a nudge against her slippery woman's place and his erection slid inside.

"Or a bewitching."

The sensation bore no resemblance to that experience, best forgotten, of eleven years before. Her body coiled tightly around him.
She squeezed and moved her hips instinctively. He seemed to touch
some place inside her she'd never been aware of, and every time he
surged inside he sent her burning higher.

His tongue thrust deeply into her mouth with each pistoning of
his hips. Water splashed to the lip of the tub and washed over the
edge. She devoured his mouth eagerly, her hands sliding up and down
his heavily muscled arms. When she needed to be even closer, she
pressed her torso against his, feeling his chest hair abrade her tender
breasts. Her arms clasped around his neck. The water was warm but
he was incandescent.

"Can't hold on," he gasped.

She licked his lips. "Michael, oh Michael."

"Alys, are you ready? Be ready, sweet, be ready."

He moved his hand. She protested, wanting to fit herself to him,
but then she realized he was doing something with his fingers, like he
had before, something she liked. Eagerly, she moved not just against
his penis, but his fingers. Her body broke around him.

He pressed his face into her hair and thrust fast, so deep he'd have
hurt her if he'd moved like this before, though now it felt exquisite as
aftershocks clenched her around him. He cried out hoarsely and
shuddered. She felt him relax. His hands cupped her shoulders as he
breathed heavily.

The water level in the tub had dropped. After a moment Alys realized she felt cold air on her back. She pressed her torso tightly to his.

Michael did not yet seem capable of speech. He pulled her head to
his shoulder and nuzzled her wet hair. She sighed and relaxed against
him. When would an opportunity come like this again? Soon his family or hers would arrive at the Farm and they'd never have an opportunity to steal a moment, unless she blatantly became his mistress,
with some kind of arrangement. Her family would cut her from their
lives. But she couldn't think of that right now, with her brain fogged
by newfound pleasure. The novels had it right. How foolish attraction
could make a woman. And to think she hadn't wanted to come to the
country.

"I had thought leaving London meant leaving you," she whispered.

"Not when your home here is so convenient to mine," he said, yawning.

"I didn't know. So much has changed in my life. I cannot wrap my thoughts around it."

His muscles bunched underneath her. She was shocked by the power he demonstrated as he stood in the tub, holding her, not a small woman. Her legs locked around his waist as he stepped to the floor and wrapped a towel around her. He kissed her forehead, then set her back on the stool and secured the towel.

"You need a good rest," he said. "I should not have taken advantage of your exhaustion so. I've not been a good host."

She could do nothing but blink at him. Her passionate lover dissolved into a mere host? Did he often treat guests so? She'd heard of such things at country estates but had never considered the truth of them before. Perhaps it was common to have relations with visiting ladies, at least those who did not arrive as virgins.

"I am tired, but most pleasurably so."

He smiled. The hunger in his gaze had faded, and his expression was uncommonly sweet. "As am I. I cannot express how pleasant this has been."

"Yes," she agreed. But was that all it had been to him?

"Do you need help dressing?"

"No. I will be fine." She watched limply as he dressed, then unlocked the door and opened it a crack to check the passage.

"I'll duck out now."

She stayed on her stool until he was gone. Her life suddenly seemed like a carriage with a broken wheel. Some level of certainty had been lost to her and she didn't know how to restore equilibrium. At least she had a memory of heat to carry her through long, dark nights.

Early the next afternoon she was wondering if Michael was purposely avoiding her when a note was delivered to Rose's room, inviting them to a dinner at a neighboring farm.

"How exciting," Rose said, from the chaise where she lounged by the fire. "I think I'll wear my pink."

"Are you sure you are ready to leave the room, much less go outside in the cold?"

"I have been trapped here for days," Rose declared. "This is our chance to be a part of the best society in the area. We cannot miss such an opportunity. Guests of Hatbrook Farm will have a greater entry than daughters of Redcake Manor."

"I don't wish you to relapse, Rose."

"I came here because the air was healthier," she said with a little dance of her slippered heel against the chair. "It will be fine."

"At least you have a few days more to rest before we enter society," Alys said, noting the dinner was three days away. Though she knew society would not accept her if they knew the truth about her relationship with Hatbrook.

Three days had never been spent in such dull occupation. Rose continued to struggle with her breathing, so all of their meals were served in their room. Michael did no more than look in late in the evening, after days spent with his tenants. Alys noticed his waistcoat did not fit as tightly as it had, so he was taking brisk exercise. Rose's cough worsened at night, so Alys found herself napping next to the fire in the afternoons. At least naps passed the time. But Michael appeared in every dream, making her feel hot and restless.

Otherwise, her primary occupation was making repairs to a gray sateen evening gown for herself, and helping Rose take in her favorite pink gown, since she'd lost enough weight for it to be noticeable.

Finally, the evening came and they were dressed in their finery. Rose's cough had improved or she was hiding it better.

"At least I no longer sound like a farm animal braying," Rose said. "If I can drink tea I should do quite well."

"I'll make sure you have it," Alys agreed. "I'll tell the marquess that wine makes your wheezing worse. I'm sure he'll know who to tell."

"Are you sure he's coming tonight? We haven't seen much of the marquess this week."

"Like Father, he's a busy man," Alys said. "We can't expect him to entertain us when we are unexpected guests." No matter what had passed between them.

"You are right of course," Rose sighed. "But it does lift my spirits to see such a handsome man, even if I don't think I've ever seen him smile."

"We shall watch him tonight and see if he is more at ease around country landowners."

"Do you think there will be eligible men at the dinner?"

"I do not know any more than you."

"I am sorry you've been cooped up here with me all this time. I know you prefer to be occupied in more active pursuits. You haven't had a minute to yourself in days."

And well she knew it, but she resolved not to be selfish anymore. "Your health is my chief concern. But if you are ready now, we should go downstairs."

Forty minutes later a footman helped them dismount at Dickondell Farm. Michael did not join them in the carriage or ride alongside, so they entertained themselves by speculating about the family who had invited them. The house was a large, old pile of local stone, but inside was quite inviting and modern.

"Aren't you a pretty little thing," exclaimed Mrs. Dickondell to Rose as they were ushered into the drawing room. She nodded politely to Alys and took Rose's hand, patting it as she led Rose to a seat by the fire. "We've heard all about your illness, dear. I hope a bit of dancing won't set you back any. I have three sons who are looking forward to it."

Rose smiled widely. "I'm certain I will be fine, thank you."

Alys was surprised not to see Michael at dinner, but their hosts didn't mention him. She was seated next to the youngest Dickondell brother on one side, all of seventeen years of age, and an elderly deaf aunt on the other, while Rose carried on a brisk conversation with Mrs. Dickondell and the Dickondell heir, Clement.

After dinner, the rugs were rolled up in the drawing room. The gardener and one of the stable hands, both talented musicians, were brought in to play alongside Mrs. Dickondell at the piano.

Clement Dickondell spoke for Rose, the middle Dickondell brother took the hand of a fetching cousin who lived with them, and the youngest squired his fifteen-year-old sister, leaving Alys to perch on a chair on the wall, alongside the deaf aunt. She tapped her toes as a reel began, wishing Michael would appear so she might have a partner. But two hours of dancing went by. The aunt snored on Alys's shoulder. Rose drank half a cup of tea between each dance to keep her wheezes at bay, occasionally sitting out to whisper with the heir by the fire.

Rose was a palpable hit at the Dickondells' house. Alys had never felt more like an old maid, and a ruined one at that. If her father thought there would be potential husbands to overlook her advanced age in the country, he seemed to be wrong. Perhaps word of their dowries hadn't reached this part of the area. Certainly, the family did not treat her like she was in the market for a husband.

At least they had been invited out, but surely they were expected to bring their host along.

"I do hope his lordship feels better soon," said Mrs. Dickondell, wiping her florid face with a handkerchief during a break.

"Is he ill?" Alys inquired. "We did not see him today."

"I understood your sister was in fragile health. He probably did not want to overly tax her with visiting today."

"He has been most thoughtful," Alys agreed.

"I did expect to see him this evening, however. How do your families know each other, Miss Redcake?"

She gave the simplest answer. "My brother served with the marquess's brother in India."

"I see. And your brother?" Mrs. Dickondell paused delicately.

"Was wounded, but he's home safely now."

"Ah, that is good to hear." The lady patted her hand. "We are cousins of the Shield family, to the third degree. I do love genealogy and have traced our family tree back to the royal House of Wessex."

"How fascinating." Alys heard a guttural cough, and glanced up sharply to see Rose doubled over, holding her ribs. Her dance partner looked frantic. "I think it is time to order the carriage."

"Yes, of course." Concern knotted the lady's forehead.

Alys wondered if Rose had lost her chance with the Dickondell heir. But she did not always sound so bad. If only she had danced less. The exertion had done it.

When Alys had Rose home and in bed, sleeping with a warm flannel on her chest, she decided to go looking for Michael. After all, after what they'd done together, searching for him wasn't any more improper.

She found him in the library. He still wore boots despite the late hour. They were thrust in the direction of the fire. She'd never seen him slump before, but he did so now in his chair, with a piece of paper in one hand and a glass of some amber-colored liquid in the other.

Spirits, as she could smell.

In his lap rested a letter. She could just see an envelope peeking out from beneath it, with the words "On Her Majesty's Service" in typescript.

"It is with deep regret," Michael said in an ancient voice, so at odds from his usual confident tone.

"What?" Alys asked, dropping to her knees next to the chair so she could see his face.

"That I write to inform you," was all he said, in the same sepulchral tone.

Alys clutched the shawl she'd wrapped around her sateen. Oh, this was bad. "Your brother?" she whispered.

Michael continued inexorably. "Of the death," his voice broke. "Of the death—" He bent his head.

She put her hands on his knee. Her shawl fell around her, tangling in her skirts.

"I should have made him come home," he whispered. "My God, what a desolate place to die."

She blinked back tears. "What can I do?"

"Everything changes now," he said. "Everything."

"I'm so very sorry," she said, wondering what he meant. His brother hadn't been in England for a very long time, and Michael was the marquess, not his brother. So what would change, really, other than a chance of having Judah home again someday? His heart must be breaking at the loss, and he had to inform his mother and Beth.

"Go to bed, Alys. I need to think."

She got to her feet and nodded. "Is there anything I can bring you?"

"No, thank you."

After a moment's hesitation, she kissed his forehead, just a quick peck he could scarcely have felt before it was over, and ran out of the room to make sure the staff knew.

Chapter Thirteen

Rose was too excited by her triumph to feel ill the next morning. By the time they went down for breakfast, out of respect to the household both in gray dresses and black shawls, the closest thing they had to mourning, the mirrors were already covered in black. The curtains were drawn and the clocks silenced.

Michael was nowhere to be seen, but the housekeeper came in when they were finished eating.

"His lordship would like to see you in his study, Miss Redcake."

Alys nodded, guessing it was time for them to leave. Since they had been at the Farm for nearly a week at least some new servants would have been hired, and cleaning done at her family home. Rose was better, even if their night at the Dickondells' had ended somewhat badly. She left Rose with a cup of coffee and went to learn their fate.

From the pure, pale color of Michael's skin, she doubted he'd been to bed the previous night, but he smelled beautifully of mint and rosemary, and wore fresh clothing. The black band on his arm blended into the dark fabric, and his waistcoat was purest ebony.

Even his hair had been slicked back with a pomade of some kind, blending the blond highlights into the darker hair. He looked forbidding yet utterly exhausted. Alone, but powerful. Desolate, but resolved.

The only sound came hissing from the gaslight sconces along the walls, necessary due to the pulled curtains. Perhaps it was their light that made him look so white.

She twisted her hands behind her, thinking how her work-roughened hands didn't fit into a place of such purity, such grief, such elegance. Too loud and healthy for this place she was, with her flaming hair and sturdy body. How had her father ever thought she'd fit into the country gentry?

"Will you have a seat, Alys?" Michael asked with quiet formality.

"No, you must be busy, my lord. I've started the packing, so we can return to my father's house as soon as will be convenient."

"Why would you do that?"

She furrowed her brow. "Surely you don't want us underfoot. You must have preparations to make. Is family coming?"

"For what, Alys?" he asked.

"A funeral?" she queried.

He folded his hands across his chest and bent his head for a moment. "I am waiting for word. He may have been buried where he fell."

"Of course, I see."

"There is really nothing to be done now, except write letters."

She nodded. "You asked to see me. Can I be of assistance, then? Writing the letters? Are you going to go back to London to await word?"

"No. It is Saturday. There won't be anything to discover in London right away."

"I suppose not." She waited, wondering why he'd sent for her.

"Alys, in light of recent events, I feel I should make a change in my circumstances."

"How so, my lord?"

"I realize this is a bit irregular, but then our situation has ever been that." He scrubbed his face with his hands.

Poor man, his head must be aching from sorrow and his overindulgence of the night before. "Indeed," she agreed.

He put his hands, palms out, toward her.

"To be clear, as one must be in these circumstances, I wish to take you to wife."

Alys felt as if she'd been struck in the heart so forcefully that her hearing extinguished, to be overlain with a dull buzz. She sat abruptly. Had he really said those words? She put her hands to her breast. "To wife?"

"Yes, I'd like to marry you, as soon as possible. Special license. Under the circumstances, you know. We shouldn't wait six months or a year. What if you were already, well, expectant?"

Alys felt her cheeks color. "You didn't ruin me. I explained."

"I wish it," he said firmly. "I like you, and it is really the best thing for you."

"Oh?" she said in a small voice so unlike her. Why did everyone seem to know what was best for her before she could decide for herself?

"And for me too, of course. I need an heir now."

"If I am expectant, of course you'd want the child," she said, seizing on his reason, that bit of sanity. "Yes, of course."

"I can get a license from the local vicar. We could marry in as soon as a week," he said. "That will allow our families time to arrive and for you to make the necessary arrangements."

"And if I discover I am not with child in that time?" she asked.

"It makes no difference," he said, the faintest of twinkles returning to his gaze. "We shall have other opportunities. But I think until then we should stay apart from each other, for propriety's sake."

She colored again when she realized he'd planned to continue with her. When she had seen him so little over the past week she'd assumed he had experienced a moment of madness with her never to be repeated. It appeared the madness had all been hers. She covered her mouth with her hand, hiding the inappropriate smile that came with the realization that he hadn't meant to be done with her. Her body would receive his glorious caresses again.

"What say you? Shall I obtain the license? Are you willing to marry in a week?"

"I wonder if I have a choice, unless you are willing to wait longer."

"You don't want me?" His expression reverted to blank remoteness.

She did not want to heap rejection upon mourning. Of course she wanted him, but marriage? She'd never thought it was for her. "I need time."

He stared at her. "I understand it is common for young ladies to refuse, or demur at first, but surely you realize you'll never have a better offer than this."

She wondered if his arrogance came from his title, his money, or his own sense of worth. "Marriage was not in my plans."

"It most assuredly was in your father's plans. He terminated your career. You are at his mercy."

She steeled her spine, angry now. "You are all but my third offer, my lord, in less than a month."

His eyes slitted. "I see. Then why the dalliance with me?"

"You are not a gentleman for mentioning it."

"Then perhaps you are not a—"

Thankfully, the next word didn't come out of his mouth, but she knew what it was. *Lady.* She was not a lady. "I think it is clear what I am, my lord."

"Stop calling me that. My name is Michael. At least call me Hatbrook. We are friends, are we not?"

She tried the name on her tongue, unfamiliar for all that he'd become "Michael" in her thoughts after they'd made love. "You are under great stress, Michael, and perhaps are making decisions that you will think twice about in the future. In giving myself time to make this decision, I give it to you as well." She wanted his hands on her body, but the rest? The title, responsibilities she was completely unprepared for? The censure of his peers?

"And that is all you have to say on this matter?"

"For now."

He stood, his large body looming over her. "I am not satisfied."

In his dark clothing, with his distant expression, he looked dangerous for the first time. But this was her life. Her spine stiffened. "Why? Do you have some other candidate for this great honor waiting in the wings?" Another lover, perhaps? No, she didn't even want to have that thought. She stood.

A muscle in his cheek jerked visibly. "I did not plan for any of this."

Plan for what? He certainly hadn't said he loved her. Plan for his brother's death, obviously not. Oh, her head was in such a whirl.

"I must go," she said, her voice cracking. "I need to check on Rose."

He nodded. "I'll expect an answer soon, but I can't get the license until Monday at any rate. You have two days."

She turned and ran away, like the most abject coward. Rose was not in their room when she arrived. She knew she should look for her sister but she'd much rather fling herself on the bed and cry. What a mess she'd made of the proposal and she couldn't talk to anyone about it. Rose would think the best response would be to throw herself at Michael's feet and beg his forgiveness and accept him immediately. In her heart of hearts she knew that would be best. She wasn't a fool. A little shop with her name above the door was hardly likely. She probably would be refused a shop lease. Maybe she should have accepted Lewis, but she didn't love him. Or Popham. She couldn't imagine offering her body to either of them.

These thoughts stopped her cold in a hallway. Michael didn't love her, but how did she feel about him? Passion, certainly. But nothing so strong that she had no trouble throwing away all her dreams of a career in favor of being his wife, no matter how elevated a position it might be.

Was her mother at fault, for not filling her head with appropriately feminine dreams? No, she saw her father far more than her mother and all he'd wanted of her until recently was hard work. He had created for her the wrong dreams, the wrong goals. She could not change as quickly as he could. She had molded herself into the perfect Redcake daughter, but then the rules of the family had altered.

She shut the door with a bang and went to look for Rose, finding her in the long gallery, hung with old family pictures interspersed with an alarming selection of ancient chairs.

Rose's profile looked gray. Alarmed, Alys took her arm, turning her from the Jacobean portrait she stared at. "You overexerted yourself last night. Come back to bed."

"Just after you left we had a telegram from Mother. She and Father and Matilda will be here Monday."

More complications. "Really, why? Did something go wrong with Matilda's courtship?"

Rose coughed. "I don't know. You wrote and said I was ill, didn't you?"

"Yes, but I'd have thought husband-catching was more important."

"Alys!"

She sighed. "You're often ill."

"But they thought I'd be better in the country."

"I suppose you are right. Perhaps they mean to see the condition of Redcake Manor for themselves. Now, come and lie down."

Rose complied and they spent the afternoon with their embroidery hoops. Alys rarely made a stitch, torn by her situation. She knew she had to marry if she was expecting, but if she hadn't conceived eleven years ago, what were the chances now? When she thought about what her heart desired, it wasn't life buried in the country, as a marchioness or not. She wanted the bustle of London, the satisfaction of hard work.

Eventually, Rose threw down her hoop and Alys was glad to follow. "Do you think you could find a chess set?" Rose asked.

Alys snatched the bell pull, glad for any diversion.

Alys had expected Michael to send for her, but she didn't see him at all during the next two days.

"Shut himself away in his room, he has," the housekeeper said when she inquired. "Grieving for his brother."

Or too embarrassed by his foolish proposal to see her. Alys wondered if he hoped she'd simply go away. Perhaps he was being courteous and giving her the time she desired.

While Rose napped, she went for a long walk after services on Sunday. The bitterly cold air made her long for a shop to duck into, but of course there was nothing open. She didn't know any of the villagers or tenants. If she married Michael she'd meet them, but not as their equal. Whom would she associate with? She was used to the close connection of her sisters, brother, and cousin, fellow employees. Would his sister live with them? No, she'd likely marry in a year or two, and Alys didn't enjoy his mother. All together, marriage to him didn't seem a pleasant proposition.

Perhaps she could busy herself with a child, if there was one. As she walked, she spun a pleasant fantasy of making a cake with her little girl, a red-haired moppet with Michael's serious eyes, but would you be allowed to bake with a marquess's daughter? Probably not. The kitchen belonged to the cook more than it did the mistress.

By the time her parents and Matilda entered the door of Hatbrook Farm early Monday afternoon, she'd resolved to refuse Michael. She didn't know what her next step might be, but the life she envisioned as his wife frightened her.

Michael joined her family for tea in the shrouded morning room. She noticed his hands shook a bit as he passed a plate of scones, and he was again very pale, but after he ate he seemed to regain strength. Had he been sleeping well?

"I understand Miss Rose Redcake cut quite a swath through the Dickondell brothers at dinner the other night," Michael murmured in a near monotone, stirring himself when her mother asked him about local doings, once they'd exhausted the news of his brother's death.

"And what about Alys?" her father said.

"I believe the brothers are more of an age with Miss Rose," Michael said.

Her mother furrowed her brow. "I had thought the eldest son was twenty-six."

Michael didn't respond, other than to tighten his lips. Was her family irritating him?

Her father sighed. "Well, Alys isn't the pretty one either, I suppose. Perhaps we've expected too much of her at her age. She's left with little more to choose from than my own widower employees."

Alys set down her teacup, which had rattled in its saucer nearly as much as Michael's had when he first sat down. How could her father say such things? Her mother's head was bent as if trying to avoid her father's words.

"No," her father continued. "It's all very well. She can care for her mother and me in our old age. Very proper to have a daughter unmarried. Why, the queen herself held back a daughter as long as she could, and them all princesses."

Alys glanced at Michael and found him staring quite fixedly at his plate of apple tart. Her embarrassment at this improper conversation was acute. No doubt he'd change his mind about his proposal of marriage now, when he realized what her family thought of her.

"You know them, don't you? All those princesses?" said her father.

"Yes," Michael said.

Her father squinted as if he'd just realized how little Michael cared for the path the conversation had taken.

"It's so kind of you to shelter our daughters in their time of need," her mother said. "I never could have expected such kindness, my lord, but I'm very grateful for it."

"I'm sure you were not aware of the situation at the Manor," said Michael, his cool pitch rising above his previous monotone.

"No, I had not realized they had only a skeleton staff," her mother agreed. "In the last week they have found some suitable people but the kitchen is so outdated."

"You are lucky to have a daughter who knows so much about their design."

"And a husband too, my lord. No, the situation is insupportable and again, I must express my gratitude."

"Will you be staying at the Manor for long?" he inquired distantly, as if the subject pained him.

"No, we merely came down to collect Rose and Alys. Matilda has engagements to attend to in London, and we can't impose upon you any longer."

"But Rose's health," Michael said.

"She's better off in London than at the Manor right now," her father interjected. "A bit of work on the kitchens, get a good cook installed. We should be back down in spring."

Alys felt Michael's gaze on her. She lifted her eyes to his and offered a tiny smile, all she felt able to manage for the moment. Her breath had quickened at the mere mention of a return to London. Not long ago this had been her fondest wish, but now she didn't know if she wanted to escape.

"Perhaps you'd like a tour of the kitchen here?" he suggested. "I can give you the name of the architect who did some modernizing here last year."

"An excellent idea," her father said.

"Very good. I'll ring for the housekeeper. She knows much more about the subject than I do."

Her mother looked a bit disappointed to be foisted off on the housekeeper. "Alys, I'm sure you'll find the kitchens fascinating."

Michael cleared his throat. "If you don't mind, I'd like a word with Miss Redcake before she joins you."

"I should supervise our packing?" Rose said tentatively.

"I'll help," Matilda agreed, almost leaping to her feet.

Alys could feel the jealous waves oozing off her middle sister, who hadn't spent the week at a marquess's home.

Her father's gaze narrowed, but he allowed the housekeeper to lead everyone but Alys out the door. She watched Michael shut and lock it behind them.

"Why are you locking it?"

"I don't want anyone popping back in to ask a question."

"It's very improper."

"Proper doesn't seem to be part of the vocabulary of our relationship, Alys," Michael said. "Though I kept a civil tongue with your family."

"We are not genteel," Alys ventured. "I am sorry they are so intent on mundane items when you are mourning."

"That doesn't make me want you any less," he said roughly. "Have you an answer for me?"

She had woken that morning with one answer, but now she saw the future her father had planned stretching out even more bleakly. He must be desperate to put her firmly on the shelf due to Matilda's prospects with Theodore Bliven. If she was still considered marriageable, Matilda would have to wait for her to announce an engagement first, since she was the eldest daughter. His plan meant she'd be expected to fade into the background for the remainder of her lifetime. A lifetime of nights like the one at the Dickondells'.

"Have you had any communication from Mr. Bliven?" she ventured.

"About your sister?"

"Yes."

"Not since I left town. No one will be offering me anything but condolences for a long while."

She circled back to the matter at hand. "Isn't it disrespectful to your brother's memory to marry in haste?"

"He was practical enough to see the need for it," Michael said. "Come now, you know I'm your best option. You'll have a great deal more freedom as my wife than an unmarried Redcake daughter. And you ought to be married."

She swallowed hard as his meaning became clear to her. If she took another lover in the future he might not offer as generously for her as Michael had. Not that she intended to take a lover in future, but boredom and loneliness could make a woman do strange things.

"I don't want you to regret marrying me," she said.

"No one will second-guess me," Michael said. "Men with titles have been marrying wealthy merchants' daughters for some time now. These large homes are expensive to manage."

She blinked back tears at his calm assurance. At least she knew he wanted something of her, her body, not just money. "You don't need my dowry."

"I would have two years ago," he said. "A few bad harvests and I might be right back to where my father left things. Most men will think me smart to marry you."

"Despite my advanced age?"

"Your father doesn't see you like I do, Alys," he countered. "Come now, you know that I find you attractive. And you are younger than me besides."

She swallowed hard. Her father's plans for her were impossible. A kind of tunnel vision centered her gaze on Michael's face. At least he offered her passion. "Then I accept your kind offer, my lord."

He let out a breath and rubbed his hands together. "Excellent. Do you want an engagement ring?"

"The wedding will be so soon. You can dispense with that sort of thing."

"Then you don't mind if I take your leave and hunt down the vicar?"

"No, of course not. I can join the kitchen tour." Not even a kiss?

"If you see any improvements that can be made, please let me know." Sudden humor crinkled the corners of his eyes. "We had best serve the most famous desserts in the county with you as marchioness."

A feeling of hope bubbled to life. "You'll allow me to train a pastry chef?"

"You may even perform that office yourself, if you like, until your attentions are taken with other duties."

She blushed. Oh, this would be an improvement over her father's house. "Yes, of course. Thank you, my lord."

"Michael, or Hatbrook, remember?"

"Yes, Michael."

He took a step toward her and tucked a finger under her chin. "May I have a kiss to celebrate the occasion?"

"Of course," she whispered. Thank heavens some romance remained to her.

He bent his head and matched his lips to hers. His mouth, faintly gritty with crumbs, tasted delightfully of lemon and tea. But it was only a moment before he left her, lips pursed and eyes half closed.

"I have much to do if we're going to be married next week," he said, not noticing.

She touched her lips. "Should I tell my family?"

"No, I'll pull your father aside first, so he doesn't think I'm being underhanded."

"I'm sure he'll be delighted." Her tone was sour.

"Once he gets over the shock," Michael snorted.

Alys clasped one of her hands over the other, tightening her fingers together.

He must have seen a change in her expression. "Don't worry about what they think, Alys. Honestly, they'll be happy for you. Ecstatic."

"I expect so." Jealous too, but pleased by the new opportunities her alliance would bring them.

"And perhaps we'll have Theo as a brother soon," he suggested. "That wouldn't be bad at all."

She wished she liked his friend better, but it was Matilda's opinion of Theodore Bliven that mattered. As he unlocked the door and stepped out, she sank onto a fainting couch and tried to breathe. What had she done?

Only Sir Bartley Redcake returned to London that day. A week later on Monday morning, Alys married Michael in the breakfast parlor of the Farm, with her family, Lady Hatbrook and Beth, and Theodore Bliven in attendance. Her mother had insisted the room be decorated appropriately, despite the family's recent loss. All black was removed from the room. Pots of ferns decorated with white bows were brought in from the conservatory since the time of year precluded flowers.

Lady Hatbrook's lips were thinned in disapproval during the entire ceremony, but Beth seemed transported, her face shining above her black bombazine.

Alys wore a dress of navy silk, constructed quickly by her mother and sisters. She had made her wedding cake herself, which, though small, had kept her occupied and away from her bemused relatives.

After they signed the parish registry, she and Michael were seated for their wedding breakfast. Conversation was stilted among the few guests, with Lady Hatbrook speaking exclusively to the vicar. Only Beth seemed to enjoy herself, in animated conversation with the female Redcakes. Alys was pleased to see the color back in Rose's cheeks. An additional week in the country had served her well and she hoped the family's return to London wouldn't cause her sister to become ill again.

While she was speaking to Gawain about the condition of Redcake Manor, Michael approached her.

"Are you ready to depart?"

Alys looked up at her new husband. "Depart?"

"We are taking a honeymoon trip."

"We are?" She hadn't expected it.

He nodded. "It will be a less oppressive atmosphere away from the Farm."

Alys noticed his gaze had drifted to his mother. She had hoped that lady would return posthaste to London but didn't know exactly what her plans were. "Do I need to prepare?"

"No, your sisters and mother have it all arranged."

"Very well." Her heart fluttered at the idea of being alone with him. It had been so long. She'd been surrounded by family for the past week and, in truth, had scarcely seen Michael since he received the news about his brother.

What kind of honeymoon trip could they have under these difficult circumstances? The only thing she knew for sure was he wanted an heir immediately.

Chapter Fourteen

Michael brought Alys to a small cottage near Beachy Head, on the property of an old family friend. The views were famously spectacular and he wanted his new wife to be familiar with the highlights of this part of the world.

But here, with the only light coming from candles and firelight, the windows nearly dark with midwinter twilight, the only view concerning him was the new Marchioness of Hatbrook, holding her hands in front of the fireplace to warm them. Alys, to be precise, whose blatantly red hair caught the firelight and took on a flame of its own. Her tea-colored eyes pulled in the shards of light and seemed to burn gold, more chamomile than Assam.

Had he really married her to get an heir as soon as possible? Yes, in his grief it seemed the wise thing to do, but looking at her now, it was hard to remember a better reason than simple animal lust. She didn't offer the purity of skin of some untouched society miss. No, her cheeks seemed permanently reddened from years of standing in front of ovens. Her hands were covered in tiny scars and he remembered feeling calluses against his chest the night they'd been together. But, the beauty of her curvaceous form and the knowledge of how she'd come to have the marks of hard work on her body enticed him. Despite his city polish and education, the last years had turned him into a farmer, after all. He appreciated hard work.

Alys, who had labored all last week making and decorating her own elaborate wedding cake, complete with entwined marzipan swans on top, even though her father suggested he have one brought down from Redcake's. Most brides-to-be would have spent the week primping. Alys? She'd made pastries and other desserts too. He'd had to try a bite of the chocolate groom's cake and was amazed by the depth of flavor.

He cleared his throat. "Would you like some dinner? It will have to be cold tonight, but the hamper is still full. Someone from the main house will bring us meals tomorrow."

She stared at the fire. "No, I'm not hungry."

"I'm going to change out of these dusty travel clothes. Would you like to retire first?"

When the footman let them into the cottage, he'd pointed out cans of hot water that had just been brought in and lit the fire in the parlor for them.

Alys didn't look up. Michael realized she was staring at the wedding ring gracing her hand.

"I can scarcely believe we are wed either," he said, guessing her thoughts.

"Two weeks ago, when that night happened, I'd never have expected this to be the result," she said in a low voice.

"Me either. But everything has changed."

Alys's mother had made sure to supply a mourning wardrobe for Alys, which she'd have to wear for the next six months in honor of Judah. Before they departed Alys had changed from her wedding gown into a black travelling outfit finished with a flowerpot hat of velvet topped with a tall crepe bow. Michael thought the hat looked spectacularly uncomfortable and was not surprised when Alys rubbed her temples now as if they ached.

"For the past two months it has been one change after another. I've always considered myself practical and steady. I knew my place in the world."

His fingers itched to pull out the pins holding the silly hat to her head. "It takes time for any new bride to become accustomed to her new life."

"I never expected to be a bride. I'd given that dream up so long ago."

"You'll be fine, Alys. Come, let's remove your outer clothing. It's damp."

She ignored the suggestion. "Will I? I don't fit into your world. Your mother detests me."

"We'll see her as little as possible. And Beth adores you. Rose can live at the Farm. She'll be healthier there. We'll find her a husband locally."

"You are an organizer."

"I've had to be. Everything was a mess when I inherited. I know you are experiencing immense change, but after all, you've been at the Farm for a couple of weeks now, so at least your new home isn't new to you." He decided she must disrobe so the fire might have more benefit on her damp skirts, which had swept through a puddle on the way to the cottage door. Stepping close enough to smell her orange-flower-water scent, he pulled at the damp ribbon holding the front of the cloak closed. He couldn't risk her becoming ill, not when she might be carrying his heir.

She allowed him to take the heavy cloak from her shoulders and slid the sleeves down her arms to display the front of her slim-fitting crepe dress. His gaze was caught by her rounded breasts, lifting with each breath. A bolt of lust sizzled through his lower extremities, hardening him in an instant.

"I wonder if Gawain will find the same financial mess to be true of our family someday. I don't understand my father's goals anymore. Why can't he be happy with all his achievements? He wanted us to become something we weren't."

He knew what she'd stopped short of saying. Alys had soared beyond her father's wildest dreams when she'd married into the aristocracy. Although with Theo courting Matilda there might be a second title in the family someday. "He should be very proud of you now."

"Why? Because his daughter whored herself and by a tragic turn of events that led to an advantageous marriage?"

He winced, not at least because he desperately wanted to repeat the act sooner rather than later. Slowly, he unbuttoned his greatcoat

and hung it on a hook by the front door, then took a seat on a long settee. Since her back was turned, he was able to subtly rearrange himself before the pain became too intense. "Please don't think of our
night together like that."

"Why not? We didn't come together out of love."

He struggled to keep his expression unchanged at that bald remark. Of course he'd known she didn't love him. She'd have accepted
his first proposal if she did. But to hear it stated so plainly was unpleasant. "If all we have together is lust, my lady wife, then we may
as well take advantage of it."

Her back straightened and her head tilted. With a cry of pain she
righted her head and turned to him.

"We are here for an heir, after all. Unless you feel you are already
increasing?"

She blinked.

"Alys?" He stood, wincing as the motion rocked his pulsating
erection against too-tight clothing. He put his fingers to the first black
glass-topped pin holding her hat to her head, not able to stand her obvious pain anymore.

"I don't know yet." Her voice was uncharacteristically plaintive.

He held back a smile. "Then let us not waste another opportunity."

He pulled away the pins holding the hat to her head, then found
the comb anchoring it to the back of her head and pulled the contrap-
tion away from her hair. Orange strands straightened into the air, giving her a look of a disheveled orange hedgehog.

His erection subsided somewhat as his focus went to containing
his laugh. He turned away to set her hat on a table by the fireplace and
noticed most of the space was taken by a quilted lump that turned out
to be a teapot under a cozy when he investigated.

"Exactly what we need," he declared. "Will you pour, my dear?"

"I don't think you've ever used an endearment for me before," she
said shyly, her hands flattening her hair as she joined him at the table.

"I cannot imagine how that dashed servant forgot to mention the
tea. How remiss of him." He glanced at her, saw her flush. "Sorry, er,
my dear. I plan to use many endearments for you in the future."

Her lips quirked. "You made a robin's nest of my hair, I'm afraid."

"I did think of calling you my little hedgehog." When she shook a
fist at him he laughed. "I did think better of it."

"In terms of the animal kingdom, I believe my hair is far closer to a mane than spines, Hatbrook."

"My mistake has me relegated to Hatbrook, I see," he observed, taking a fragile cup of tea and downing it in one gulp. "Ah, still warm."

She took the cup from him and filled it again with a dark, fragrant brew, then sat with her own beverage. He could tell she was thinking hard about something as he seated himself at the other end of the settee.

After a couple of moments' pause, she ventured, "Was some provision made for a maid? This new style is so fitted that I don't think I can manage myself."

"I will play maid tonight."

She rested her cup on her lap and began to cough.

"My dear?" he inquired.

"I do not think so, Michael."

"Why not?"

"You have no idea," she said, her voice hoarse. "The strings and buttons, the hooks and tapes. Very tedious."

"But it will be my pleasure to disrobe you."

"I cannot allow you to," she said in a faint voice, staring down at her hands. "Really, Michael."

"I've seen all of you before."

"I was in the bath," she said, even fainter. "I was a wanton, not a wife."

He liked the idea of a wanton Alys, hungry for him. "I shall restate," he said, polishing off his second cup of tea. "I would like to see all of you."

He watched her swallow hard. Her cheeks had pinkened and both hands were clutching her teacup so tightly he was afraid she'd break the thing. He leaned forward and plucked it from her cupped palms. "We are husband and wife now."

"Most husbands would not take such a liberty."

"But we are in lust, not love," he reminded her. "In some ways our relationship is more of mistress to master, not wife to husband. Therefore more liberties than are usual are to be expected."

"Because I was born so common?"

"No, of course not. Because we were lovers, first. Don't you want your naked skin to slide against mine when we make love? Want our bodies flesh to flesh, rather than separated by uncomfortable layers of cotton?"

Her fingers flexed into the thin topmost layer of her dress, bunching the fabric together.

"You are usually dressed much more comfortably than that. You must be chafing."

"You must not remark on that," she said sharply.

He sighed. "Must we have an aristocratic marriage, Alys? Cannot we be at ease with one another?"

"It would be preferable." She plucked at the skirt again. "Very well. I loathe this dress. I hate this wadded petticoat, my skin is being rubbed raw by the chemise under my horridly tight corset and I feel as if I cannot breathe. But I must be respectable and this is how respectable women in mourning look, or so the dressmaker told my mother. She had my measurements from making my court dress last year, but I seemed to have gained weight since then, though I cannot imagine why, with all the fretting I've done these past weeks."

He felt his shoulders relax with each word of her outpouring. "I always gain during the holidays," he told her. "It's all the sweets."

"You do eat quite a lot of sweets," Alys observed. "Whenever your hands shake I see you reach for them."

On one hand, he was pleased by her close regard. On the other, he was afraid his bride had far too searching a gaze. "Perhaps you are increasing," he suggested delicately.

She flushed again. "I had no idea you would be so frank about these things."

He smiled, pleased her attention had left him. "Shall I play maid now? You can spend the next few days clad only in your dressing gown, if it pleases you."

"What will I do in a dressing gown?"

"Read novels, dance, make love?"

"Dance?"

"It will be easier to dance with me if you can breathe." He held out his hand. When she took it he pulled her to her feet.

"Wait." He sat her back down. "Where is your buttonhook?"

"I have no idea. I didn't pack for myself."

"I'll go hunt for it. You relax." Swiftly, he left the room to paw through her baggage, wishing they hadn't been in mourning so that he might have seen something more exciting than unrelieved black.

Not even a red petticoat or a pair of fancifully worked stockings decorated her trunk, but he did find her buttonhook.

He reentered the sitting room and knelt at her feet so he could work off her damp boot. She sighed with pleasure as her black stocking-clad toes were released.

"New shoes?" he asked.

She flexed her feet. "Yes. The latest style, I believe. My mother had great fun at my expense. Usually I insist on choosing my own clothes."

"I think you are quite fetching in that cakie uniform."

"I could wear it around the house," she offered. "It is the appropriate color."

"I doubt your sisters packed it." He discarded her second boot and tucked the buttonhook under a cushion to be retrieved later. Then, he took one of her small feet into his own and lightly stroked her sole.

She shrieked and pulled away from him.

"What?"

"I do apologize," she wheezed. "That tickled."

Feeling mischievous, he took her foot in hand again. Through trial and error, he discovered a firmer grip made her toes unstiffen.

"Are you enjoying this?" Alys asked, yawning.

The fire gave a loud pop as one of the logs cracked. He turned. "I had better put another log on."

"Perhaps you should light the fire in the bedchamber instead," she suggested.

He swiveled his head back around. "Tired?"

She stood, wincing as the cold floor soaked through her stockings. "It is late."

"I do not wish to overtax you," he said, mindful of her possible pregnancy.

"Pish posh," she snorted. "If I am a mistress more than a wife, I demand my mistress rights first, before sleep."

"Mistress rights?"

She all but marched the three steps separating them, and reaching to his chest, smartly divested him of his topcoat. "Pray light the fire, my lord, and let us be off to bed."

He detached his watch chain from his waistcoat and set that on the mantelpiece. "Perhaps you ought to remove my clothing as well."

Her fingers shook slightly as she unbuttoned the close-fitting garment. "And your shirt?"

"I don't think I wish to risk a singeing," he said. "But once I've laid the fire."

A few minutes later, he had a small fire going in the bedroom. He tested the sheets and was pleased to see a warming pan had been placed at the foot of the bed. When he stepped out of the room he saw Alys had snuffed most of the candles.

"Come." He held out his hand. "There is a rug in front of the bedchamber fireplace. Your feet will be warmer there."

When she stared at him uncertainly, holding a candlestick, he bowed to her and held out his hand. "My lady?"

"I'm to be a mistress tonight," she whispered.

"My red Venus," he replied, the phrase coming to him with the inspiration of her tumbled hair. "Let me see those lovely curves of yours."

She stepped forward and, after handing him the candlestick, set to work on his clothing. Before he'd have thought it possible, he was standing in front of her, in the doorway of the bedchamber, in nothing but his drawers, his erection poking a tent into the woolen fabric.

Her cheeks blazed with color, but she lifted her head into an elegant pose. "My lord, I believe you are ready for me."

He set the candlestick down with such rapidity that the candle swayed on the base and nearly fell. With a curse, he righted it and pulled her to the rug in front of the fire. While she laughed softly he worked on the buttons of her dress. She hadn't exaggerated the tight fit and he had trouble pulling off her sleeves. The corset cover was easy enough but then he had to figure out her corset hooks and laces.

When his father died he'd left too little money for a mistress, and once Michael had the money he hadn't the time for one. Now he regretted how long it had been since he'd disrobed a woman. He had a feeling fashions were not so form-fitting in that distant past.

The shadowy recess between Alys's full breasts deepened as she took her first full breath of the evening. He kicked aside the rest of her petticoats.

"Ah, the chemise."

"Don't make fun of me. If I'd known I was to be a mistress I'd have found some decadent underthings, rather than these matronly pieces," she said.

He smiled at the thought of her in frills and lace under the severe dresses she must wear. As it was, the tartan combinations might have been off-putting to one less aroused. "My tartan Venus?" he suggested.

With a rude word, she tugged and pulled until the offending combinations were on the rug. "I ought to throw them in the fire and stay naked until you can send for proper mistress attire."

"You desire me to send a maid to London? To some scandalous shop known only to the demimonde?"

She turned to him, hands on hips, then seemed to realize she hadn't any clothes on. With a gasp, she put her hands to her breasts. The motion only served to plump the delectable mounds. He groaned.

Her eyes widened. "What?"

"What you do to me, sweet Alys." He took one of her hands away from those orange-flower-water-scented breasts and put it to the front of his drawers. Her fingers formed a loose fist automatically and he stroked himself through it.

"Does this feel as good to you as it did to me, when you touched me before?" she asked, repeating the movement.

He felt dots of sweat break on the small of his back, though whether from the fire or her loving attention he couldn't say. "Yes, my Venus. It feels so good."

"I'm glad. I liked the way you touched me."

With action rather than thought, he picked her up, straddling her legs around his waist, and walked her toward the bed. She fell back but he scarcely noticed because he was feathering his fingers through the orange silk between her legs, searching for the hooded pearl hidden there. When he touched her she gasped. The sensual exclamation made him want to kiss her so he did, hot and open-mouthed as he stroked between her legs. When she moaned again he slipped his mouth to her neck, then moved down her breastbone between her magnificent breasts. She bucked against his hand so he tested and found her already damp and heated. Touching him must really have excited her. With his free hand, he unfastened and pushed down his drawers. His erection pressed into her leg. He slipped between her thighs. She moaned in approval and said his name. This was no virginal wife but his lusty mistress. He pulled her legs to his hips and found her channel with his erection, thrusting inside.

Her back arched and she cried out, then tightened her legs at his hips, locking her feet together behind him. His hands moved to her breasts and he stroked her there, her cries rising when he found her nipples.

"This is so naughty," she moaned.

"So good," he said, following his hands with his lips, kissing her breasts with abandon.

She moved her hips against his. The tentative motion sent a surge of white-hot lust through him. He grabbed for her hips and helped her pulse against him. They rocked and rocked until he thought his heart might explode. Just when he thought he might die of the pleasure, she stiffened and arched, crying out. Her hot sheath throbbed around him and he lost all control, pouring himself into her as he sagged forward. Never had his life seemed so gloriously complete.

When he regained a sense of himself he realized her arms were cradling his head. He looked up at her and saw a sleepy smile tinged with wonder.

More gentlemanly this time, he lifted her into his arms and tenderly placed her on the sheet, her head properly centered on a pillow.

When he had the covers tucked around her naked body, she said sleepily, "Your hand is shaking, Michael. Perhaps you'd better find that hamper."

"Yes, my dear. I'll find it and be back in a moment."

By the time he'd returned with a hastily prepared napkin full of bread and cheese, she was fast asleep. He wouldn't dare wake her, so he found a dressing gown and sat in an armchair by the fire to eat his repast.

Considering how his wedding night had gone, he had a curious realization. As sensual as the delights had been, lust had only been a small part of it. Yes, he lusted after his new wife, but his feelings were equally tender. He wanted her happiness. He wanted her as she was, not what she or her mother thought she should be. He loved Alys, though he hadn't understood that before.

It did not escape Alys's keen managerial eye that her new husband's hands often shook. If he hadn't eaten in a while, even his thoughts seemed to drift. Needless to say, their honeymoon meals were not exactly regular as they ignored the clock and did what they liked. When Michael pawed at the buns in the morning, or sliced off a hunk of cake in the evenings, it wasn't more than an hour before his hands were shaking again. The afternoon meal, which never had a sweet, seemed to regulate his body better. A few days in, she dared to specifically request that nothing sweet be served with their evening meal either.

He grumbled when he wanted something to eat after a postprandial bout of lovemaking, but nibbled some cheese and an apple instead of the usual cake. An hour later, as his head nodded over an American novel, she noted with satisfaction that his hands were still.

How ironic that a Redcake husband was ill served by sugar.

The next day, maids from the big house descended to pack them up for the carriage ride to the train station. They had shared four nights of wedded bliss.

As they jostled against the walls while the carriage rolled up the track to the main road, Michael promised, "We'll have a proper honeymoon trip in the spring. Go to Italy, perhaps. Or to winegrowing country in France. Would you like that?"

Alys thought she'd likely be increasing by then, whether or not she was now, and the trip would not happen for some years, but she smiled politely and agreed. "Of course, Michael. You can combine research with pleasure, always an excellent notion. I wonder if your mother will be in residence when we arrive at the Farm?"

"No, she's in London. I had a telegram from Beth yesterday."

Alys remembered the footman delivering it but had assumed it was related to business. "How is she doing?"

"She said Mother had contacted a cousin of ours in the War Office to try to get more details about Judah but none were forthcoming."

"I see."

"She'd promised to let me know if she learned anything. We are still awaiting the official army form."

"Of course. Very kind of her. So vexing."

"The telegram said our cousin was no longer speaking to Mother."

Alys put her gloved hand to her mouth in an attempt to stifle commentary. At least she was free of the termagant for now. "I have much to do when we arrive."

"Will you take over the running of the house?"

"With your permission, of course."

"I would expect nothing less. I look forward to some of your splendid desserts. You shall have to train a pastry chef. There are several likely lads in the village. The vicar and his wife run an excellent school but there isn't much for work around here, except what I can provide."

"Could I train a woman?"

He smiled at her. "Perhaps one of each? Of course a girl would marry eventually and leave us. A male pastry chef will create continuity."

"I believe I provide the continuity, Michael."

He waved a hand. "I won't interfere in the running of the house. It is merely a suggestion."

Alys simply wished he wasn't correct. She was ready to accept her career was over, but girls did need to learn a trade. What if they married a drunkard, or their husband died? They had to support their families somehow.

For now though, her concerns were smaller. Michael needed to eat less sugar. An in-house pastry chef, or two, for just their small family, could spell disaster. He wasn't the man to accept a fruit and cheese course for dessert every night without argument.

"Your groom's cake was divine, my dear," Michael said dreamily. "I've been thinking of it all week. Do you think you could reconstruct it for our one-week anniversary on Monday?"

She sighed. "I'll have to send to London for the special Belgian chocolate I used. Perhaps for our two-week anniversary?" He might have forgotten by then.

Michael nodded. "Perhaps a sponge then, with a delicate cream. I do look forward to berries in season."

"I hope your housekeeper has plenty of jams put away," Alys said. "I can do great things with good jam."

The carriage lurched as the horses conveyed them onto the main road. She found herself leaning against Michael. He put his arm around her and pulled her close, then bent his head to hers for a kiss. She forgot about menu planning as she kissed him back.

On Sunday night, Michael pushed back his plate of Stilton and stewed prunes with a frown. "I know it is Cook's half-day, but surely there is a pudding."

His wife smiled at him beatifically. "I quite had my fill of sweets over the holidays. Doesn't it feel good to eat lightly?"

"I keep myself trim through hard work, madam," he said, his jaw clenching. "I do not need to be abstemious at table. Did I not marry a cake expert?"

Her eyes narrowed. "I thought you married me for lust, not cake."

Michael was thankful he had told the footmen they could retire. "You cannot deny that the cake came first."

She looked down her nose at him. "I think I should be insulted by that remark."

"But you aren't, my dear. Cake is important to us both."

"You are the veritable Marquess of Cake, my lord. One would think you had no other interests."

Michael considered the truth in that remark. The first thing he'd attended to on arrival wasn't farm or winery business, but the Redcake's transaction. Still, it was winter and the rest could wait. "I like my sweets."

"We have been married nearly a week, no?"

One of Michael's eyes began to itch and he rubbed at it. "You know our wedding date as well as I do."

Alys leaned forward. "Do you need a handkerchief, my dear?"

He waved her away. "You were making a point?"

"You may not like to hear this, Michael, but I've noticed something about you."

"What is that?"

"Your hands shake rather a lot. Even your conversation changes at times, when you are underfed."

"And then I eat and everything is fine," he growled.

"Yes, dear, of course. But when you eat sweets, you are shaking again in an hour, whereas other kinds of food seem to restore you for a much greater period."

"And your point, my lady wife?"

"I think you should reduce your sweet consumption." She held up a hand. "I would never presume to remove them from your diet. But perhaps we should reserve them for special occasions. Friday night dinners, parties, that kind of thing, instead of a daily indulgence."

"You presume greatly."

"Wouldn't your life be easier if you weren't finding it necessary so frequently to restore your thoughts and hands with food?"

He opened his mouth, then closed it again as her words sank in. "What do you propose?"

"Instead of reaching into a box of chocolates, or having a bun, perhaps a slice of cheese or ham. I'm certain upon experimentation we could find other solutions."

"I could agree to not reaching for sweets during the day, but I must insist upon a sweet after dinner."

She coughed delicately, her face flushing. "I did notice, my dear, that your stamina is improved when desserts aren't available late in the evening."

He gritted his teeth. "Dash it." He slammed his hands onto the table and stood, striding away before he could even explain his own actions. Didn't he expect a wife to keep close attention on her husband? But why did he have to marry such a keen eye? Hadn't he had enough change for one year already?

Chapter Fifteen

Michael had not trusted himself to test his "stamina" the previous evening after he had behaved in such ungentlemanly fashion. He'd climbed into his wife's bed late into the night, long after she'd fallen asleep. Alys was, thankfully, not a light sleeper, so his tossing and turning had not seemed to trouble her.

When he woke, she was already out of bed. He suspected she still kept bakers' hours and it would take time for her to be able to stay awake for social events and then sleep later in the morning. Since farmers' hours were not so different than bakers' hours, it wouldn't be a problem in the country. No doubt she had already ordered an earlier breakfast.

When he arrived downstairs after giving his valet orders, he discovered the sideboard in the dining room held the usual bacon and eggs and rack of toast, but nothing whatsoever in the bun family.

He bit back a savage curse and dumped so much sugar into his tea that the brew was fouled beyond his ability to drink it. When he pushed back the morning libation to attack his eggs, the cheerful blue-and-white china tipped, spilling tea onto the tablecloth. He clenched his hand into a fist to stop the shaking, then realized his fingers weren't shaking at all. Mere temper had caused the spill.

Perhaps Alys had a point. Could his physical infirmities, which had slowly been becoming more troublesome over the past half-decade, be cured so simply? And yet he craved the sweet.

How could he have married a Redcake baker and be denied the fruits of her trade?

"May I bring you a fresh cup of tea, my lord?" inquired a footman as he entered.

"Yes, thank you, but have it brought to my study. I'm done here." He pushed back from the table and stalked out of the breakfast room, wondering if he should see a doctor to verify Alys's claims. Foolish to give up something he enjoyed based on her opinion, but then he'd always considered doctors to be of limited use.

His mother had called in a baker's dozen of the fools as his father began to complain of head pain and slowly declined. None of them had done him any good, merely addicted him to laudanum. Though, perhaps that had been the best thing at the end.

He turned at the door. "Any idea as to the whereabouts of Lady Hatbrook?"

"I believe she is closeted with Mrs. Hall, my lord. Candidates for the position of her ladyship's maid are arriving this afternoon."

"From where?" Did she apply to a London agency so quickly?

"Eastbourne, sir. Mrs. Hall said there was a good agency there and her ladyship wanted to keep the hiring as local as possible."

He nodded. "Very good." Feeling dissatisfied, he went to his office, making sure to throw the contents of his chocolate box into the waste can before he was tempted to have a truffle. He set his pocket watch on his desk, determined to ascertain how long it would take for his hands to shake without a morning bun.

Two hours later, he was pouring over the Redcake acquisition papers again, writing final instructions for his new man of business, when a knock came at the door.

He stared down at the papers as if awoken from a dream, wondering if purchasing Redcake's had been a mistake. Alys seemed committed to living here in the country because of her sister's health. But he'd have to spend time in London until he had a competent manager in place. No suitable candidates had been found as of yet. Redcake's would be an onslaught of temptations, that, if Alys was right, could be considered a danger to his well-being.

Plus, he needed to focus on the getting of an heir.

The gentle knock came again, one he didn't recognize.

"Come."

The door opened and Alys's copper-bright head poked in.

"You were up early this morning."

"Mrs. Hall had much to show me. What is keeping you at your desk today? There is a sun blazing outside despite the cold. I thought we might take a walk."

"I'm working on my London papers."

"Oh? Anything of interest?" Alys asked eagerly.

He looked down and saw her father's name, and set his arm over the papers. "It's my business, Alys," he said more abruptly than he intended. "Yours is the running of the house. Surely you have plenty with which to occupy yourself?"

Her lips lost their upward curve and tightened. "You will not share your concerns with me?"

"Not in matters of business. Different spheres, my dear."

"I was very involved in my father's business."

He stood. "Not to hear Sir Bartley tell the tale. I understood you'd be occupied with staff interviews today."

Her eyes narrowed. "No doubt my father was attempting to make me sound silly enough to be marriageable. Good day." She turned away from the door and it swung closed behind her, too well oiled to make more than a subtle *snick* as the lock met the doorjamb. But he knew his wife would have slammed it if she could.

He looked down, expecting his hands to be shaking on top of the Redcake papers, but they weren't. Though he didn't want her wrapped into his business life, especially since he needed an heir from her, not a bakery manager's skills, he couldn't underestimate her intelligence.

He stared longingly at the pitiful heap of chocolates resting on crumpled papers in the waste bin, craving the smooth, deep flavor, the soft melt on his tongue.

Turning away resolutely, for he needed all his wits about him as he negotiated his new life, he eyed his papers instead.

* * *

Late Wednesday afternoon, as Alys conveyed her final instructions on the hiring of her maid to Mrs. Hall, a footman knocked on the open door of her study.

"Lady Redcake and Miss Rose Redcake have arrived, my lady," he said.

Alys nodded. "Thank you."

After the footman departed, Mrs. Hall said, "I can have the matter investigated. If Miss Hortense Turner is supporting a child as is rumored in the village, her moral character is thrown into question."

"Her references were excellent. And certainly supporting a child is better than abandoning it, or turning to lesser forms of work than service to pay for the child."

"The other servants won't accept a fallen woman."

Alys kept her expression neutral. Little did the woman know what kind of past her new mistress had. "They don't need to know. I can rely on your discretion, of course."

Mrs. Hall, stone-faced, nodded.

"Bring her in for a one-month trial and we'll see how she does." Miss Turner was the only experienced lady's maid able to begin work this very week. With Rose being in residence Alys knew they needed more help. Her mother's maid, Edith, didn't know the house and would have her hands full.

"Yes, my lady. I'll send word to her aunt's cottage in Polegate. Miss Turner will be here tomorrow if not tonight."

"Very good." Alys stood and smoothed her black crepe skirts, then followed Mrs. Hall out of her study so she could greet her mother and sister. At least the new maid wouldn't have too much clothing to manage for the next few months. Her mother had only had time to procure two crepe mourning gowns, though she probably had brought more along with her, possibly even the black silk gowns Alys would wear once it had been three months since Judah's death.

When Alys entered the front parlor, Rose immediately stood and flew into her arms, vibrating with so much excitement that she could scarcely contain her sister within a hug. Within thirty seconds though, her sister had begun to cough.

"That's enough," her mother said. "Edith, take Rose upstairs and help her into one of her new aesthetic garments."

"Mother!" exclaimed Rose between coughs.

"We agreed you would wear them at the Farm," her mother said.

Rose hung her head, but Alys, seeing her pallor, tilted her head toward the door. Edith opened it and Rose followed her out.

"I cannot understand that girl. We found some lovely silk twill dresses at Liberty, and Edith fit them perfectly. So much more comfortable for her than those constricting fashions."

"She has definite opinions of herself."

Her mother's arm fluttered gracefully. "She should throw them out the window after what has happened to you. And Matilda, for that matter. Who would have thought you would do so well for yourself and pave the way for Matilda besides. I expect we'll have a second engagement to announce in the family by summer."

"Things are moving that quickly for Matilda?"

"Why shouldn't they? How long did you know the marquess before you married?"

"About two months."

"Exactly. It doesn't take the right man very long to decide." Her mother leaned forward and took her hand. "My dear, I am so happy for you. You couldn't have done better for yourself."

Alys knew her mother was right, but she was living Rose's dream, not her own. If it wasn't for the heat between her and Michael, none of this would ever have happened. How long would that heat last if the friction between them continued?

In the two days since Alys had drastically altered the menus and they had quarreled in his study, they had scarcely spoken. She knew he'd been busy with affairs of business. Telegrams had been leaving and arriving steadily over the past two days.

He hadn't avoided her bed at night either, though he hadn't made advances. Since she'd already been asleep when he retired both nights, she supposed he was being considerate.

At her mother's expectant look, she said, "I thought I would invite the Dickondells to dinner soon. Will you be staying for a while?"

"I thought I would stay a month, until I feel certain Rose is on the mend."

"Then perhaps I can invite them in a couple of weeks? That will give her time to find her bloom again."

"I'm not sure we need to announce a third engagement this year," her mother said uncertainly.

"I'm sure Rose wouldn't accept anyone until she's investigated all the eligible men in the neighborhood, at least, but I should invite them soon."

"I shall be happy to meet them," her mother pronounced.

A maid brought in a tea cart and Alys poured. She and her mother were just sitting back with their milky tea and a low-sugar seedcake Alys had prepared when a knock came at the door and a footman entered.

"The Dowager Marchioness of Hatbrook and the Lady Elizabeth Shield," he announced.

A hunk of buttered seedcake fell into Alys's tea. Hastily, she set the mess down as Michael's family swept into the room.

Lady Hatbrook looked jaundiced despite the cheery sun streaming through the large windows. She could have been Beth's grandmother rather than her mother, though Michael had told her his mother was only forty-seven. The mourning gown did her complexion no favors. She had aged in the past two weeks.

"I was not expecting you, my lady," Alys said, rising to greet them.

Lady Hatbrook nodded stiffly but Beth flew to give her a hug, her healthy glow undiminished by the black crepe she wore.

"I have had no satisfaction from the War Office and my nerves could not take another day in London," Lady Hatbrook announced.

"You have had a most trying time," Alys agreed. "I do not know if my husband has learned anything more."

Lady Hatbrook sniffed. "It is unlikely. We shall not stay for long, but a few days of fresh air will do us good. Will you pour?"

Alys went to the bell pull, but the staff knew the routine when Lady Hatbrook descended and were bringing in a tray before she could touch the tassel.

Lady Hatbrook sniffed as Alys offered her seedcake. "I would have thought you could do better. I hope you aren't trying to reduce when you have an heir to produce."

Alys's mother hid a smile behind her napkin at the lady's inadvertent rhyme.

Alys didn't want to discuss Michael's health concerns, especially since she suspected his mother had similar issues, so she merely said, "We are experimenting with the menu."

"You must have a cake about here somewhere," Lady Hatbrook said. "I'll ring for one at once."

Alys sighed as her mother-in-law took the initiative. She supposed there might very well be cake in the house, prepared for the servants, but when the maid who came shook her head, Lady Hatbrook demanded Mrs. Hall.

Alys refused to create a scene, so when the housekeeper arrived she agreed that cake would be available for the next day's tea. Pudding wasn't mentioned, nor breakfast, but she wasn't going to bring that up. They'd simply have fireworks at each meal. Perhaps twenty-four hours without sugary foods would soften her ladyship's temper.

By Friday, pastry had been added to all menus again, but Alys was gratified to see Michael refusing to partake of most of it, patting his stomach whenever his mother made rude remarks. She felt quite in charity with him as they retired together that night for the first time in days.

"How are you feeling?" he asked. "I imagine it is difficult to have all these guests when you are scarcely accustomed to your new role."

"My family is no trouble, any more than your sister, who is a delight."

"But my mother is another matter."

"She looks so unwell," Alys commented. "I cannot help but think ill health troubles her disposition."

"She was never pleasant," Michael said.

She hadn't been looking at him, but she turned, surprised by his bald statement. "That must have been hard to deal with as a child."

He shrugged. "In aristocratic households, servants raise children."

Visions of teaching her child to bake diminished. "Then what are the mothers supposed to do?"

"They are very busy. Parties, calls, charitable works, especially on properties their family owns, supervising households." He put his hand on her nightgown-clad thigh. "Pleasing their husbands."

When she didn't push it away, he slowly moved his hand higher. Tired as she was, she felt her body softening and warming under his touch. Despite the early February chill outside, the fire and warming pan kept the room warm enough. When she removed her nightgown, her husband's grunt of admiration heated her everywhere the fire had not.

He reached for her breasts, whispering endearments and praise.

For the first time, he avidly suckled her nipples, and Alys found a new level of sensual pleasure. He scarcely had to touch her between her legs before she was spiraling into ecstasy. The feel of his erection nudging its way into her body only heightened the feeling, and she rode a wave of delight, circling complete abandon as their bodies moved together.

It was only when they lay together, intertwined, that she wondered what her life would be like. At least there was no thought that she was merely to be an ornament on Michael's arm. With his mother being so difficult, surely plenty of work existed for her, in charitable affairs if nothing else. She considered what occupations would have filled her time had she been born wealthy.

When Michael's breathing deepened, she tugged her assorted parts from underneath him and reached for her nightgown, flung on the opposite side of the bed. She went to bathe, feeling sticky from all the heat they had generated.

When she lowered herself into the tub, she saw streaks of blood on her inner thigh. *Not this.* Her hands shook as she covered her eyes and hunched into the hot water. No babe grew inside her. She pressed her legs together. All of this had been for nothing. What would Michael think of her? She turned her head to the wall and sobbed.

A couple of minutes later, the door opened. She jerked up with a cry, then saw Michael, his hair tousled, fingers struggling with the belt of his dressing gown.

"What is wrong? Did I hurt you?" Looking more awake now, he knelt by the tub.

She sniffled and rubbed her nose.

"What?"

"It's too horrid."

"Tell me," he commanded.

"I have bad news."

He took a washcloth and wiped her cheeks. "So?"

Her lower lip trembled. "I'm afraid there is no child."

"You're not—"

"Exactly. I'm sorry."

He poked his hand into the water and found her hand. After squeezing it, he said, "It was unlikely, my dear, that you would have that expectation so soon."

She sniffed again. "I suppose you are right. Thank you for being kind."

"Of course I am right." He found a towel and held it out. "The water is quite cool. Come out of there and we'll go back to bed."

When she stood, he lifted her out and carried her to the fire, then helped her into her nightgown. Remembering her condition, she went into her dressing room to find what she needed, then joined him back in bed where he held her all night.

He was right. She would navigate the early days of marriage better if she didn't have to hide a pregnancy. Now, everyone could delight together when it happened and she wouldn't have to hide anything. Still, a part of her regretted the loss of the child who had never existed.

A couple of weeks later, she was inspecting her wardrobe with her mother and Hortense, her new lady's maid, when Beth ran into the room, followed closely by Rose.

"Gawain is here!" Rose sang out, then coughed.

Her mother frowned. "I wonder why? I thought he had business in Bristol."

"It does seem strange," Rose agreed, her voice croaking. "But I saw him in the hallway. He asked to see the marquess."

"Not his own mother?" she said, frowning.

Alys knew how attached her mother had been to Gawain since he returned home and didn't want her to be upset at the slight. "I'm certain he is simply greeting his host to make sure he is welcome, which he is of course. I'll go and see him."

Her mother smiled gratefully.

"Beth? Would you ring for Mrs. Hall and make sure a room is prepared?"

Beth nodded. "I know just the room for him, too. It's quite military. Crossed swords over the mantel and lots of family portraits of fighting men. Judah used to stare at them for hours."

Alys shared a look with her mother. Gawain would be unlikely to find the sight stirring, but perhaps it was better than one of the many rooms decorated in shades of rose, a color the dowager must have favored in the extreme.

While Alys had no interest in decorating, even she knew something needed to be done with at least some of the rose rooms. She plucked at the laddered silk on a faded rose pillow next to her on the divan. Starting with this room.

"Mother, this room needs a fresh eye. I'd like to make some changes."

Her mother's petulant expression changed immediately. She clasped her hands to her chest. "I do agree, darling. William Morris. That's what this dressing room needs, some of his papers. I must make sketches." She lifted her skirt and ran to a writing desk tucked in the corner like a girl half her age.

"I'll leave you to it then," Alys said. "And see to Gawain."

With a wave to Beth, Alys went down the staircase at the end of the hall and headed for the newest part of the house, which looked out over a paddock. Michael's study was at one corner. She opened the door to the first room, where his secretary worked sometimes, then started toward the open door leading to the inner chamber.

"But when did the War Office say he was killed?"

She recognized Gawain's gravelly rasp, wondering why he was using that almost belligerent tone with Michael, especially about a death. Judah's?

"The telegram said January second, nearly two months ago now, but we haven't received any further information. Our cousin at the War Office hasn't been able to confirm any details. I believe there has been a great deal of unrest in the area."

Alys peeked around the door and saw her brother pull a letter from his coat. He unfolded the pages.

"I think the facts are wrong," her brother rasped. "Look at this."

Michael frowned. "What is it?"

"A letter from an herb trader I befriended. I'm working on an import business of my own."

"What about your father's factories?"

Alys could just see the sneer on her brother's face from the side view she could catch from her angle. "That's his business. Only Alys ever cared about it. I have my own plans."

"And what? You want me to invest? This trader has something of value?"

"No man, you aren't listening. It's about your brother. Here." Gawain pointed at the top of the first page. "Look at the date."

"January sixteen," Michael read. "That's the day I received the telegram from the War Office."

"I just received this letter last Friday," Gawain said. His voice rose to a command. "Now read it, this paragraph here." He pointed again.

"I had the pleasure of conversing with your old comrades in arms. I took tea with Captain Shield and Lieutenant Cross in Lahore, after we met at a market where they were purchasing dried fruit. This city has very fine fruit, though it is best known for carpets. Perhaps this merchandise may be of value to you? I have good contacts in this city, better than in Kabul. The captain bought some very fine silk, another specialty of the region. He hoped to ship it to his sister to be made into gowns. Since you have so many sisters this may be of interest to you as well."

Michael set down the letter. "That is all very well, but it doesn't mean Judah is alive."

"Read further," Gawain said impatiently.

Michael picked up the sheet again, muttering his way down the page. "Wait." His index finger poked the page. "January fourteenth. He says he arrived at Lahore on the fourteenth."

Gawain nodded. "Exactly. Zahir Khan, the trader, mailed this letter from the city on the sixteenth. You probably were notified of Captain Shield's death within a day of Khan meeting him at the market. Since I received my letter on Friday you might see something from your brother soon."

"He'd have sent it straight to London, but my family is here," Michael muttered. "I'll write my butler and see if anything has arrived from India."

"An excellent notion."

Michael started to crumple the letter in his fist, then handed it to Gawain. "What if this has all been a mistake?"

"It does happen."

Michael thumped the desk. "Everything, a mistake?"

Alys stumbled as her hand slid from the door, then, instinctively, she turned and ran. All a mistake? Not just Judah's death, but the marriage too. After all, she wasn't carrying his child. He was a marquess who'd married a baker, all for nothing.

Now what? He didn't need her after all. But he couldn't ask for an annulment. The marriage was consummated. Had he ruined his family for nothing? She knew it was his opinion that mattered, not hers. He'd been sanguine when told of her courses. But they didn't love each other. The marriage had been a convenient one, and not approved by his mother. They had made no attempt to enter society in the weeks since the wedding.

Good heavens. The dinner party tomorrow would be her first attempt with a local family since the wedding. Would Michael even attend her dinner, or would he head to London to try to find out the truth?

If she were him, she'd leave for the train station immediately.

Chapter Sixteen

When Alys rose the next morning, she saw Michael's side of the bed had been slept in at some point during the night, though she had missed his entrance and departure. The news about Judah's possible survival had given her a terrible headache on top of the stress she felt, and a strong cup of willow bark tea had allowed her to sleep, though very heavily.

When Hortense came in with her tea tray, she asked the young woman about the marquess's whereabouts.

"I'm sorry, my lady, but I am so new to the Farm I don't pay much mind to the toings and froings yet."

"How have your first five days been?"

"Oh, I'm very happy for the work, my lady, and in such a fine house too." Hortense turned to pull open the heavy wool and silk curtains of dark rose. The view displayed gray skies obscured by rain.

"I'm glad to hear it." Alys's hearing, sharpened from years of dealing with employees, noted that Hortense left out any commentary about her fellow servants.

"Would you like me to check for you?" Hortense asked.

"Perhaps you could ask Mrs. Hall to come to my study after breakfast," Alys said. "We need to review the final details for the dinner tonight."

"That should be lovely," Hortense said. "I understand there is a greenhouse with flowers here. So nice to have flowers during the winter, I always think."

"Did you hear talk about bringing in flowers?" Alys asked. That might make Rose feel worse. They never had flowers in the family rooms in London in case they aggravated her asthma.

"I heard talk of a display on that big table in the front hall," the maid said.

"That is very well," Alys said. Rose wouldn't be in the hall.

"And something for the dinner table too. I believe the dowager marquess ordered a display, as she always had flowers on the table for parties."

So Michael's mother was trying to give orders for Alys's first dinner party? That would not do. Alys's left temple throbbed in distant memory of yesterday's headache. Well, she'd suffered through worse, like when she had three society weddings the same day and a new employee put rose water into the buttercream rather than the orange flower water ordered for all three cakes. Her ladyship could decorate the house as she liked for her own party, but not for Alys's.

She pushed back her quilt and took a sip of tea. "It will be a busy day. At least we don't have to fret over what I'm going to wear today."

"No, my lady, your mourning dresses are very much alike."

"Save the cleanest one for tonight and bring me one of the others for now."

"They are all clean, my lady," said Hortense, her mouth rounding into a horrified O. "You and I are too careful for any troubles of that sort."

Alys took another sip of tea. "I'll take your word, but I am afraid my habits may disappoint you in future. Bring one quickly."

Hortense curtsied and went to the dressing room to select a gown. Alys wished she could wear cakie attire today but the days of that being acceptable were over.

Michael entered the drawing room rather late for that evening's family dinner, but he was followed in, to Alys's surprise, by Matilda and Theodore Bliven.

"Is Father coming?" she whispered to her mother.

"I had a letter from him this morning saying he'd caught a chill and was sneezing too much to leave the house," her mother said.

"Matilda looks well, at least," Alys said. So did Mr. Bliven, though she thought his expression too coy.

"I do hope she brought Lucy with her," her mother fretted. "Surely she wouldn't have come alone on the train with Mr. Bliven."

"I can't imagine she'd be so foolish," said Alys. Matilda had been trained to be a lady.

"I did wonder if you'd want to take Lucy with you, but then you found the local girl. Is she suitable? Edith said there was talk."

"I'm very happy with my choice." Alys wasn't about to gossip about her maid to her mother. For one thing, she didn't know what her mother would think about a lady's maid with a bastard child. Hortense was so eager to please, so much friendlier than an imported maid from France or the like, that Alys felt quite comfortable with her. She didn't want a maid who put on more airs than she did.

Her mother rose and gave Matilda a hug while Gawain pulled away from the Dickondell brothers to shake Theo's hand and introduce him around. Matilda soon joined Rose, Beth, and Maud Wilson, the Dickondells' pretty cousin, while young Adela Dickondell sat with her parents, and stared at Gawain's eye patch. Lady Hatbrook conversed with the Dickondell aunt, whose name Alys had missed. Michael's aunt stayed in her room, but Alys had taken Mrs. Dickondell for a brief visit earlier.

As soon as Alys had greeted her sister, she caught her husband's eye and joined him under a large portrait of three cocker spaniel puppies in a ribbon-trimmed basket, favored pets of a previous marchioness.

"You look very somber," she observed. "Some news?" She couldn't reveal the extent of her knowledge, though her head fairly throbbed with it.

Michael held himself so tightly in check that he was white around his lips. "I do not know if you've spoken to your brother today, but he presented me with some evidence that the report of Judah's death is incorrect."

Thankfully, Gawain had shown her the letter today. After he'd shared the news about Judah, he'd gone on to explain that the trader had a line on an Indian herb reputed to do wonders for vision problems. She had not realized her brother dreamed of restoring the vision in his damaged eye. She was so glad he was trying to help himself. He'd been angry and grim when he first arrived home, so unlike the boy she'd known.

"Were you able to learn more today?"

Michael scratched under his nose with his thumb. "I sent a telegram to Lieutenant Cross's family. I was at school with his older brother. You may recall the younger brother, who fought with Lord Mews at the ball last year."

"Oh, yes," she said, remembering with sickening clarity the blood and smell of burning flesh. "Did they know anything?"

"They were also mourning the death of their soldier."

"They received the telegram as well?"

"Yes." He tapped the nail of his thumb against his teeth.

Normally, his control over himself was absolute. He was a still man in general, not tending to all these small movements, but at least she saw his hands were steady.

"How very strange. Was anything reported in the papers about a battle or skirmish or anything last month?"

"No," he said. "Nothing new. It is very strange. The War Office has been most unhelpful. I have had thoughts of leaving for India myself."

"Good heavens," Alys exclaimed. "It is so savage there. I wouldn't be surprised if Gawain returned to India on business someday but I've never understood you to be a traveller."

"Any thoughts I've had of adventure were in trade," he said, "which is surely as savage as any Asiatic tribe. But I must know the truth about my brother."

"Of course." Alys agreed instantly. "I will go with you, if it comes to that."

He raised an eyebrow. "Would you?"

She nodded. He regarded her for a moment, still as an untamed beast considering his prey. She had forgotten he probably didn't want her anymore, not now that he had an heir again. They must find out the truth before they could plan their future.

"I didn't think you'd appear tonight," she said, ignoring her mother's gesture to come.

"It is our first dinner party as husband and wife."

"You must prefer to be with the Cross family, storming the War Office or some such."

"I believe they have an assault planned tomorrow," he said with wry humor. "I shall await their news. I do wish we had a way to reach your brother's trader friend."

"There must be some way, if he hopes to provide goods to Gawain. He showed me the letter." Good, she'd managed to mention that.

"No doubt he will attempt to become a businessman on a large scale if Gawain can provide the capital, but until that time, he sounds rather itinerant. Gawain sent a telegram to a shop in Lahore who takes messages for this Zahir Khan chap, offering financial incentive to learn more."

A moment of quiet settled over the room, punctuated by Lady Hatbrook's plummy tones. "The nerve of that girl, travelling with a man. She is no better than she should be."

Mrs. Redcake appeared at Alys's elbow. Alys felt her face flush red. Her mother must have been trying to warn her that the nasty woman was saying things about Matilda. Now the entire room had heard her poison.

Matilda's face had gone as red as Alys's, the freckles on her nose showing through her powder as her nostrils pinched.

Michael strode quickly toward his mother, seating himself next to her and bending to her ear. She, innocent as a lamb, looked around as if she couldn't understand why anyone would be staring at her in mute shock.

Alys forced herself to glide toward the bell pull, rather than to run. A footman appeared at the door and she hissed at him to have them called for dinner. Then, she went toward her sister.

"Lucy came with us," Matilda said fretfully. "She was in the third-class car, of course, but we were never alone, I promise you. There was an entire family in the car with us, the Carneys, I believe. Do you know them?"

She directed this remark to Alys.

"No, but if they are a Polegate family I'm sure I will become aware of them eventually." Alys searched for Mr. Bliven, but he was engaged in a boisterous discussion with Clement Dickondell, the oldest son, who was laughing as Mr. Bliven waved his hands.

Men, she thought disgustedly. Did nothing improper touch them? Then she remembered Mr. Cross, falling under Lord Mews's fist, and shuddered. She wondered who would play white knight to Matilda. Her father? Gawain? They both seemed far too fond of Theodore Bliven.

"Will there be a happy announcement soon?" she inquired to her sister.

Matilda's only response was a closed-lip, secretive smile, but their mother put a hand to her breast and sighed happily. Alys narrowed her eyes and stared at Mr. Bliven again. He was Michael's friend, and she knew too well what *he* was capable of in the department of impropriety. She could only hope Matilda was far more sensible than she had been.

The butler appeared in the doorway and announced dinner. Alys wasn't sure what the correct order was, but Michael and Mrs. Dickondell had everyone arranged in moments and they went into the formal dining room.

Conversation was subdued at first but free-flowing wine and Mr. Bliven's jokes loosened the crowd a bit. Michael, not surprisingly, was lost in thought most of the time, eating sparingly and not touching sweets at all, not even a course of lemon sorbet.

Alys saw Lady Hatbrook staring at Michael often and wondered what he had said to her to prevent further outbursts. She didn't speak, but ate rather heavily, even taking Michael's cake for her own.

Rose was the belle of the dinner, and Alys had ensured the floral centerpiece had been replaced by a topiary of studded oranges from the greenhouse, so she had no breathing difficulty. Ernest Dickondell, the middle brother, spent far more time speaking to her than to Aunt Dickondell on his other side.

"Another romance on our hands?" her mother whispered to her when they had moved to the music room, after the men had their coffee and cigars. Rose had agreed to play the piano, with young Ernest turning pages.

"I don't know if Rose would be pleased with a second son," Alys had to admit. "At least not at eighteen."

"I suppose you are right," her mother said. "Do you suppose Mr. Clement Dickondell is courting his cousin?"

"Maud Wilson is just seventeen and seems younger than her age. I wouldn't think it likely, not now at least."

Her mother waited until Rose had completed her sonata before speaking again. "And then there is Lady Elizabeth, but she is looking for a husband in London."

"I believe so, but that is not to say this is the one family with sons in the area, simply the only family who I've met in the short time I've been here."

"They are very pleasant," her mother said.

"Yes, I like them even better upon this second meeting. I was quite distracted by Rose's health the first time." She heard a snore behind her.

"She does look well. I am so pleased you can give her a home for now. Staying here in Sussex may be the perfect solution for her."

Alys glanced back discreetly and saw Michael's mother had fallen asleep during a Mozart piece. "What will you do with yourself, once we are all married off?"

"There is still Gawain, and Lewis, poor man. And I'll be able to throw myself into the dress reform cause. I'm very passionate about that."

"Understandably," Alys said, then applauded as Rose finished her last piece. Lady Hatbrook woke up with a loud snort. Maud agreed to sing next, then Adela and Samuel Dickondell, the youngest of the family, did a duet on flute and violin.

"What a talented musical family," her mother said to Mrs. Dickondell, who flushed with pleasure.

"We are much in each other's society," the lady said. "I'm so pleased your daughters are here at the Farm now. We had no idea a romance was brewing."

Or that the new Lady Hatbrook had not been on the shelf, when they had treated her so. But despite her pique at that first night's treatment, she enjoyed the family. "I hope we shall have many such evenings," Alys said.

"I agree. It is such a comfort to have family visit during times of grief, even if one cannot formally entertain or be entertained. But I must say, there are such rumors of telegrams flying in and out of the Farm today."

"My husband is hoping for better news than he has hitherto received," Alys said.

"I am glad," she said, clasping her hands to her heart. "Such a comfort for his mother, of course."

"We hope to know more soon."

"Yes, yes. We will not breathe a word, but will pray for the best."

The Dickondells soon called for their carriage, pleading country hours. Lady Hatbrook had already retired, muttering about the lack of sweets.

Alys found her way into Michael's arms in the wee hours, flush with the success of her first dinner. Perhaps she wouldn't be such a bad hostess after all. They made love until gray light seeped around the windows. Then he muttered something about a horse and left her to sleep.

Hortense had the curtains drawn the next morning by the time Alys pried open her eyes. "Good morning, my lady. The kitchen is buzzing with news of the party last night."

She yawned, covering her mouth with her hand. "A good buzz?"

"Yes, ma'am. Everyone wonders if your sisters will have happy news soon."

"I have no idea," Alys admitted, reaching for her dressing gown, which Michael had draped over the bed when he left.

"And then there is much to question about Captain Shield."

"I would dearly love to know the truth there," Alys said, feeling as if she'd bit into a lemon. Her entire new life was built on a sad fiction if he was alive.

"A telegram boy came this morning," Hortense said, pouring a cup of tea and adding cream and sugar.

Her heartbeat pounded audibly in her chest. "Did the marquess give any clue as to the contents?"

Hortense shrugged. "He isn't here. I believe the telegram is waiting for him in his study."

Alys ignored her tea. "Help me dress at once, please." How she wished she could put on one of her simple gowns.

A half hour later, she slipped into Michael's study, tiptoeing gingerly to the window because it was too dark to see.

"Ow!" She barked her shin on the edge of the desk, despite her layers of skirts.

Finally, she found the edge of a navy velvet curtain and pulled it aside until sunlight streamed in. She'd slept until midmorning, an unheard of state of affairs only a few months ago. The aristocrat and the working girl did not keep the same hours.

The telegram was on a silver tray, centered on Michael's desk. She wished she could see the contents, but it was still folded shut.

Collapsing into his desk chair as the adrenaline-fueled curiosity diminished, she glanced at the rest of his desk, and ran her fingers along the ancient wood.

The top page of a stack of papers caught her attention, as she recognized her father's handwriting. Apparently Michael's secretary had yet to file away her dowry settlement. She stood, and leaned over the paper. At first, she couldn't believe what she was reading. This wasn't about her at all, but about Redcake's.

Her father had sold the tea shop and emporium to Michael? His London flagship? How could he have done this and not told her? How could *Michael* have purchased it and not told her?

She snatched up the sheath of papers and read rapidly until a cough at the doorway distracted her.

"What are you doing?" Michael asked, stepping into the room, still in muddy riding clothes.

"I was told a telegram had come for you from London, so I came in to see it, and found this." She waved the papers at him. "My father sold Redcake's to you and you didn't inform me?"

"You have no place in my business life, Alys. I've made that clear to you already."

She slammed the papers to the desk. "But Redcake's is my business too. My toil, my ideas."

His expression remained patient, remote. "Once again, my dear, your father has disputed that point of view."

"Even when a woman is providing value he can't see it," she spat. "I might have hoped you would be more enlightened, but you are all the same, brothers under the skin."

He took a step forward. "Didn't you enjoy your party last night? Despite your lack of experience you did a wonderful job."

"Thanks to outsmarting your mother at her game," Alys said. "She changed my arrangements without consulting me, and if I hadn't discovered this Rose would have been too ill to stay."

He frowned. "I'm sorry to hear that."

"This is my sphere," Alys hissed. "Daily battle with your mother for supremacy? Taking my mother's role with her daughter? Meanwhile doing nothing that I want because my husband's health prevents me from even using the skills I've spent years honing."

His gaze sharpened. "I'm happy to have your desserts on my table."

"I'm not happy to make you sick, Michael. I am impressed by your self-control, but I see no purpose in testing that control continuously. Nor do I think it is in your mother's best interests to have pastry ever-present, given that she looks to be at death's door herself."

Michael's mouth closed into a thin line. "If you think that, then why deny her pleasures?"

She leaned forward, glad they had the desk between them. "That's tantamount to giving me permission to kill her."

"You are not a doctor. Your theory about sugar is merely that."

"And you deny the truth?"

He hesitated. "Not for myself. If I didn't feel better I wouldn't play along. With all of the present difficulties it has been a great boon to have a clear head and steady hands. I am grateful to you."

He stepped closer to the desk. Alys wrapped her arms around herself as much as her tight bodice would allow.

"Managing me is a large task of its own, wouldn't you say, wife? Cannot your success with me satisfy you?"

"My heart has not yet sacrificed Redcake's." She turned away, blinking back tears. How had business become so emotion-filled? "To think you kept this a secret."

"No secret, simply none of your business."

"I cannot believe that," she said. "When you know what it meant to me. You are most unfeeling."

He tilted his head. "As are you, for taxing me with this when I have my brother's very life to concern myself with."

She gripped the edge of the desk. "I will leave you to your concerns then, husband. I believe I shall take the train to London with my mother and Matilda since you are so busy. I need to order dresses again and I would prefer to choose the fabrics myself."

"Whatever you wish." His cold gaze swept hers for a moment, then fixed on the telegram on his desk.

Would he open it in front of her? She wished to know if Judah had sent mail to the London address, too. But Michael didn't move toward the telegram. Very well. He had resolved to shut her out. She lifted her chin and swept out from behind the desk, making sure not to touch him with any part of her mourning skirts.

* * *

Alys ignored her mother when she asked if Alys would be staying at Hatbrook House, and no further comment was made as she followed her mother up the steps to her family's St. James's Square mansion two days later, Matilda giggling behind her as she clutched Mr. Bliven's arm.

She thought his behavior was too joking, and Matilda's far too sensual, but who was she to judge? She had little experience with men, and none of it successful.

Ten minutes later she was back in her old room. Lewis's mechanical bird still perched next to her bed, its plumage dampened by dust.

"They must have shut up the room," Hortense said, looking around.

"It appears so," Alys agreed. "I share a dressing room with my sisters, just down the hall. I suppose you should hang my clothes there. I'll have to keep wearing the crepe until we're certain Judah is alive."

Hortense opened the door as a sharp rap came from the other side. Alys recognized the knock instantly.

"Hello, Father." Alys didn't bother to keep the cool tone from her voice. Affection still bloomed instantaneously from her heart at the sight of his bushy, fading red hair, but anger filled her mind.

Hortense lowered her head. "I'll be down the hall then, sorting out the luggage, my lady." She scurried out and shut the door behind her.

"My lady," her father said, leaning against the door with his arms crossed over his chest. "I never thought to hear one of my daughters called a lady."

Alys mimicked his pose. "I imagine you thought exactly that, when you gave your two youngest daughters a lady's education."

He sighed. "Not this again, Alys. You'd never have wanted lessons in elocution or deportment, much less painting or the piano. You wanted to be in the kitchen."

"And yet you forced me out."

"To find your proper place in the world."

"What would that be, stuck as I was between the kitchen and the boudoir? Do you have any idea how narrowly I escaped ruin?"

"Why do you think I let you stay in the kitchen as long as I did?"

She stared at him, noting he'd lost weight in the month since her wedding. How serious had his illness been?

"It seemed overnight you went from a bubbly girl as interested in young fellows as the next lass, to a frozen, cake-obsessed mite. At first I thought you were simply following your old father, but something was missing behind your eyes."

She scowled. "Do you want to discuss what happened?"

"No, daughter. I want to tell you that I saw you come back to life last fall. A sparkle had returned to your eyes that I hadn't seen in a decade. I didn't know why, but I noticed that men at Redcake's began to show an interest in you that had never been apparent. I thought it was time for you to find a husband."

"You didn't think that spark was there for one man?"

He scratched his head. "You would have told me."

"I did not," she pointed out.

"I didn't know a marquess was involved."

She rubbed her eyes, still gritty from the train, then went to look in a drawer for a handkerchief. "Why did you sell him Redcake's, Father? I cannot understand that impulse. I had no hopes of marrying Hatbrook. I wanted to stay where I was."

"I did it for Rose, primarily, and Matilda too, though her situation appears to be resolving differently than I'd planned."

"You did?"

"Yes. Rose doesn't belong in London. And a girl needs her mother. Your mother will not leave me, so we all need to move." He scratched his head again. "I set out to conquer London and did exactly that. Now I can move on, for my family's sake."

She wiped her eyes. "What do I do? I'm not prepared for the life of a marchioness. I'm prepared to be a baker."

"I would have married you to Ralph Popham or Ewan Hales," he said. "You made your choice."

"Then why did you bring Theodore Bliven to dinner?"

"His father suggested he was in need of an occupation and I thought I might hire him as a manager for Redcake's and keep ownership. But he is too light-minded to manage it. Your marquess has the sense needed, but of course he will have to hire someone. I have faith he'll find the right person, however."

"So you thought I might marry Mr. Bliven and he would run Redcake's," she said flatly. "Why not Lewis?"

Her father wrinkled his nose. "Lewis is good with machines, not people. He wouldn't give any daughter of mine the attention she deserved."

She laughed sourly, glancing at the bird and thinking of all the hours Lewis must have lavished onto his love token. "And Hatbrook will?"

"You chose him. Clearly this business with his brother has blackened his outlook for now, but the situation will eventually resolve."

"If Captain Shield hadn't been declared dead, Hatbrook never would have married me." She wiped her eyes again.

"No one is to blame for that, unless you want to call out the army," her father said. "You and Hatbrook are bound together now and you'll have to make the best of it. I'm just glad you'll be living near Redcake Manor."

"Which is uninhabitable."

"An unforgivable oversight on my part," her father admitted.

Alys knew that was an apology. "At least Rose didn't suffer for it, thanks to Hatbrook."

"And now you've left her in the country? Is Hatbrook on his way here?"

"I am certain he will have to come eventually, to straighten out this business with his brother."

Her father sniffed and found his own handkerchief. "A difficult business. I am glad we never had this trouble with Gawain."

"Yes. In fact it was him who brought the news to Hatbrook."

"Yes, he informed me before he departed, since he was supposed to be at Redcake's."

"What is he going to do with Redcake's sold?"

"I offered him the factories to manage. He didn't refuse."

She met her father's gaze, and knew he realized Gawain wouldn't stay for long. He wanted to make his own successes. But she understood her father was simply happy Gawain was alive, given how close they'd come to losing him. And Arthur was already long lost. He was worried about Rose.

With so much to consider, she was surprised he'd given thought to her future. Just a few months ago she hadn't anticipated anything changing, but her father had been planning. Maybe she didn't have the business acumen she had thought she possessed after all.

"Eighteen-eighty-seven is shaping into quite a different year than eighteen-eighty-six, is it not?"

He nodded. "It is indeed, my lady."

She laughed, then put a hand to her temple as the vibration made her head throb.

"Are you ill?" Her father led her to a chair in front of the fireplace.

"No, the train made my head hurt. Hatbrook is angry with me for looking at the papers on his desk," she whispered. "But I don't want a life where I am supposed to stay strictly in the home. He won't even share information about his brother with me! I do not know my place, except that what he wants is too narrow for me."

"Marriage is an adjustment."

"For the woman."

Her father perched on the edge of the bed. "No, Alys, for the man, too. Have patience. A soft manner and tolerant heart will help greatly. When he learns how strong and capable you are, he will relent and include you where appropriate."

"You think so?"

"In family matters, certainly. Your mother had no interest in business. But over the years I wanted to tell her things, and she listened to me. Hear what Hatbrook has to say. Follow his lead. The rest will come."

"He just disappears," she confessed.

"He doesn't appear to meals?"

"Not when I do."

"Then alter your schedule to fit his. Eventually, he will talk."

"Who would have thought you would be the one to give me sound marital advice?" She winced as the headache took stronger hold.

"I'll ring for your maid," her father said. "Rest now. I'm sure your husband will be on his way soon."

Alys closed her eyes and rested her head on the back of her chair when her father departed. She thought she'd misled him about the actual nature of the situation. Michael didn't care where she was and she didn't really know if he planned to come to London.

Matilda burst into the room, slamming the door into the wall. "I've just sent a note to Lady Lillian. We must have a council of war tomorrow, to help me with Mr. Bliven. You will help me figure out how to catch him, won't you, Alys?"

Chapter Seventeen

"Your visitors have been shown into the Rose Room, my lord," said the footman.

Michael thought irritably that most rooms in the house were rose-colored. Alys had chattered about redecorating once her mother arrived but all the Redcakes except Rose had decamped to London the day before. He hadn't asked Rose how she felt about her name matching the Farm's decor. She'd been shut away with Beth, pouring over fashion plates. Which left him to hide from his mother as much as possible.

That lady had changed the menus again the moment Alys left. The night before the table had groaned under cream soups, fancy French sauces, and a seven-layer cake. He'd hardly slept last night as a result, even though he hadn't touched the cake. It was as if, after a month of abstemious eating habits, his body had rebelled.

He was in too foul a mood to receive visitors, but nonetheless his boots ate up the hallways between his study and the Rose Room. These men were from the War Office.

His mother met him in the hallway. The high ruffles on her dress angled her head even more arrogantly than usual.

"Is it about Judah?"

"I would imagine so, Mother."

She took his arm. "Then I will join you."

He examined her for a second, trying to see her through Alys's eyes. Did his mother really look ill, or did the color black disagree with her complexion? He had no idea, but the anxious look in her eyes had him opening the door without further perusal.

He wished Alys was on his arm instead. He'd known it would be difficult to turn a baker into a marchioness, even one with money and relatives eager for the transformation, but he hadn't expected her to find her new role this difficult. He needed to remove his mother from the Farm if he had any hope of domestic tranquility.

Two gentlemen dressed like civilians in black-checkered suits stood at the fire. Their military bearing gave them away, however.

"I am Hatbrook," he said, and helped his mother sit in a rose-colored armchair. "And this is my mother, Lady Hatbrook."

The gentlemen bent their heads.

"Be seated," his mother instructed.

They all sat in a half-circle grouping at an angle to the fireplace.

"I would imagine you are here regarding Captain Shield?" Michael asked.

"Yes, my lord," said the elder, stroking his oiled, graying mustache.

The younger man unsnapped a valise and pulled out papers.

"Is he alive?" quavered Lady Hatbrook, in a rare show of tender emotion.

"Yes," said the younger man.

Michael's queasy stomach from the night before returned, along with a sense of elation that had him clamping his lips shut so that he didn't smile in front of these men.

The elder narrowed his eyes. "What Captain Nettles means is he was alive two days ago, when we received a telegram from his regiment."

"Dreadful series of errors," said Captain Nettles.

The other man took the top paper from the captain and handed it to Michael.

210 • *Heather Hiestand*

He read over the reassurance carefully, then passed it to his mother. Fighting against the urge to bash their uncaring heads together, he drew in his chin and placed his hands on his thighs. "Why the confusion regarding my brother and Lieutenant Cross?"

"Bombay mixed up a death list and a discipline list," said the captain.

"I'm afraid," said the elder man, "that they made an unapproved excursion to Lahore. This resulted in disciplinary action, but a dreadful paperwork error ensued. We deeply apologize and will visit the Cross family upon our return to London."

"I can scarcely believe two experienced officers would jaunt off many miles just to buy fruit and carpets," Michael said.

His mother tittered harshly, then covered her mouth with her hand and sank into her chair.

"Even so," began the elder man.

"My brother is a gentleman," Michael said, injecting steel into his voice. "A man of honor, bred from generations of fighting men. And you tell me he has done something worthy of discipline?"

The elder man shifted in his chair, spreading his feet apart. "It was all rather a misunderstanding."

"Then he was under orders when he went to Lahore?"

"Unclear," said the captain.

"From this distance, you know, my lord," said the elder man. "Hard to say what is happening in India. But his career is secure, you need not worry about him."

"And the lieutenant?"

The captain cleared his throat. "Resigned his commission."

"Then he's on his way home?"

"Believe he's taken a civilian appointment."

Michael tapped his fingers against his chin. "Why don't you start from the beginning? I can see there was some incident."

"Nothing that reflects poorly on your brother," insisted Captain Nettles.

"Can you not see, Hatbrook," interrupted his mother, "that we were meant to think Judah and this other fellow were dead, and it is only the stink we caused that has brought them back to life again?"

The older man's eyes widened. "Now, Lady Hatbrook. I assure you—"

She waved her hand. "Do not try to pull the wool over my eyes. I can see the situation clearly enough. If it wasn't for my son's new brother-by-marriage finding out the truth quite by accident, we'd have gone on thinking Judah was dead. My own cousin would not tell us the truth."

"Madam—"

She sniffed. "I hope you have not turned my son into a spy. I will not tolerate such nonsense. I shall write him at once. Yes, and write the Cross boy's brother too. For all their birth and noble relatives, that family has never been any better than they should be."

The younger man sat stone-faced. Michael could see he was the real power of the two men.

"You may do as you wish, of c-course," stammered the older man, stroking his mustache.

"War is a dangerous business," interrupted the captain. "The border region is full of petty tribes. Do not expect your mail to reach him."

Michael stood, his fists clenched at the implied threat. His mother's hand had flown to her throat and he noted the trembling, so similar to his own. "As you can imagine, I have many pressing affairs. Good day, gentlemen."

His mother started to rise too, but couldn't support her weight. Michael took her arm to assist. The officers stood instantly. He pulled the bell pull on the way out, and didn't stop walking until he had his mother upstairs in her own parlor.

"You are not well, madam," he said, pushing aside thoughts of possible actions to focus on for the sake of the problem in front of him.

"How could I be with all this worry oversetting me?" she said irritably, sinking into a flower-patterned armchair next to an open box of chocolates.

He watched as she reached for a chocolate. After she had chewed and swallowed, she rested her head back. Her shoulders lowered.

"Ah, that is better." She put her hand to her stomach.

"Do you have pains, Mother?"

"Sometimes."

"I'll send for the doctor."

"No one locally is any good," she said irritably.

"Then we'll return to London."

"I do not want to travel."

He leaned over the chair. "Mother."

She fixed him with a glare. "Let me rest. I am always better after a rest."

"Very well." As his mother's maid entered the room, he said, "Her ladyship is not feeling well."

"Shall I ring *pour une tasse de thé*, my lady?" the woman asked in her exaggerated French accent.

"Idiot," his mother muttered, but nodded.

"Also, you can put away her ladyship's mourning clothes," he said, wanting the reminders of this terrible time gone. "Captain Shield is alive."

"*Mon dieu,*" squeaked the maid, clasping her hands together. "*Vraiment?*"

"*Oui,*" his mother said in an arch tone.

He bowed to his mother and left the room. As long as she continued to be rude, he couldn't worry too much about her.

When Lady Lillian called, Alys and Matilda were helping Edith put the rest of Rose's winter wardrobe into trunks. Their shared maid, Lucy, had stayed at the Farm, and Alys's maid, Hortense, had already come down with a cold and headache. Matilda was afraid Edith would pack up some of her clothes by accident if she didn't supervise.

"Put her ladyship in the afternoon parlor," Alys told the maid. "We'll be down in a moment."

"Those are the final two gowns, I believe," Matilda told Edith. "You don't think Rose will need her pink silk in the country, do you? I'd love to wear it to the musicale at the Canders' next week."

"No pink," Alys said. "You know you look frightful in it."

Matilda put the gown to her cheek. "Are you quite sure? I think it is delightful."

"It is not," Alys said firmly. "You sent a note to Lady Lillian, so let us not keep her waiting."

When they walked into the parlor, Lady Lillian's dark sausage curls were vibrating as she paced in front of the fireplace. Alys had never seen her so animated.

When the younger woman saw her, she smiled and hop-stepped toward her, reaching for her hands.

"Lady Hatbrook, I wish you happy!" she said, giving Alys a kiss.

Alys had always been a wallflower at best when her sisters' friend had visited in the past, but now, it seemed, her triumph had brought her out from behind the metaphorical potted plants. "Thank you, Lady Lillian."

"Will you and Lord Hatbrook be out and about in town for the Season?" she asked.

"We're in mourning for his brother," Alys said, gesturing at herself.

A frown creased Lady Lillian's pretty, plump face. "But I had a letter from my cousin, Magdalene Cross, this morning, saying he was alive all along."

Matilda gasped.

Alys put a hand to her chest as her heart thumped wildly. "What?"

Lady Lillian fluttered her eyelashes. "Some mistake in India. One of those native clerks, no doubt. Why, Lady Hatbrook, you are still in mourning. How is it that I heard this news before you?"

"The Cross family was intimately involved, since one of their sons was reported dead along with the captain," Alys said. "I left my husband at the Farm."

"Surely he sent you a note," Lady Lillian cooed.

"It would not reach me as quickly as one from Miss Cross, here in London," Alys said, though she was not sure Michael would bother notifying her. Would he consider his brother his own business, or a family concern she might need to be aware of? She honestly did not know.

Lady Lillian toyed with a fat curl. "Of course, silly me. I am so grateful to be the bearer of such news then. Why, you can throw off your crow black and dress fashionably again!"

"I'm so pleased," Alys said in a monotone.

Matilda cleared her throat. Alys knew she wanted some attention. She gestured to the seating arrangement closest to the fire as a maid brought in a tea service.

"Your note said it was urgent," Lady Lillian said to Matilda. "I assumed you wanted assistance consulting on your sister's new wardrobe." She turned. "Of course you haven't been able to dress to your new position in life, what with the mourning."

"I wanted advice on Mr. Bliven," Matilda said with a pout. "Oh, Lily, I know I could have him, if I could just cipher how to make it clear I am prepared to accept."

Alys wanted to throw up her hands in an echo of her sister's dramatic behavior. "You wouldn't be so forward."

"I know I must be subtle, but we are allied to the marquess now." Matilda grinned.

"With that and your dowry, your capital on the marriage market has gone up considerably," Lady Lillian said. "Wouldn't you rather set your cap on a title?"

"Mr. Bliven expects to inherit a title someday," Matilda said. "None of the men between him are likely to have a family. At the very least his son is likely to be an earl someday."

Lady Lillian tapped her chin. "I see. But there is Viscount Hortley. He has a title now and he did seem very interested in you at the Mewses' party."

"Besides, I believe Mr. Bliven is no longer assured of the title," Alys interjected. "Father said his cousin is engaged."

"I have not heard that," Lady Lillian said thoughtfully. "Well, that ought to make him an easier catch."

"The viscount is balding," said Matilda. "Whereas Mr. Bliven is too handsome for words."

"And too charming," muttered Alys.

"You do not like our Mr. Bliven?" Lady Lillian asked.

"I find his tongue to be overly sharp," Alys admitted. "And I think he takes liberties with my sister."

Matilda did not look at her, but faced Lady Lillian resolutely. Alys wished she had been a better role model. Her own adventures with Michael could have ended so badly. While she could offer counsel, it could not be specific to a properly conducted courtship.

"But your husband is his close friend," Lady Lillian said. "Certainly he cannot be too bad."

If Mr. Bliven knew from Michael what had happened, he might indeed think he could take the same liberties.

"I would counsel caution," she said. "Mr. Bliven is clearly enamored of you. You have no need to rush a declaration."

Matilda's right eye half closed. Alys felt a frisson of alarm. Matilda was always hiding something when she did that with her eye.

"You haven't been compromised?" she whispered.

Matilda flushed up to her carroty hair. "No."

"You did seem quite familiar at the Farm."

Lady Lillian leaned closer.

"You need not worry, Alys," Matilda said. "I have not been foolish."

"A little foolishness can sometimes help," Lady Lillian advised. "With an honorable man it can be just the thing."

Alys felt her fingers digging into the fragile fabric of her mourning gown. "I do not think that is sensible advice. I am ready to pour. Would you care for tea, Lady Lillian?"

The door opened and a maid said, "Mr. Lewis Noble is calling for you, my lady."

Alys handed a cup to Lady Lillian, who was staring at her. She realized the maid meant her. She shook her head. "Thank you. Could you direct him to the library? I will join him shortly."

"Oh my goodness. You haven't seen him since the wedding," Matilda said.

"Or spoken to him since Father refused his suit to marry me," Alys added. "Heavens, that was months ago."

"He must have heard that you'd returned. At least he and Father are speaking again."

"I'm glad to hear that. Well, I had better go see him." Alys poured quickly for her sister then rose, wishing she had time to change, but she couldn't keep her cousin waiting. How exciting that her brother-by-marriage was alive after all. The entire Shield family would be so relieved, and Michael would not be so busy.

She ventured down the hall slowly, wondering about Lewis's mood. He had thought she refused him because she never planned to marry. It had been true at the time. She couldn't possibly reveal the reason behind her sudden change of heart. Where Michael was involved all of her reason disappeared as quickly as a soufflé could collapse.

With a sigh, she pushed open the door to the library and found Lewis perusing a book on natural history.

"Not your subject," she said, moving toward him. She wished to give him her hand, but he held the book open on his palms.

"Did you know ants carry many times their weight? If I could replicate that strength using machinery, I could save a great deal of heavy lifting."

He glanced up as she nodded, and shut the book. "But that is not important. I cannot believe that I have not seen you since last year. How are you, Alys?"

She smiled tentatively. "Well enough. How are you?"

His mouth pulled to the side. "I suppose I should call you Lady Hatbrook now."

"Don't be ridiculous. We are too close for that." She took the book from him and placed it on a shelf.

"Are we?" he asked. "I didn't come here to accuse you of anything, or to fight with you, but I wonder now if I ever understood you at all."

"I had similar thoughts when I heard you were here," Alys admitted. "How did my life change so drastically? It was very sudden."

"You couldn't refuse the title," Lewis said. "Your father would have had an apoplexy."

Little did he know that she almost had. "He had nothing to do with it. The decision was made without him, as he has made decisions without me."

"He sold Redcake's."

"Yes." That was one thing about Lewis. He could never have kept a secret from her.

"I considered removing my machinery from the bakery," Lewis said, "but it probably would have taken some kind of legal action, and besides, my best innovations are in the factories."

"You didn't lose any secrets, then?"

He shrugged. "It's all in the family anyway, right? Your husband bought the place."

"He did, but I only found out by accident. I am completely shut out of that sort of decision making."

Lewis smirked. "He is a traditionalist then, the marquess?"

"More so than you."

"You should have run off with me, Alys. I know I don't have anything, but I could. All I'd have to do is ally myself with one of your father's rivals and I'd have two thousand a year. I've had offers, but stayed loyal to the family."

"We weren't loyal in return."

"Your father was not," he said. "I am done with him. I am formulating my work for a different industry now, so at least I will not enrich his business rivals. I do not wish to hurt your sisters."

"And Gawain?"

"He will be fine. He has plans of his own."

"I hope you and my father make amends."

"He is a stubborn old man." Lewis shoved his hands into his trouser pockets and began to pace.

"He counseled me to patience very recently. You must have patience with him."

"He is the one getting old, not us."

"We will have our turn, Lewis."

He turned away. "Are you happy?"

"I am sorry that you cannot look at me when you ask."

"I do not like to see you dressed like a crow for a man you never met."

"I just heard that my mourning is premature," she said lightly. "The captain has been found alive."

Lewis sniffed. "Then you should change your gown."

She didn't like his tone. "I plan to, as soon as I leave you. I have plenty of clothing here still."

"Where is your husband?"

"In Sussex."

"If we were married I'd never want to be apart from you."

"I left," Alys admitted. "But I won't attempt to rewrite the past, or what might have been. What is done is done. We need to go our separate ways."

"Will I ever see you again?" He waved his arms.

"Don't be melodramatic. We are family."

"As you say."

She took his hands in hers, finding him to be chilled despite the fire. "I wish you happiness, Lewis. And success. You are most deserving of it. I know your capabilities. And if you ever want to set your sights lower, you could do an amazing line in curiosity shops."

"You like my birds?"

"I adore them. You could sell thousands."

He squeezed her hands, then pulled away. "I shall keep that in mind for the future."

"I must leave you now. I'm afraid Matilda is going to be up to some mischief on Lady Lillian's advice."

He nodded, and she realized he would have no idea of Mr. Bliven's courtship, since he'd been exiled from the family.

"Do you have enough money for now? Until you've signed contracts?"

"I'm fine, Alys. I don't need your husband's money."

She was embarrassed to have asked, especially since he looked beautifully tended and healthy, despite the machine oil permanently marking his clever fingers. Quickly, she kissed his cheek and left the room.

Feeling unsettled, she decided to have Hortense help her change before she rejoined her sister. None of her old clothes were as confining as this mourning, not even her court presentation gown. She couldn't wait to put black away, hopefully for a very long time.

The next day Matilda claimed a headache and stayed home from church. After services, Lady Redcake remained behind as planned for a charitable sewing circle, but everyone knew of Alys's limited sewing skills so she was not encouraged to join. Sir Bartley went to his club as always.

She arrived home, dressed conservatively in gray sateen, resolved to spend the afternoon looking over fashion plates with Hortense so she could order new gowns more suitable for a marchioness. Her mother had sent a note to the dress designer they had used for court gowns the previous year and she would arrive tomorrow to consult with Alys. After that, she knew she needed to return to the Farm.

Her place was with Michael. Angry as she was with his strict line between the home and his business affairs, she'd had trouble sleeping since returning to London. And, difficult as it was to admit, she missed his caresses. She missed seeing him regularly. Her life here had lost any sparkle it once had.

A servant removed her mantle when she arrived and she ordered a tea tray to be brought to her shared dressing room. A few minutes later she was just outside the door, longing for her buttonhook so she could remove her damp shoes. At least the arms of this dress were loose enough that she could manage her own footwear.

As she opened the door, she heard what sounded like a gasp. Had Hortense dropped something? She pushed the door open farther, but the curtains were closed. The only light came from the banked fire. Frowning, she walked slowly into the room, careful to avoid furnishings, and threw open the curtains.

There. That was a definite gasp this time. She turned to find not her maid, but her sister, holding a lap robe to her naked chest, and Theodore Bliven, standing over her, quite naked from the waist down.

So naked, that she could see the state of his manly parts. The turgid state of his oversized manly part. She clenched her fists so tightly that her glove-covered nails dug into her palms. With such rigid self-control that she reminded herself of her husband, she addressed her sister.

"Do I need to call for the constable?"

Mutely, Matilda shook her head.

"What do you have to say for yourself, Mr. Bliven?" Now, she smelled the tang of lovemaking in the air. "How long has this been going on, and under my father's roof, no less? I knew something seemed off when you came to the Farm."

"This is the first time," Matilda said, pleading in her voice.

Alys turned back, noting how pale her sister looked. "Why?"

"We're going to be married," she said.

Alys moved her gaze to Mr. Bliven.

"I n-never said that." He tugged down his shirttails with a smile, as if he'd waited for her to look at him first.

A gasp came from Matilda. Her lover's expression hardened.

"How dare you," Alys gasped.

"She offered herself freely," he said coolly. "How was I to know she'd claim to be a virgin after?"

"Claim?" Matilda's voice squeaked. "You know very well I told the truth."

"If you don't mind, ladies, I shall go behind that screen there and right myself."

Alys watched, open-mouthed, as he casually scooped up his clothing, clustered around an armchair, and walked over to the screen, his pale buttocks flashing with every step.

Matilda made a choking sob, then began to cry in earnest, making no attempt to push down her petticoat.

"Go to my bedroom, Matilda. I'll speak to you later."

Hortense ran into the room. "My lady! We were told not to disturb the room, but then Jerry said you were home and coming up here."

"The servants knew what was transpiring?"

"Someone must have," Hortense said darkly. "And those deeds which are committed behind closed doors in the middle of the day rarely come to anything good."

"Take my sister to my room and help her to dress."

Hortense curtsied and wrapped Matilda into the blanket, then took her arm, pulling her from the room.

When Mr. Bliven emerged, Alys reached deep into herself for a cool tone. "What do you have to say for yourself?"

"Only that I am on a boat to Bombay next week, on your brother's orders." He pulled out his watch and checked it.

"My brother's orders?" What had Gawain to do with this?

"I have gone into partnership with him."

"Perhaps my brother does not care about his sister's honor, but my husband will."

"Your husband, my lady, is my oldest friend. He is aware there is a lady in Bombay, whose family has had an understanding with mine for years."

"Then why did your father offer you to my father?"

"That was before the lady suffered a recent bereavement." He smiled. "Her husband, while not approved of by her relations at the time of her elopement, left her most comfortable."

"You are a scoundrel, sir."

He sneered. "Do not claim to be more than you are."

"What do you mean?"

"That you are no better than your sister. I did wonder why Hatbrook married you so precipitously, and now I have the answer. The Redcake sisters are seductresses and adventuresses."

Her eyes narrowed. He was so unutterably vile. If Michael had shared any intimate details she would be utterly shocked. "How dare you. You seduced her."

"Quite the opposite, I assure you. She must have thought I'd fold as easily as the marquess did for you. But I have other plans." He bowed. "I shall take my leave."

Alys stood mutely in the room for a moment, until she found her lungs needed air. Then she ran down the corridor and took the stairs to the entrance hall as quickly as her skirts allowed. "Pounds!" she cried.

"Yes, my lady?" said the butler, appearing at the base of the stairs.

"Mr. Bliven is no longer welcome in this house."

"Yes, my lady." His expression remained serene.

"Where is my brother?"

"He went to Bristol last week, my lady. I'm not sure when he is expected back. I shall ascertain this information for you." He nodded briskly.

"Thank you." Feeling so weary then, Alys climbed slowly back up the stairs, to see Jerry holding a heavily laden tea tray. She opened her door a crack and saw it was empty, so she gestured to her desk and had him set it there.

Shaking, she poured herself a cup of tea. Her sister had been ravished, and Theodore Bliven had had a very good notion that she and Michael had relations before marriage. Matilda had offered herself to that horrible man, a man who would not think twice before ruining their good names, and Rose with them. And Gawain had probably given him money.

Her maid came into the room, her arm around Matilda. "It was not rape," she said.

Alys looked up from her tea. "Were you raped, Hortense?"

Her watery blue eyes met Alys's gaze. "Yes, my lady."

"I am sorry for that."

"I am grateful you took me on despite my past."

"As you no doubt have heard today, my past is no more unstained than yours. Or now, Matilda's. Let us hope she does not suffer the consequences you did."

"I love my daughter," Hortense said, her eyes fierce.

"I am glad. It is not her fault."

"No, my lady. I do all I can for her."

Alys wondered what happened to the children without resourceful mothers like Hortense. At least foolish Matilda had family to aid her.

Chapter Eighteen

"How could you have thought seducing Mr. Bliven was a smart thing to do?" Alys asked Matilda, as she set her cup back on the tray.

"Rose told me that was how you ensnared the marquess," her sister said. She was swathed in a pink dressing gown, which clashed alarmingly with her hair. Her color was high and her wet hair dripped onto the fabric of the gown, staining it darkly. "She saw you in the bathroom with him."

"I wasn't raised to be a lady, unlike you." How had Rose known? Hadn't Michael properly locked the door behind him?

"I thought I had an understanding with Mr. Bliven. He was courting me most assiduously." Matilda pulled at the cuffs of her gown, as if she wished to hide her hands.

Her maid shut the door. Alys said, "I never thought the marquess wanted to wed me. That isn't the reason for what happened between us."

"That's even worse! You made yourself his mistress?"

"I made a mistake, one that was not repeated," Alys said. "And I was not a virgin."

"You had done this before?" Matilda's freckles sharpened as she scrunched her face.

"I was forced, more than a decade before, when our circumstances were quite different," Alys said, fighting to keep her voice even. "I do not care to think of it, and unlike Hortense, there was no permanent evidence of the misdeed."

"I thought we'd be married by special license," Matilda whispered. "Lady Lillian thought it was the best way to keep Theo from leaving for India."

"You are never to see Lady Lillian again." The effort it took to keep her voice calm made her jaw sore.

"You didn't come back after Lewis arrived," Matilda whined.

"We were in the same house all night. You made this plan, sent a note to Mr. Bliven. You were a little fool and what if there are consequences? Not just a child, but Mr. Bliven has a vicious tongue. He may share your adventure with him all over London!"

"He wouldn't dare," she said in a kitten's voice.

"Why not? He clearly has no respect for either of us."

"Won't the marquess intervene?"

"How? He is not here."

"Father? Will he not force Mr. Bliven to marry me?" Matilda's plump lower lip trembled.

"Why would you want him to marry you?" Hortense asked, with an air of disgust. "He's a devil, that one. Black-hearted and nasty."

"I did not ask your opinion," Matilda snarled. She flopped onto Alys's bed, her foot hitting the pedestal Lewis's mechanical bird rested on. The pedestal rocked and the bird crashed to the floor. Alys ran to it and found one of the delicate wings had been corrugated into a lump of metal. She picked it up, cradling it in her arms.

"I am as broken as that bird," Matilda cried.

"Do hush up," Alys said. "You brought this on yourself."

Her sister sniffed. "At least I do not think he finished. I might escape without consequences."

Alys turned away and gently placed the bird back on the pedestal Hortense had just righted. In a testament to Lewis's skill, it still balanced, despite the damaged wing. "How is it that you know anything about relations? Lady Lillian?"

Matilda didn't answer.

"You are not to leave this house today," Alys said. "I do not know what to tell our parents."

Matilda swung into an upright position on her knees in the center of the bed. "Nothing! At least, unless you think Father can force the situation somehow."

"You want him to know what you did?"

Matilda shrank back. "I made a mistake?"

"You do not sound very sure of yourself. I suggest you retire until you decide exactly how you feel about your actions."

"I'm hungry," Matilda said.

Alys couldn't tolerate the childish tone of her voice. How could her sister be twenty-one years old? She might have understood this behavior from someone fresh from the schoolroom. But her sister was too old to be this naively calculating.

And she had chosen the wrong man.

"Why didn't you think Mr. Bliven would not propose?" Alys asked. "Why couldn't you have been patient?"

"He said he had needs that he didn't want to satisfy elsewhere, but I made him unable to think of anything else," Matilda said in her little girl voice.

"You were afraid you'd lose him to someone else?"

"Magdalene Cross," Matilda said. "Have you seen her bosom? She goes about practically naked from the waist up at every gathering. Theo could scarcely take his eyes off her."

"But you have a dowry," Alys said. "Did you think of that? Mr. Bliven, by all accounts, could have used that. It's of more value than a deep bosom."

Matilda didn't respond. "I think I shall retire now. I do not feel very well."

Alys shared a glance with her maid. "I am not surprised. Hortense, would you have a tray sent to Matilda's room, please?"

Hortense went to the bell pull as Matilda climbed off Alys's bed.

Michael opened the afternoon post as he sat at his desk in the study. He had insisted his mother see the doctor after she'd felt so ill she'd had to leave church during the vicar's sermon the day before. The vicar had called late yesterday to make sure he hadn't done anything to offend. When the doctor came out of his mother's sitting room he'd told Michael he was very concerned about her.

But, as his mother had said, the local medical man was not much use for anything beyond childhood injuries, and he had suggested they see their personal doctor in London. So, he'd asked Beth to supervise the packing, insisting that she return as well, rather than staying with Rose Redcake as she'd requested.

Beth didn't want to admit anything was wrong.

He set down a terse note from Alys, suggesting that she planned to return to the Farm by midweek. Michael realized he didn't know her well enough to understand if that was an apology or not. But, he had a feeling they would be spending some time in London after all. At least winter was almost over.

Next, he opened a letter from Theo. He scanned the contents, not being in the mood for casual gossip. However, the contents were useful. He hadn't realized Alys was at her father's home, rather than at Hatbrook House. The letter kept him from looking a fool when he arrived with expectations that his wife was in residence.

He read on. Theo in partnership with Gawain Redcake? What had possessed his friend to actually take on work? He was leaving for India? Ahead of creditors, no doubt, and with a healthy chunk of Redcake funding in his pocket. Frowning, he dashed off notes to his butler, his physician, and his wife, then called for his valet and a footman. He had a great deal to do in order to travel the next morning.

While he was worried about his mother, eagerness put speed into every move. He could not wait to mend the situation between him and his wife. They needed to find a level of accord which left her unable to feel storming off and leaving was reasonable.

He wanted Alys beside him, no matter what the future brought. Even if she wanted to spend hours poring over papers on his desk.

"Surgery?" Michael repeated to the physician, disbelieving his ears.

"It would be best. This procedure came into practice four or five years ago. I do not like the look of Lady Hatbrook's skin. If the gallbladder is not removed soon, her liver could be compromised due to blockages."

"How did she respond?"

"She said she would consider it. As her son, my lord, you need to counsel her that it is for the best."

Michael nodded. "Thank you, Doctor." First, he would let her rest from the ordeal of the examination.

A footman opened the door, handing the physician his greatcoat.

"Bring me my coat as well, and have the carriage brought around," Michael directed. He needed a walk in fresh air, or at least as fresh as it came in London. This was the first day of March, and with any luck the townsfolk would begin to burn less coal as the weather warmed, making the air more wholesome.

But, first, he had business at Redcake's, and later, he promised himself to dinner with the Cross family, to discuss the situation in India. He also sent a note to Gawain Redcake.

Most importantly, of course, he needed to see his wife. He had sent her a note to inform her that he would be in London with his mother. However, the train had been delayed coming into town and he had neglected the morning's post so he had no idea if she responded. Certainly, she hadn't arrived at his door, ready to take up residence.

He knocked on the roof of the carriage with his umbrella a couple of blocks from Redcake's, deciding he could take the time to walk the rest, and exited into a light drizzle that was, at least, preferable to yellow fog.

He pulled his top hat a little lower, to shield his eyes, but decided not to unfurl his umbrella. There were already so many open on this main shopping thoroughfare.

He was a few yards from Redcake's when he spotted Alys. The only other woman he'd ever met with that insistent shade of orange hair was her sister, Matilda, and she wasn't as tall or curvaceous.

As he slowed to watch, his wife, dressed in a shabby black mantle and dowdy gray dress, turned to her companion and gestured. Her male companion.

Alys turned sideways to let a portly businessman go by. Michael could not doubt his eyes, but the man was still facing ahead of him.

As Michael blinked away raindrops, a memory flashed through his mind. While out on a walk with his governess, he'd seen his mother gesturing to an unfamiliar gentleman, just like this. Only, she'd thrown up her hands and, wait, kissed him?

Michael squinted. Had he really just remembered his mother kissing someone, not his father? He must have been very young as his governess had been replaced by a tutor when he was five. Judah had stayed with the governess, being some three years younger.

He tried to place the memory. Not London, but Eastbourne, perhaps? He put his gloved hand to the back of his neck, feeling his fingers begin to tremble.

Alys put her hand through her companion's arm and they began to walk again, passing Redcake's without a glance.

Feeling sick and shaken, Michael went into the tearoom as soon as they were out of sight, and, without thinking twice, ordered a plate of scones and jam from a cakie who didn't recognize him.

Instead of settling him though, the treat made him feel even worse. He clasped his hands together. Even if he had just remembered some summer-soaked evidence of his mother's infidelity, surely that didn't mean Alys was up to the same game.

His parents' marriage in 1857 had been all but arranged. His mother was of good birth and good dowry, his father of better birth and dwindling funds. Already he had been a gambler. He knew his parents had lived separate lives, but had they gone their own way so soon? Where was Judah in that memory? Not walking on the other side of the governess, not trailing behind in a pram pushed by a nursemaid. How old was this recollection?

He flagged the cakie again. "Have a meat pie brought up to the manager's office as soon as possible."

"Sir?" the girl said, looking confused.

"I own this establishment. I'm the Marquess of Hatbrook."

"My goodness. I'm so sorry, my lord."

He waved away her shock. "There is no cause for concern. I am going upstairs now."

"Yes, my lord."

He hoped the meat would make him feel better. Perhaps he would scrape away the deliciously flaky pastry outside and focus on the beef and vegetables. He knew Alys would suggest such a thing.

When he reached the desk, he put his head in his hands. Had he married a wanton? Why had he thought she only responded to his caresses?

A knock came on the door and he straightened, his head throbbing. It seemed, ever since the false report of Judah's death, that his

228 • *Heather Hiestand*

life had come crashing down upon him. His mother's health, his new marriage, his concerns about what was really happening in India along with a forced connection with the unsuitable Cross family, a new business he had no time to run, and even his friend's defection to India, had all created an unholy mess.

The door opened. It wasn't his meat pie, but Ewan Hales, the secretary Sir Bartley had bequeathed him along with the business. Michael found the man quite competent, though too young to run the entire enterprise without guidance.

"Mr. Hellman and Mr. Popham are waiting with their reports, my lord," the secretary said. "I have a report as well."

"Send in the cakie first, and give me a few moments. I need to collect my thoughts."

"Very good, my lord. I shall attempt to find the cakie in question."

"I don't need the cakie, just my food," he said irritably. "And give me your report while you are at it. I shall peruse it while I am dining."

Hales bowed slightly and backed out of the room, as if Michael was ruler of the company instead of just its owner. Thankfully, Hales delivered his food and the first report within minutes.

Three hours later, Michael was clear of Redcake's, but mindful that the place desperately needed a manager. Alys needed to be replaced too, since Betsy Popham was completely overwhelmed with orders. They were turning away business, which could be very bad. A couple of the cakies had announced engagements and new girls needed to be hired and trained. Apparently one of the ovens wasn't working, and Lewis Noble had refused to fix it, though it was his own design, and the oven expert brought in to replace him had thrown up his hands in confusion.

Michael had a long list of tasks to complete, but at the top of the list was finding someone competent to manage. He resolved to write a note to Mumford and Egglesworth, asking more urgently for suitable candidates, as soon as he could find the time. He missed Sir John's robust competence.

Now though, he had a couple of hours in which to confront Alys before he had to be at home to dress for the Cross dinner. His carriage pulled up in front of Sir Bartley's mansion and Michael alighted, grateful that the meat pie had done its duty and calmed his nerves and hands.

When he rang the bell, the butler answered.

"What a pleasure to see you, my lord," said the man.

Michael handed him his hat, gloves, and greatcoat. "Is my wife here? I have not had time to check the post and came here in between business matters."

"Yes, my lord, I believe the marchioness is with her sister. Would you like to go into the drawing room while I ascertain her whereabouts?"

"Thank you, Pounds." Michael allowed himself to be directed into the drawing room, which, thankfully, was not decorated in an abundance of rose, but wallpapered tastefully in a blue, white, and yellow floral motif, echoed in its soothing furniture and discreet tapestries. He'd be pleased to have Alys redecorate the Farm accordingly, now that her dowry made the funds available for niceties.

He placed himself in an armchair and stared into the fire. Half in a doze within moments, he shot to his feet when the door opened, not quite sure where he was.

"I received your note," Alys said, walking into the room, still in her dowdy gown.

He drank in the sight of her, then hardened his heart with the memory of that morning. "I see you have left off mourning. I am glad of that."

She smiled. "I'm so happy that your brother is safe."

"As safe as one can be in India, I suppose. I'm to dine with the Cross family tonight."

"Perhaps they know more. I heard about your brother from a connection of theirs initially."

"I am sorry you didn't hear it from me first," he said stiffly.

"News travels fast in London," she said. "How is your mother? I am sorry to hear she is so unwell."

His thoughts flashed for a moment on a sight of her, young and laughing, her hand on a strange man's chest. "She requires surgery. I am to persuade her."

"I'm sure she will have the best medical assistance."

"Of course." He cleared his throat. "Will you be seated?"

"Thank you." Alys worried at her lower lip as she sat on a settee. Michael seated himself at the opposite end.

"I was going to return to the Farm," Alys said. "But I am so angry with what happened on Sunday that I have not had the heart to organize my things."

"Sunday?" he asked, uncertain of what she referred to.

"The business with Theodore Bliven."

He rubbed the back of his neck. "I am sorry if there was some unpleasantness, but really, Alys, I have more important things to discuss."

"How can you say that?"

"I can say that because I saw you, not three hours ago, arm in arm with some man on Oxford Street. And frankly, you should not be appearing in public in such shabby clothing. It is a poor reflection on our position in society."

Alys stared at him, the corners of her lips faintly tilted, as if she found his speech amusing.

"Really," he said, all the words he wanted to say quite failing him. "But I must say, your hair is lovely today. I like the curls."

"Hortense has a special technique," Alys said. "I did meet with a dressmaker just this morning, Michael. I know my wardrobe is frightful, but Mother ordered the mourning clothes, which were very appropriate, and I haven't had time to plan."

He waved his hand. "I do understand. I'm sorry." But as he rubbed his chin, he remembered that man.

"I was simply out walking with Gawain, you know. I can't imagine anyone would assume he was an inappropriate companion. I realize we do not look very alike, since he takes after Mother and I take after Father, but the limp and the eye patch make him quite memorable, I'm afraid. No one could possibly mistake him for anyone else."

"I only saw him from the back," Michael muttered, feeling a fool. That forgotten scene from his past must have predisposed him to suspicion.

"I had to take him out to yell at him. Matilda has been in bed with a sick headache since Sunday evening. She simply cannot cope with the consequences."

"Of Theo going to India?"

"Of the seduction, of course," Alys said sharply. "You do know what transpired?"

Michael felt his left hand tremor. "I believe I do not."

When he saw the look she gave him, he wished he had the power to read minds. She entwined her fingers in her lap. The tips of her fingers reddened from the pressure. "I do not wish to put the events into words."

He reached over and quickly patted her hands, then folded his arms across his chest. "I am afraid you must if you wish me to understand."

She shut her eyes. "Rose discovered our secret, Michael. She gave Matilda her own interpretation of why you married me. Apparently she thought it was the seduction that was key, not your brother's death."

He lifted a brow. He'd welcomed a nasty, gossiping traitor into his home. How despicable to gossip about your own sister. "I had no idea."

"Yes, well, Matilda decided that since Mr. Bliven was your friend, he would be willing to marry her if she provided the same, er, service to him."

"I see." While his face stayed calm, he felt red-hot rage sweep his thoughts.

"But she is not me. Our family fortune changed so greatly between our respective youths. She was not prepared for the consequences."

No matter what Alys thought, she would not have been either. How could he have served the woman he loved so ill? "And he left?"

"Yes, feeling no responsibility whatsoever. He claimed he was previously engaged to a woman who lives in India." Her eyes filled with tears. "Oh, Michael, it was terrible. I don't know how to help her."

He rose and reseated himself next to her, then put his arm around her and pulled her close. "I am so very sorry, my dear. Do you want me to try and catch him before he gets too far afield? He didn't send me his itinerary but Gawain must know it. I am afraid I cannot recall the lady in question's name."

She sniffed. "Gawain doesn't. Mr. Bliven has vanished. He must plan to send word once he's reached India."

He reached for his handkerchief and wiped her eyes with it, wishing he could take some immediate action.

She leaned her head into his shoulder, muffling her voice.

He spoke. "I think Matilda should go to the Farm. We can put it about that Rose requires her. If there are no consequences, then she can return for the Season if she feels herself capable." He didn't want either sister on his property, but for now it was best.

"Lady Lillian Cander suggested her actions to her," Alys said. "Who knows what she will gossip about?"

"I will call on her father," Michael said. "I cannot leave London now, because of my mother, so I might as well make use of the time."

"I will stay here with you," she said.

"Do we need to file a breach of promise suit?"

"I am afraid the commitment was all in Matilda's head. She thought to force a declaration, rather than acting in conjunction with one. I am simply appalled, and I feel terrible that this could soil your reputation as well."

"I did not introduce Mr. Bliven to your sister. Your father did that," he said.

"But he is your friend." She took his handkerchief and dabbed at her eyes.

"That does not mean I would consider him a responsible suitor. Nor would anyone who knows him, I am afraid."

"I knew his behavior was incorrect when we saw them at the Farm," Alys confessed. "But my mother is not used to high society, even less so than I am. She must have thought they were secretly engaged or some such. I was too focused on my own concerns to do anything."

"You could not know what your sister was planning. You haven't lived in the same house for much of the courtship."

"And Gawain! Supporting that man. I am afraid I have a very unsuitable family."

"Theo probably told him only what he wanted to convey, just as he did in the letter to me. Anything to get enough money to flee your sister's demand." That memory of his mother's hand flashed through his mind. "Every family is about the same, I believe. For every Victoria and Albert there must fall a Prince of Wales."

"Then your brother must be a scoundrel, since you are not."

"Only where you are concerned." He found her mouth with his own, then licked the seam of her lips with his tongue until she opened to him with a little moan. He plundered, pulling her close until she was half across him, before he came back to his senses.

She panted as he set her back in her place. "I missed you."

"I like to think I am the scoundrel, but I never should have let you leave."

"We do have a certain effect on each other."

"Then we are lucky to be husband and wife."

She smiled tentatively. He reached into her hair to toy with one of the springy curls.

"You shall have to pay your maid well, so that she does not leave you."

"She has an illegitimate child," Alys whispered. "I hope you aren't disappointed with me for choosing her."

"What happened to the father of the child?"

"He forced her," Alys said simply.

He felt a surge of love. "And you wanted her because she so easily could have been you?"

Alys nodded. "And now my sister."

"I still think we could file for breach of promise. Matilda is connected to my family. Theo could be shamed into marrying her, or he won't be received anywhere in England, and that is not good for his family, despite what he claims about the other woman."

"Maybe he truly loves her. I didn't have the impression that he cared about Matilda."

"Perhaps not. Certainly he is attempting to start over far away. But India is full of younger sons, and even better, their wives. Ultimately, we can kill his prospects in India almost as easily as we could in London."

"Has he done this before?"

"Perhaps you should ask Lady Lillian that. I vaguely remember some scandal at school with an innkeeper's daughter, but we were so young then. I have never made it a practice to involve myself in the love affairs of others."

"I can't imagine an innkeeper's daughter would have thought a student at Eton would marry her."

"One would think not."

Alys sighed. "Should I begin packing, then, and move to Hatbrook House?"

The clock on the mantel signaled the hour. He patted her hand. "I do apologize, but I am late."

"To go to the Crosses'?"

"Exactly. Do your parents know what has happened to your sister?"

"My mother does."

"I'll schedule an appointment with your father then, and tell him that Matilda is welcome to go to the Farm. I can't imagine he will disagree."

"Rose will not be pleased if it hurts her chances in local society."

"We can shut Matilda away and claim she is ill, if necessary. No one near us could be surprised, given Rose's history." He rose. "I am sorry to leave you, my dear. May I claim another audience tomorrow? I must persuade my mother of the surgery, which is of some urgency, according to the physician."

"Then I should go south with Matilda, and you will come home as soon as you can? Should I hire a nurse for your mother?"

"We shall decide all after I meet with your father. I imagine my mother will convalesce here at the start. And I do not want you to be run ragged by her. She does not improve, I'm afraid."

"She is my family now too, Michael. I know my duty."

He caressed her curls again. "How I wish I could be your seducer, my lady."

She leaned her cheek into his hand. "I know."

"I realize we were not in accord when we saw each other last."

"I must learn patience," she said.

He appreciated the thought. "As must I. I have not been a good husband, but I will improve. I am not used to help, you see." He caught her lips in his, letting his hands slide from her curls to her slender back to her curvaceous hips.

"I wish we could start over," she whispered.

"Life insists on forward movement." He cupped her cheek. "But if we are in charity with one another all will be well."

Chapter Nineteen

"Have you nothing better to do than stare at me?" his mother asked, grimacing for a moment before she returned her gaze to the fire in her sitting room.

Michael pulled her rose afghan over her leg, brushing it with his fingers in the process. How long had it been since he'd touched her?

"Mother, I have a most indelicate question."

"Trouble in the marriage bed, Hatbrook?"

He lifted his gaze to her face instantly. But she wasn't sneering. Her tone did not contain its usual venom, not that she sounded prepared to be helpful, either.

"As you may recall, my bride is not in residence."

"Where is your cake bride? Dashed if I can understand why you would marry a girl who bakes and then stop eating cake."

The older his mother grew, the more her speech sounded more like a young man's than a mature lady's. He wondered if she, like Alys, strained at the bonds of feminine behavior. He remembered now, that he had compared Alys to his mother on the day he met her. Strange that he'd forgotten that.

"She is with her family. Her sister suffered a shock."

"How disagreeable."

Now his mother sounded like a petulant widow again.

"What was this indelicate question?" she queried as she reached for a chocolate and popped it into her mouth, chewing with it slightly open.

Michael closed his eyes. "I have a memory of you kissing another man when I was quite young. It was summer and Judah must have been a babe."

"Judah was not born at all," his mother remarked, licking her fingers. "That would have been Judah's father you saw, though I am amazed you have a memory of something that transpired when you were two."

Judah's father? "What are you saying?"

"I am saying that your father transgressed one too many times, and with a dear friend of mine, no less, and I retaliated. I did not expect this to result in a child, but thankfully the timing was such Judah might just have been his, so there was no trouble in society's eyes." Her eyes closed, and the skin around her eyes tightened as if she had momentary pain. "Though there were enough whispers that it affected our reputations. Neither of us were liked enough to overcome scandal."

"Mother, you need to have the surgery," Michael said.

She opened her eyes again. They were watery. "Is there no other way? I could stop eating chocolate."

"You look very, very ill. I think we must take the doctor's advice."

"I do not want to die. I have enjoyed these earthly pleasures far too much."

He blinked rapidly, almost overset by the plaintive tone in her voice.

"But what is left to me in my old age if I cannot have rich foods?" she said.

"You are not so old. Why, your hair is not even gray."

"It is kind of you to say so, but I went gray half a decade ago. My maid is artful with techniques to disguise my voyage to the grave."

"Good God, Mother, have a heart! You will shock me into mine with all this talk."

"You have too much to live for. Do you know, last winter was the first time I saw you come to town and not gain a double chin? Though

I didn't realize it, you were fairly wasting away from love with that unsuitable girl. At least she has been bred to stand up for herself, but she desperately needs a new wardrobe." She shuddered. "And that hair. Not to mention her appalling taste in maids."

That was the mother he knew so well. "Hold your insults, madam. My wife has had a difficult transition."

"It was rather sudden. I expected happy news."

"I am sorry we could not provide that for you."

She waved a yellowed hand. "She has a good build. She will give you children. I have no doubt."

He needed to get his wife back into his bed, first.

"Do you know, I think I shall have the surgery," she mused. "I would not like to die before seeing my first grandchild, knowing there most likely will be one within the year. And I do suggest you persuade her to choose her husband's comfort over her sister's, so this will be possible."

"I thought to suggest her sister return to the Farm with us."

"If that is what it takes. Good heavens but these Redcake chits are a needy set."

"At any rate, we will not leave London until you are recovered."

"Do not delay your happiness on my account. Now, go send word to the surgeon. I have letters to write."

"Very well, Mother." He stood and kissed her on the cheek.

She put her hand to the spot when he was done. "You haven't kissed me since you were a boy."

"I do not want us to have such a difficult time anymore. I shall need your advice."

She let out a low chuckle. "Simply repeat nothing I have done. That is the best advice I can give you. I cannot take credit for anything that has gone well for you, and much that has not."

"I blame Father for everything, not you."

"I did not make his life easy, for all that he repaid me in kind. If you love that girl you married, by all means, keep loving her. Do not let the love turn sour. Ignore every fault and live in blissful ignorance that she is anything less than an angel."

"Thank you, Mother. I shall make the necessary arrangements."

"Call for my maid, will you?" She reached for her chocolate box, then left her hand hovering there.

"I will." God keep her safe, he prayed as he left the sitting room.

He didn't want this surgery any more than she did, but she looked all too close to death.

Her maid hovered in the hall outside, so he sent her into the room before he went downstairs. His mother should not be alone.

When Alys entered Matilda's room, she found her flopped on her bed, looking like an abandoned puppet dressed in the latest fashion. She remembered all those years of sharing a room with her sisters, before they came to London. They had grown apart since, even more than she realized.

"You are not going to feel better until you take some action," she told Matilda. "Staying in your room, focused on your disgrace, will accomplish nothing."

"I thought he'd send a note," Matilda squeaked, then burst out sobbing. "Lady Lillian has not yet responded to me either!"

"If Mr. Bliven had planned to contact you, you would have received word at the same time Gawain and my husband did. As for Lady Lillian, the marquess said he would speak to her father about her appalling advice to you. She is no doubt in disgrace herself."

Matilda snapped upright as if someone had taken up her strings. "You told Michael? He spoke to the earl?"

"Of course I did. If not for your situation, I'd have removed myself to Hatbrook House by now. The Shields came to town Monday night."

"Then everyone knows," Matilda whispered, her tear-stained cheeks losing their flush. "Earl Gerrick is a bigger gossip than his daughter."

"I am sure the marquess knows that and approached him with appropriate delicacy."

"The Canders are frightfully intelligent as a clan," Matilda said, sniffing. "Lady Lillian may have used me as entertaining conversation at the dinner table."

"I doubt that."

"It was a plot!" Matilda gasped. "She has always liked Rose better than me. She wanted my disgrace. Oh, Alys, I must leave!"

"I am all for that." Alys glanced around her, hoping Matilda would not want to bring all of her bric-a-brac with her to the Farm. Her room had always been spartan in comparison. She did not want to direct the packing, and hear the hysterics, when inevitably, something broke in transit. Matilda would simply give orders and not be bothered otherwise.

Matilda wiped her eyes. "Where shall we go? India, after Mr. Bliven? Or Bristol, perhaps, to the scene of our spotless childhood? Perhaps Brighton, for the diversion. Or Italy?"

Alys broke into the reverie, feeling quite sharp. "How long until you know if your disgrace will, er, bear fruit?"

Matilda wiped at her eyes again and shrieked.

Alys pressed on. "I want to be clear on the timing, Matilda. Are your courses regular?"

Some of the color popped back into her sister's cheeks. "A couple of weeks, I should think," she whispered.

"Then there is no call to plan a trip abroad, I think. You would not want to be ill on a ship."

"Just Bristol or Brighton then," Matilda whispered. "Or do we know anyone in Edinburgh? The climate would suit my great sorrow."

Alys wasn't sure if her sister was hoping they had acquaintances in Scotland, or not. Had she been such a ninny after she and Michael had joined for the first time? In her head, perhaps, but certainly not out loud. She still wasn't sure how Rose had known what transpired. Or why Rose had revealed her secret.

"My place is with my husband," Alys said.

"Don't be silly, Alys. He doesn't need you now that his brother has been found alive. And you don't love him. Come away with me. I hardly ever see you, since you were always busy working, and I can't possibly travel alone. Mother won't leave Father again, since he's been ill."

"As pleased as I am by your sisterly desire to spend time with me, I cannot appreciate your consideration of my marriage."

"He married you because you pleased him in a marital way," Matilda said defiantly. "And you married him to escape from under Father's thumb. So why not go with me now?"

"Because I do love him," Alys snapped.

They stared at each other. Matilda, because of the vehemence behind Alys's words, and Alys, because she had never realized her feelings until now.

"You do?"

She felt lighter, as if she'd swallowed a cloud of meringue. "Yes. Ever since he came to that dreadful, falling-down house Father bought, and rescued Rose and me. I'd never have been so foolish as to become his mistress otherwise."

"You've lost your head," Matilda observed. "I always thought you such an odd, cold thing."

"I never had the time to sit around reading romantic novels."

"No, you were too busy disgracing the family with your employment," Matilda sneered.

Would Matilda never stop insulting her? "At least I was happy with myself."

"I am quite pleased with my life, thank you very much."

"Really?"

Matilda shrank back a little. "Until I miscalculated."

"I think you should stop reading novels and find some suitable friends."

Matilda slid off the bed and came around to Alys. She clutched at her older sister's hand. "What if I bear a child? Could you pass it off as yours? If we go away it would be so easy."

"I am not passing off a Bliven as a Shield," Alys said, pulling away. "I would never do that to Michael. If you have consequences, you shall have to live with the result."

"Are you sure you wouldn't go away? We have plenty of money. We could live in luxury."

Alys shook her head. "You do not understand me at all, and clearly you are too upset to think of anyone but yourself. I shall leave you to reflect, for a time." She straightened her sleeve, in disarray from where Matilda had grabbed her, and made for the door. Her steps were punctuated by Matilda's reoccurring sobs.

Alys put her hands to her temples, realizing as she walked down the hall that her interview had given her a terrible headache. She decided to go to the salon and look at some of her mother's magazines.

Really, she simply wanted to stare into the fire and think about Michael. About the first time they'd kissed, when she'd noticed the tiny mole on his cheek for the first time, because she'd finally been so close to him. So close that she'd smelled the gingerbread on his breath.

And now, she could call him her own, though she had yet to really claim him. With all of the sorrow and madness surrounding his brother's supposed death, they had never found the time for the simple pleasures of marriage.

Perhaps those moments she'd witnessed her parents sharing didn't happen in an aristocratic marriage. Did you not sit close in a parlor, reading and sharing bits of news? Maybe you didn't cover your husband's sore hands with unguent, to soothe the burns from a day's baking, or massage your wife's shoulders, because they were sore from a day spent bending over the bed of a sick child. Or play cards with relatives, but still find the opportunity to touch.

Was an aristocratic marriage all cold formality, dancing once or twice at a ball, sitting at opposite ends of an enormous dining table with disapproving relatives making rude remarks? And your husband always at his club?

No, she didn't want her marriage to become that. She had all the time in the world to spend with him. He was terribly busy, of course. She simply needed to make herself more interesting than his business concerns, or his clubs, or his friends.

An easy companion, that was what she wanted to be. Now that she was married, and to a man she loved.

How could she never have realized it before? Perhaps she had never let herself. She had been frightened, had been hurting, and had not wanted to make it worse with any declaration of her own.

Even now, with his mother so ill, she could hardly have expectations. But if he would let her come home to him, she could be there in the background, ready to start anew when there was time.

She stood and paced in front of the fire. Had she not already proven her worth? She should learn more about what ailed him, so she could refine the household menus further, to give him stamina for his work. For his nights, she mused, remembering how unexpected the pleasure she'd found with him was.

And she wanted it again. A warm rush softened her entire body as she remembered.

A knock came at the door. It opened before she could speak. And there was Michael, as if she conjured him, dressed in a jaunty houndstooth check suit that was definitely not mourning appropriate.

She lifted her skirts and ran toward him, unable to keep the smile from her face. His quizzical expression softened into a smile as she took his hands and squeezed.

"What news?" she asked, feeling small and feminine since he had to bend down to kiss her.

"I have spoken to your father. I did not reveal the totality of your sister's disgrace, in the hopes that it would not bear fruit, but I have suggested she take charge of Rose for now and he agreed."

"And Earl Gerrick?"

"I told him his daughter had been offering quite unmaidenly advice and he muttered something about it being past time for her to wed. He is writing to Viscount Bricker in Yorkshire immediately, to set a date for the wedding."

She clasped her hands between his. "Will he ship her off there?"

"Oh, yes. Special license, wedding in the chapel on the estate in Yorkshire. If the man isn't willing, Earl Gerrick said he'd marry Lady Lillian off to Viscount Hortley."

"Thank you."

He squeezed her hands. "My mother will have her surgery on Friday. I don't mean to suggest that you wait on her as I will hire sufficient staff, but would you consider coming to Hatbrook House soon?"

"I'd like nothing better," Alys said. "I am so happy you asked. It was foolish of me to leave the Farm without you."

"You were worried about your father." He offered her an excuse but she dismissed it.

"No, I was afraid."

"That he was seriously ill? He seemed well to me, other than a sore nose."

"No, I was afraid of our life together." She lifted her hands from his grasp and moved her fingers up his chest, hoping he would embrace her. "I didn't know how to make it work, to have the loving relationship I know I want."

His gaze was intent on her. She snuggled closer and his arms found their way around her.

"I love you, Michael. I didn't know it before. I've been such a fool. I should have been patient and kept putting myself in front of you, so we would have time to know each other. I don't know how to be still."

"I love you too and I'm sorry I never told you. I thought you regretted our marriage terribly once you discovered there was to be no baby."

"I have wanted you desperately since you rescued us from Redcake Manor. You are my hero, Michael. But I lived more like a man than a woman. I didn't know how I felt because I never let myself feel."

"You have never lived like a man," Michael said, pressing his lips against her hair. "But you did lock your sensibilities away. That I can believe. Every tender moment with you is like an explosion before you lock yourself away again."

"I want to change."

"I want to change too," he whispered, his breath tickling her ear. "You have made my life so much better already. Who would have thought that War Office telegram would become a blessing?"

She found his lapels and tugged until his lips met hers.

"Everything has changed. Even my mother and I had a moment, yesterday. It is as if your presence in my life spun everything on its axis and everyone and everything came down in a slightly different place."

She agreed wholeheartedly. "In a very different place for me."

"I can see that. I have asked you to make an incredibly hard adjustment."

"That is what women have to do," Alys said. "That is the way it is."

"It does not have to be. Do you want Redcake's? I'll give it to you, even if you want to manage it yourself. It needs a steady hand."

She considered his words carefully. "You want me in your business?"

"I'll sign it over to you as your own personal property, if you like. It is up to you."

She felt a smile brighten her face. "Are you certain you do not mind? I love Redcake's so much, but being your wife in every way is important to me."

His gaze stayed intent on hers. "I am proud that you consider our families in this decision, but I want you to be happy."

She stared into the flames for a moment, her brain whirring with plans. "Will you help me find a good manager for Redcake's? Then there will not be so much for me to do. I can make cakes and be happy if we can employ someone with the right sensibility to report to me," she said. "They must be perfect for the establishment."

"I like your fierce spirit." He feathered a finger over her hair. "It comes with the red."

"Is your temper as bad as mine?"

"In times of stress. I am sorry I snapped at you about my business affairs. I should have realized how capable and knowledgeable you are about many things."

She flexed her fingers, already poring over options. "I shall make a list."

"We shall live in London most of the time," he mused. "But I will be needed at the Farm now and then. However, I promise I shall never hold a hunting ball."

She glanced up and saw his wink. "Whatever do you mean?"

"The first time I saw you, you were telling one of the cakies that you never wanted to be an ornament at a hunting ball. I am guilty of attempting to treat you as ornamental. It shall never happen again."

She couldn't hold back her laugh. She remembered that day so clearly. "As for myself, I do not think I shall find the country so bad when we visit. Certainly the air is better, which means it shall be a better place for children."

"I cannot wait to see what kind of scamps Alys Shield produces."

She laughed again and hugged him. "An austere firecracker. I cannot wait either. We will have so much joy."

"I agree."

"And good times."

"Absolutely."

"All the pleasure in the world does not reside in cake," she mused.

He put a hand on her shoulder. "But you must promise me something."

Looking into his eyes, she said, "Anything. What?"

"Never lose that scent you have. Of orange flower water and cake?"

"Ah, there is that hungry look again, my love."

"I retract any desire I may ever have mentioned to marry a biddable girl, as long as she is as sweet as you."

He tilted her laughing face to his, and Alys surrendered herself to an endless, promising kiss. He still tasted faintly of gingerbread, though she knew it might be only a memory since his hands were steady on the back of her head. His mouth worshipped hers as if she tasted of the finest Scotch trifle. This was their true beginning, and a sweet one at that.

If you liked *The Marquess of Cake*,
look for Judah's story,
ONE TASTE OF SCANDAL,
coming in December 2013!

photo credit: Syneca Featherstone

ABOUT THE AUTHOR

Heather Hiestand was born in Illinois but her family migrated west before she started school. Since then she has claimed Washington State as home, except for a few years in California. She wrote her first story at age seven and went on to major in creative writing at the University of Washington. Her first published fiction was a mystery short story, but since then it has been all about the many flavors of romance. Heather's first published romance short story was set in the Victorian period and she continues to return, fascinated by the rapid changes of the nineteenth century. The author of many novels, novellas, and short stories, she has achieved best-seller status on Amazon's Romance Anthologies list and on Amazon UK's Romance Short Stories list. With her husband and son, she makes her home in a small town and supposedly works out of her tiny office, though she mostly writes in her easy chair in the living room.

For more information, visit Heather's website at www.heather hiestand.com. Heather loves to hear from readers! Her e-mail is heather@heatherhiestand.com.